Preface

Before the storm.

King Edward II's lover Piers Gaveston was murdered by irate English nobles in 1312. They did so because they were offended by his relationship with the king and his misuse of the ever-increasing powers the king gave him. Edward then gave his new lover, Hugh Despenser, the son of the Earl of Winchester, even great powers as his chancellor and together they wreaked terrible vengeance on Gaveston's killers and everyone associated with them. The King had earlier married the twelve year old sister of the King of France and had a son, Edward III, by her when she was sixteen and he was twenty-eight.

One of the Gaveston's murderers, Roger Mortimer, escaped from the Tower and fled to France. In 1323 Queen Isabella was sent to France to help her husband "make peace" with the French. She was thought to be the perfect emissary because she was the French king's only sister. She took her young son, Edward III, with her. She was also allegedly pregnant with King Edward's second son, John of Cornwall.

Once in France, however, the Queen refused to return to England and King Edward. Instead she took the exiled Mortimer as a lover and together they returned to

England in 1326 with an army of mercenaries from Anvers and the lowlands. They did so in an effort to make her young son, Edward III, the king with Queen Isabella as his regent and Mortimer as the boy's all-powerful chamberlain and England's king in all but name. England's nobles and bishops, sensing the end of Edward II's reign did what English nobles and bishops have always done under such circumstances—they ignored their many sworn oaths of loyalty to King Edward and rushed to join the usurpers.

Edward II and Despenser were soon deserted by almost everyone except the king's personal guards and a few die-hard supporters. In an effort to save themselves they abandoned the rank and file soldiers of the army they had mustered at Windsor and fled with their guards and what was left of their noble and priestly supporters to the powerful and easily defended Tower of London in September of 1326.

At first the embattled King and his lover-chancellor were content to seal themselves into the Tower and prepare to use their remaining guards and supporters to fight off the inevitable siege. But then, at the suggestion of a visiting bishop who had once been a soldier, they changed their minds and decided to flee westward to Wales before Mortimer's rapidly growing army could surround the Tower and cut them off from their only line of retreat.

The two men may have been in a hurry to escape and more artistically inclined than most of England's kings and chamberlains, but they were not fools; they cleaned out the royal treasury in the Tower and took coins worth sixty thousand pounds of gold with them when they left. It would, they rightly believed, buy a lot of loyalty and the mercenaries they would need to restore themselves to power.

Mortimer and his rapidly growing army of supporters pursued them. When they were about to catch up with them, Edward and Despenser panicked. They abandoned the king's guards and the wagons carrying the treasure and tried to flee by boat from Chepstow. Adverse winds blew them back to England and, now separated from their supporters and the treasure wagons they had abandoned, they tried to flee on foot to Wales.

Unfortunately, at least for King Edward and Despenser, they were soon captured by mercenaries employed by Mortimer and the Queen. Others of the mercenaries, a small company of whom appeared to be archers from Cornwall, "happened to come across" the abandoned coin wagons and were able to protect them until they could be turned over to the extremely gratefully Queen and Mortimer.

The possibility that some of the coins might have gone missing in midst of all the chaos and confusion was not considered at the time or by historians in the years that followed. That was because no one knew for sure how many coins had been in the Tower's treasure room or how many wagons had been used to carry them away when the

King fled. Even the archers who had helped load the coin chests into the wagons were not sure, probably because of the haste, hysteria, and confusion that was going on all around them.

Queen Isabella and her lover, and subsequently the scholars and historians who periodically wrote about their rise to power, initially believed all the coins had been recovered by the Queen and Mortimer. They were convinced that none were missing by an unknown bishop and several of the Angelovian priests who were attending him.

The churchmen were, quite fortuitously, on a pilgrimage to pray at a nearby Benedictine Priory and claimed to have seen everything. They swore in the name of Jesus that the Cornish archers had so well-guarded the eleven wagons that that had been proudly presented to the Queen by her supporters that not a single coin had been taken from them until she began using some of the coins they were carrying to pay her mercenaries and reward her loyal supporters.

What actually happened, in other words the true story of those events and the role of Cornwall's Company of Archers in them, was not known until recently because so many of the Company's documents from its medieval years were written on leather parchments which ended up being eaten in all or part by mice in the years that followed. Only recently when new scientific methods for analyzing microscopic bits of mice poop were developed by an interdisciplinary team of Oxford scientists funded by the

Ministry of Defence and MI6 could more of the records of the Company of Archers be brought to light and, in this case, totally change what we know about the Company of Archers and the royal family.

More specifically, the new information recovered by using powerful microscopes and artificial intelligence to piece together extremely small post-consumption parchment remnants strongly suggests that there were seventeen coin wagons and that six of them had hurriedly set out for somewhere unknown long *before* the Queen and her supporters arrived to take possession of the eleven remaining wagons. The recovered documents also provide heretofore unknown information about the royal family including the source of the red hair of some of its members.

Such an important revision of England's history and the development of a new method to obtain additional facts from heretofore lost medieval parchments will no doubt result in numerous additional government research grants and many scholarly books and articles about the origins of the royal red hair and the use of close inspections of medieval mouse poop fragments to recover medieval and even earlier writings that had heretofore been thought to be irretrievably lost. Both appear to be major breakthroughs that will keep the historians and scientists of Oxford and Cambridge funded to rewrite Britain's history for many years to come.

This then is the story of what really happened when Mortimer and the randy Queen invaded England and tried to depose King Edward.

The Windsor Deception

*Being the true story of what happened whilst
the Queen and her supporters were trying to
depose King Edward II in favour of her son.*

Chapter One

The big war galley moving slowly through the estuary
towards Fowey Village and the green forest and fields that
stretched out behind the village was only a couple of years
old. But it certainly did not look like a new-build to the
people who had come hurrying out of their hovels and the
village's little church to watch its arrival and welcome it.
They were mostly women because many of the village's men
were fishermen and out fishing. The people in the village's
two public houses and its smithy, mostly men, heard the
women's shouts and also came out to look at the new arrival
and do the same.

As you might expect from an isolated Cornish people
who rarely have anything new to talk about except the
weather, the villagers promptly began telling each other
everything they knew about the approaching galley. They
also began speculating as to who might be on it and what it

might be carrying in addition to the Commander of Cornwall's Company of Archers, John Boatman. They knew the Company's Commander was on board because they could see his well-known pennant flying on the forward mast.

On the other hand, the watchers did *not* know much about it the galley itself or who else was on board or where it had been and what it had been doing. That was understandable because the galley, Number Ninety-two, was a new-build from the Company of Archers' galley yard on Cyprus and had never before been to England.

The watchers' lack of knowledge about the approaching galley did not deter them from talking about it with a great deal of enthusiasm. Being as most of them were Cornish villagers to the bone, they quickly began making up stories to fill in the gaps about what was known about the galley and its crew, and then promptly began telling their tales to each other with the utmost sincerity. And, of course, also being mostly Cornish, their listeners courteously pretended to believe them.

In any event, people everywhere in the little village were waving and shouting out "hoys" and "welcomes" even though they were too far away to be heard by the men on the galley. It was a traditional greeting; people in the little village at the mouth of the Fowey always tended to drop whatever they were doing and come out to greet new arrivals. It gave them something new to talk about and broke up the monotony of the village's endless days.

The villagers' welcome was particularly warm in this case because the watchers could see the pennant flying on the new arrival's forward mast and knew the galley belonged to Cornwall's very own Company of Archers and had the "big man" himself, John Boatman, the Company's Commander, on board.

On the other hand, much of the watchers' talk was a bit more anxious and worried than usual. That was because of the recent and totally unexpected raid by French pirates on the shipping in the estuary that stretched out in front of the village and also because they could see the galley's badly ripped forward sail flapping uselessly in the wind. It had been an ineffectual raid because the only galley in the estuary had escaped up the Fowey and the only transport in it available to be taken, which it was, had been the Company's leaky old training cog.

What particularly drew everyone's attention and caused much pointing and many excited questions and comments that morning was the state of the galley's sail. It was unheard of for a new arrival to enter the estuary and move toward the entrance to the river with a badly ripped sail. Quite the contrary. The ripped sail combined with the previous day's visit by the French pirates caused the watchers to be much more excited and talkative than usual. Something must have happened to the Company's galley. But what?

Was the sail ripped because the Commander's galley had been in a fight with the French pirates that had recently visited the estuary or because of the recent storm? Both explanations were immediately suggested and soon became accepted facts to be earnestly argued. And why had the sail not been repaired? Could it be that almost everyone on board was down with the plague or had been wounded or killed in a great battle?

The rumour that the galley might possibly be plague-stricken spread quickly. It caused many of the watchers to make the sign of the cross and a couple of the older women to hurry to the village church. The watchers could also see and pointed out to each other the little dinghy that had been hurriedly pushed into the water in front of the village. It was being energetically rowed out to greet the new arrival despite the rowers' wet feet that resulted from having to walk out into the surf to launch it.

On board the galley, however, things were nowhere near as bad as they appeared to be to the watchers in the village. To the contrary, Galley Ninety-two had easily weathered the storm that had blown it slightly off course and it had had no trouble avoiding the galleys guarding the French fleet it had unexpectedly encountered.

In fact, Galley Ninety-two had not suffered from either event, or anything else of significance for that matter, on its long voyage from Cyprus via Malta and Lisbon. There had been the usual storms and a burial at sea and two men had run in Lisbon. But those were normal events and to be expected on every voyage. The very recent unravelling of the sail maker's stitches on its forward main sail had been a surprise, as it always was, to the galley's crew but not something that was out of the ordinary. In the real world sails periodically come apart and have to be re-sewn. It was not seen as an evil portent.

Fortunately the sudden unravelling of the stitches that held the sail together had caused the sail to come apart in the somewhat choppy English Channel just as the galley's lookouts spotted the Fowey estuary and hoyed the deck to report their sighting.

"It is a damn good thing the sail did not fail until we got through the storm and past the Frenchies," Galley Ninety-two's captain, Anthony Priest, had opined to the Company's Commander. He did so as they stood together on the roof of the galley's forward castle and looked out over the estuary and tree-covered lands behind it.

The Company's Commander, John Boatman, had been thinking behind his eyes about other more important matters at the time and merely grunted his agreement. Damage to a sail was always inopportune, but it was certainly nothing unique or special. In any event, his mind at the time had been distracted by thoughts of all the various chores and duties, both pleasant and unpleasant, that he would have to begin undertaking as soon he went ashore.

It was interesting that a large fleet of French transports and war galleys had been sighted sailing towards France, but the French fleet and its purpose did not particularly concern Commander Boatman or the men standing with him on the roof of Ninety-two's forward deck castle. That was because the leaders of Cornwall's Company's of archers, its captains and commanders, always made it a point to avoid becoming entangled in the inevitable disagreements between the nobles and kings as to who owned which lands and strongholds in England and France—unless, of course, there was a relatively riskless way for the Company to somehow profit from becoming involved.

In other words, fighting in relatively meaningless battles was something to be left to the nobles and knights of England's kings unless the payment on offer was too good to pass up and paid in advance.

Repairing the galley's forward main sail normally would have begun immediately upon its failure. But the Channel was sufficiently choppy such that the repairs would be more easily and quickly done a few minutes later whilst the galley was passing through the relatively calm waters it was about to enter. As a result, the galley's captain had conferred with the Company's Commander and decided the repairs could wait for a few hours until Ninety-two was safely rowed up the Fowey and moored to the riverbank next to the Company of Archers' training camp and depot located just below Restormel Castle.

In fact, and contrary to the fears being expressed by the villagers, the spirits of Galley Ninety-two's somewhat storm-exhausted crew were generally quite high as they slowly rowed it into the relatively quiet waters of the Fowey Estuary and began making their way toward the mouth of the River Fowey and the hovels of Fowey Village that sprawled out haphazardly next to the river's mouth.

Some of Ninety-two's crew were both pleased to have finally made it safely back in England and worried at the same time. They had not set foot on English soil for years and were looking forward to a few days of shore leave and using them to try to find those of their families and friends who were still alive. They were more than a little worried as to what and who they would find, however, since it was well-known throughout the Company that the previous two years of plague in England had taken a fearsome toll just as the plague had done several years earlier on Cyprus and in many of the Mediterranean ports the Company served.

Plague was something the galley's lieutenant knew about—he had returned to England several years earlier to find his wife and daughter dead of it and his infant son in the care of a his aunt and a wet nurse.

Most of the men in the galley's crew, however, were pleased that the voyage was almost over and cheerful as they rowed Galley Ninety-two toward the mouth of the Fowey. That was because they were primarily looking forward to spending the next few days eating food that was significantly better than that provided by the galley's cook and drinking more than a few bowls of ale and gin in one or another of Cornwall's friendly public houses.

The expectations of the galley's crew and its passengers were reasonable; even the most terrible of plagues and poxes and dangerous voyages could not stop good ale from being brewed or crushed barley corns and juniper berries from fermenting.

Indeed, and contrary to the fears of the watchers in the village and on the rocky strand in front of it, spirits were generally high amongst the men on Ninety-two. That was because everyone aboard the galley believed that the voyage's inevitable trials and tribulations of sore arms, poor food, and being frequently cold and wet, were about to end, at least temporarily. And when they did end the galley's crew would get their liberty coins and the "good times" they had been thinking and talking about for the entire voyage would begin. That is what had happened regularly in the past to the Company's crews whenever they reached friendly ports and it was what the archers and sailors on Ninety-two had every reason to expect they would see and experience in the days ahead.

On the other hand, the archers and sailors in the crew also knew the "good times" would not begin until they finished rowing Ninety-two up the River Fowey and off-loaded its passengers and the chests it was carrying; the chests that contained some of the Company's "takings" from its operations in the east during the previous year. The unloading would occur on one of the Company's three floating wharfs that were permanently moored to the riverbank at the Company's training depot that was itself located next to the river just below Restormel Castle.

Then and only then, when the unloading was totally finished, would the archers who pulled on the galley's oars and the handful of sailors who were aboard to work its sails receive their liberty coins and a few days of freedom to enjoy themselves. That was almost certainly what most of the men of Ninety-two's crew were thinking about as their galley entered the estuary and began making its way towards the gaggle of rickety hovels that were haphazardly clustered about the little church and two taverns at the mouth of the river.

The lieutenant's thoughts were slightly different. He was thinking about something he had not thought of much lately—that he would once again see his infant son who had been carried to Cornwall after his wife died and was now being raised by his uncle's childless wife. He wondered if the boy still had the same flaming red hair similar to that his own father had enjoyed. It ran in the family and seemed to skip generations and appear every so often, or so the lieutenant had been told by his father before he and the Company war galley he had been captaining disappeared years earlier on a voyage from Cyprus to Constantinople.

Some of the people watching intently as the galley headed for the mouth of the Fowey were archers and sailors stationed in the village to help conduct the Company's business and assist in the at-sea training of its new recruits. A few of them undoubtedly wished they were aboard and away from the endless hours they spent training recruits to live aboard galleys and fight at sea. Most, however, enjoyed life ashore and had "better them than me" thoughts behind their eyes that they carefully kept to themselves.

Other watchers included a dozen or more would-be passengers, mostly pilgrims and merchants and escaping outlaws fleeing from the King's justice. They had arrived in the village one way or another and were waiting for the next outbound Company galley that would carry them closer to Rome or the Holy Land or wherever else was their intended final destination. They hoped they were finally seeing it arrive after more than a few boring and idle days of waiting. And of course, as you might expect, those amongst them who understood what they were seeing were worried about the state of the galley since its ragged and flapping forward sail seemed to suggest a slack and uncaring captain and crew.

Most of the watchers, however, were villagers who had lived in Fowey Village for their entire lives. They had seen innumerable Company galleys come and go over the years; they immediately recognized, or were soon told, that the galley was one of the new and slightly larger war galleys that were now being built in the Company's shipyard on Cyprus.

The watchers also knew that the galley now heading for the mouth of the river and the Company's other galleys were mostly used to carry passengers, cargos, and money orders from port to port in the Mediterranean and the smaller seas around it.

It was not that the Company's war galleys were primarily used as transports because their crews could not or would not fight. Quite the contrary; it was well known in the Mediterranean ports, if not to England's kings and their nobles and knights, that the crews of the Company's galleys were mostly English archers. And even more importantly, archers who were so well armed with long bows and other modern weapons and so well trained and ready to use them that they were rarely required to do so compared to the sailors who crewed the galleys and transports of the Venetians and other free companies and merchants engaged in the same port to port trade.

Indeed, the fact that the Moorish pirates typically went out of their way to avoid the Company's galleys and transports was well known in the ports it served and the reason why the Company was able to charge such high prices for its cargo and passenger carrying services and its customers paid them willingly. It also helped that the Company was known for honouring its agreements and for not stealing its cargos or defaulting on the parchment money orders it issued or selling its passengers as slaves.

In any event, from the state of the arriving galley's forward sail and the fact that it had not yet been repaired the watchers assumed the galley had probably had a either an incompetent crew or an uncaring captain, both of which greatly worried those of the waiting passengers with knowledge of the sea, or it had experienced recent difficulties with either the weather or one or another of the Company's and England's many enemies.

In fact, both possibilities were excitedly talked about amongst the watchers and none of them were true. The sail's stitches had merely come undone for some reason or another just before the galley had entered the estuary. Indeed, the galley's captain and its crew were so far above average in competence that the prospective passengers' time would have been better spent worrying and praying about pirate raids and storms. In other words, the crew was in fine shape and the state of its sail, in the parlance of the day, was merely the result of the inevitable "fair wear and tear" that had occurred a few minutes earlier in the course of its normal usage.

What the watchers in the village also did not know was that the galley was arriving late because it had encountered a French fleet carrying the French army from Scotland back to France and the galley's captain, after consulting with his illustrious passenger, decided to run for safety despite his galley's speed and the fighting abilities of its well-armed and highly trained crew. It was a reasonable decision; it is, after all, one thing for a Company galley to fight two or three enemy galleys and quite another for it to seek a fight with ten or twelve, especially when it was carrying a fortune in gold and silver coins and bars in its hold.

Somewhat similarly, what the galley's passengers and crew did not know was that the dinghy was coming out to warn its captain of a potential problem that might be lurking in Cornwall and on its approaches, not to welcome it. They also did not know that some of the galleys in the French fleet they had encountered a few days earlier, and from whom they had run because they were hopelessly outnumbered, had been "visiting" England's coastal villages and towns as they made their way home with the French army they were carrying from Scotland back to France. They also did not know why the French army was returning to France or what news was waiting for the Commander further up the River Fowey at Restormel Castle and what it was that the news portended.

There was, in other words, a lot of ignorance in the air. On the other hand, the watchers were certainly right that Galley Number Ninety-two was somehow slightly different from most of the Company's other galleys: It was relatively new and slightly longer because it had an additional cargo hold forward of its upper rowing deck where the lower ranking members of the crew could take turns sheltering when they were not on duty. It also had six additional oars sticking out from each side of its lower rowing deck for a total of forty-eight on each side.

Supposedly the additional oars made Galley Ninety-two and its sister galleys slightly faster than the other galleys in the Company's fleet as well as more seaworthy and capable of carrying both more cargo and more archers to help row it. Those were significant improvements and were expected to be quite useful in the years ahead now that the Moors from Algiers and along the Spanish coast had been united under a single caliph and were making a concentrated effort to turn the Mediterranean into a Moorish sea. It was similarly significant that this galley and the Company's other new and longer galleys also had significantly larger deck castles and that the additional space on their decks and roofs meant that more archers could stand on them and push out their arrows during a fight.

Indeed, Ninety-two's improved ability to either fight or run was why it was one of the three galleys that had been chosen a few months earlier to carry a portion of the year's takings of coins from where they had been accumulated at the Company's stronghold on Cyprus to its home in Cornwall—because it was more likely to successfully run the gauntlet of Moorish pirates that was growing in the western Mediterranean. Its higher likelihood of successfully getting past the Moors unscathed was also the reason Ninety-two was carrying the Company's Commander, John Boatman, who was returning from his annual visit to Cyprus and the Company's various shipping posts east of Gibraltar.

******

Gallery Ninety-two's lieutenant, its relatively young and already widowed twenty-seven year old second in command, was up on the roof of its forward castle with the Company's commander and two captains as it moved toward the mouth of the river. The two captains standing near the lieutenant on the roof were the galley's captain, Anthony Priest, and Commander Boatman's very staid and proper senior aide, Captain Edward Robertson. Robertson was known to his friends as "Fast Eddie" for some unknown reason and had been ever since his days at the Company school.

The Lieutenant's name was William Courtenay and he was relatively young for a lieutenant. His wife and daughter had died of the plague several years earlier and he was the third Courtenay with the name of William to serve in the Company. The first had been elected by the Company's handful of surviving crusaders to be their captain more than a hundred years earlier; the second William had been the first William's grandson and the third William's grandfather.

According to the stories the lieutenant had heard at home whilst he was a young lad and what he had later been learnt at the Company school, the first William had been elected as the Company's captain by the survivors of a company of crusading English archers after King Richard abandoned them and fled for home.

After becoming its captain the first William had then somehow changed the Company from a free company of longbow-equipped archers employed by King Richard until he fled from the Holy Land into a large and powerful armed merchant company with its own galleys, transports, and shipping posts at a number of major ports. It had also acquired great strongholds on Cyprus and at Restormel Castle and in the marches along Cornwall's border with the rest of England.

Along the way the first William had somehow bought the title of Earl of Cornwall even though he was not a knight. He had also taken the name "Courtenay" as his second name, apparently because he liked the sound of it, knew he needed one to differentiate himself from all the other Williams in the Company, and could think of no other that suited him.

Not much about the Company had changed in the years that followed the first William except that the Company's strength and wealth had slowly but surely grown. It had, for example, learned how to use man-made lightning to throw stones at its enemies but still had not learned how to use the lightning to make gold. The Company was similarly still being ignored by England's latest crop of king and nobles, probably because they knew so little about its wealth and the ability of its men to fight with the most modern of weapons.

Also unchanged was the fact that the descendents of the first William still held Restormel Castle as the unknighted earls of Cornwall and the castle still held most of the Company's great and ever-growing cache of gold and silver coins. The lieutenant's elderly uncle, now retired from the Company, was the current earl and definitely not a knight. Indeed, he had never attended the King's court and almost certainly would not been allowed anywhere near the Company if he had ever attended the king's court or had been a knight or a knight's son.

What the boys were learnt in school about their obligations and futures had also not changed over the years—that the Company would be able to prosper only so long as it was left alone by the Church and by England's kings and their governments and also only so long as it recruited no sons of knights or lords into its ranks. The latter both because they did not take orders well and because they liked to fight man to man in order to demonstrate their bravery to each other instead of together as a Roman-style team in order to win battles and wars without unnecessary casualties.

So far so good as the boys in the Company school had been told over the years: The Popes continued to be placated by the Company's annual "donation" of prayer coins and the Company was still being ignored by the kings and their courtiers due to their continuing ignorance about the Company's wealth, the fighting abilities of its men, and its role in the real world across the water. As a result, the Company was still based in Cornwall and still using the lands around Restormel Castle to train likely lads to sum and scribe and to teach the boys and its older recruits to push arrows out of a longbow, use the long-handled bladed pikes produced by the Company's smiths, and put their feet down to the beat of a marching drum.

The boys were also told that if they were able to climb into the leadership ranks of the Company it would be their most important task to see that the Papal bribes and the ignorance of England's kings and their courtiers about the

Company and Cornwall were continued. It could be done, the boys were assured, because God in his wisdom had give the Church's princes vices that were expensive and England's royals and nobles especially small thinking abilities behind their eyes.

"Just keep the nobles and priests away from Cornwall, placate the Church with coins and the Crown and its nobles with ox shite, and get on with doing whatever must be done for the Company to gather coins." That was the basic instruction given to the likely lads who were enrolled in the Company school.

"We will need as many as coins in our chests as possible to get through the lean years of peace when Jesus returns and there is peace such that our services will not be needed until he decides to leave again. The problem, of course, and why we need to gather as many coins as possible, is that only God knows how long Jesus will stay the next time he visits."

Moreover, God was obviously on the Company's side for even the recent years of plague in England had not reduced the Company's presence in Cornwall or its ability to recruit sufficient numbers of commoners willing to go for an archer with the Company. Even now the number of men and boys who were willing or forced to leave England's cities and villages and go for an archer was still much more numerous than the number of archers needed to replace those who fell, ran, or retired and also provide the additional archers the Company needed to crew its ever-growing numbers of galleys, transports, and shipping posts.

The availability of England's men and boys and their willingness to make their marks on the Company's roll and go for an archer was understandable; except for becoming monks and joining a monastery and constantly chanting Latin prayers with only other monks to bugger they rarely had anything else to do except go for an archer or walk behind a lord's plough for the rest of their lives—which was often quite short because the lords of England all too often took their vassals off to fight in wars despite not providing them with modern weapons or training or transportation home when they decided to stop fighting.

Similarly unchanged was the Company's school for likely lads which had until recently been located in Restormel's middle bailey and was now located in its new quarters just outside the outermost of the castle's three curtain walls. It was still turning out half a dozen or so young apprentice sergeants each year for the twin purposes of assisting the Company's captains who were illiterate with their scribing and summing and providing the Company with some of its future captains and commanders. Indeed, Commander Boatman and the two captains on the galley had all been students at the school as had the galley's plague-widowed lieutenant, William Courtenay, and several of the galley's very young sergeants and its sergeant major.

Also unchanged was the tradition that each year one or another of the Company's higher ranking men still personally carried to the Pope a few of the coins the Company collected from its passengers "for the Pope's prayers for your safety on your voyage." They did so, took some of the prayer coins the Company collected to the Pope each year that is, in order to keep the Holy Father sweet and the Church friendly. Indeed, collecting coins for the Papal prayers was still one of the Company's biggest earners and had become even bigger and more important of late as a result of the increasing ever-increasing threat of the Moorish pirates causing the Company's passengers to feel the need for more prayers.

As the school boys all knew by the time they passed out of the school to join the Company as apprentice sergeants: "The prayer coins work well for everyone because our passengers who get through to their destinations think the coins they handed over to us were money well spent and those who do not survive their voyages are not around to complain." It was, the boys understood, a win-win situation for everyone.

******

Gallery Ninety-two entered the Fowey estuary with Captain Priest standing on the roof of the galley's forward deck castle along with his lieutenant and his two high-ranking passengers, the Company's commander, John Boatman, and the captain who aided the Commander as his assistant, Edward Robertson.

"Something is not right, Captain" Lieutenant Courtenay said to Captain Priest. As he spoke he whipped out both of his hidden wrist knives and used one of them to point across the estuary toward the mouth of the river that ran into it. "There is no training gallery in the water for the new lads to be learnt on. And the old transport where they are learnt to board prizes and fight at sea is not out there either."

"Aye William, you are right about that, yes you are." It was Commander Boatman who replied instead of the galley's captain. And he did so with an acknowledging touch of concern in his voice before Captain Priest, a slow and steady fellow, had time to think about the lieutenant's comment and respond himself.

After a moment the Commander added a comment that was directed to no one in particular.

"Well lads we should know soon enough when our port captain comes aboard. Lieutenant Chumley is probably in the skiff that just pushed off from the strand in front of the village."

No one on the roof of the galley's forward deck castle moved or said a word for some time thereafter. They all just stood silently and watched as the well-handled skiff moved through the water on a course to intercept them.

What the men waiting and watching on the deck castle's roof did *not* do was act in any way surprised when the lieutenant returned the knives to the leather wrist bindings his tunic concealed and then once again, a few seconds later, whipped them out. They ignored him because it was well known in the Company that William was obliged to always wear a double-bladed knife on each wrist and constantly practice bringing them out very quickly. It was an obligation the first William had laid upon the men of his family if they followed him into the Company. They were similarly required to always wear chain shirts under their tunics and be able to swim whilst wearing them.

Indeed, knowing that he always wore chain and seeing him periodically whip out his wrist knives and return them to their hiding places under his tunic seemed so normal to the men on the roof that they paid no attention whatsoever when he practiced. Their lack of interest was not surprising; most of them had attended the Company's school for likely lads at Restormel Castle, just as William himself had done; they understood that William had no choice. It was a well-known family tradition that had become a Company tradition for his crewmates and fellow archers not to notice; something the young lieutenant had no choice but to do and they had no choice but to ignore.

Neither tradition was unwarranted or unreasonable. To the contrary, every man on the galley understood that serving in the Company's ranks was dangerous and that being constantly ready to take an unwary enemy by surprise by sticking a knife in him was always a good thing.

Moreover, the lieutenant's hidden knives and daily practice seemed to particularly endear him to the rank and file archers and sailors of the galley's crew even though he was younger than a number of them. It seems the men liked the fact that their lieutenant had been singled out to be always be ready for a fight to defend himself—and them too since it was another well-established Company tradition that a Company man always came to the aid of his fellow archers and those who served with him and never under any circumstances abandoned them. It was little wonder that more than a few of the Company's archers followed the lieutenant's example and wore hidden wrist knives of their own.

About five minutes later the galley's sailing master shouted an order and the galley's oars were temporarily idled so the skiff could come alongside. It did so most smartly and its passenger quickly came up to the deck on the rope ladder that had been thrown over the galley's side for him to climb. As soon as he was on the ladder the order was given to commence rowing and the galley continued on its way into the mouth of the River Fowey with the men remaining in the skiff rowing hard to follow close behind.

To everyone's surprise, the man who hurried up the ladder and nervously came aboard was not Lieutenant Chumley, the elderly archer lieutenant who served as the Company's port captain and commanded the old training galley on which the new recruits were learnt how to fight at sea; it was the big and bushy bearded three-stripe sailing sergeant who should have been on board the Company's leaky old two-masted training transport, the high-decked cog that was permanently stationed in the estuary to help put the learning on the new archers as to how to board prizes and fight on their decks—the old transport that had to be constantly bailed in order to keep it from sinking and was nowhere to be seen.

"Sailing Sergeant Pew reporting, Commander," the sergeant said as he stood rigidly to attention and knuckled his forehead to salute. He was clearly quite nervous and more than a little agitated.

"Where are the training galley and your training transport, Sergeant Pew?" Commander Boatman inquired rather quietly.

The sergeant looked nervously about, and then with a hint of tears in his eyes and his voice shaky he squared his shoulders and said "The cog is gone Commander; some French galleys, five of them they was, hauled up her anchor and took her two days ago."

The sergeant was right to be worried and everyone on Galley Ninety-two's deck immediately knew it; surrendering a Company galley or transport without a fight was not acceptable behaviour. Men had been hung for less.

"Tell us exactly what happened Sergeant Pew," the Commander said quietly in a surprisingly gentle voice. "And what makes you think it was the French?"

French? The French fleet we encountered yesterday was raiding here?

Chapter Two

A day of surprises.

Sergeant Pew took a deep breath to steady himself, and then told his sad tale.

"The Frenchies surprised us Commander, yes they did. It were two days ago and everything was most normal-like before they showed up. We were anchored in our usual place over there near the mouth of river with me and all four of my sailor-men on board. The old bitch was leaking as usual and me and my four men were taking our usual turns to bail her out. The training galley was tied up at the village's little quay waiting for some new archer lads what was supposed to be marching down from Restormel to begin being learnt how to row and fight whilst aboard. It was a cloudy day and there had been some rain for about an hour.

"I was down in the hold to see for myself how the bailing was going when old Bob Brown, him what lost his eye off Cadiz, shouted at me to get my arse to the deck and be quick about it. From the sound of Bob's voice I knew I needed to hurry.

"What I saw when I got there a few moments later was some galleys, three of them they was at first, and they was rowing hard and coming straight for us. I did not have any idea as to who they might be but I knew right away something was wrong because the first thing I saw when I reached the deck was Lieutenant Chumley and some men coming out of the village. They were running towards the training galley where it was tied to the quay. At the same time I saw the three French galleys; they were about three miles out and coming fast. And there were two more of the bastards a couple of miles behind them.

"All of them French bastards was coming straight for us and rowing hard. There was doubt about it; they were coming to take us and there was no way my four lads and I could fight them off even if we had some weapons on board, which we did not; only the training swords without edges and points. So I shouted for the lads to jump in the dinghy and row like hell for the shallows over there to port where the Frenchies would not be able to follow us. I jumped in the dinghy with them and we rowed as hard as we could to get ourselves over into the shallows by the big rock on the river side of the village.

"My men are all good lads, Commander, all four of them. They only abandoned the cog because I ordered them to go. If there is anyone to blame for losing that leaky old cow and for the lads running it is only me." He said it with an apology in his voice but he held his head up with a determined look on his face as he did. *And from the way he said it we all knew he had thought about what to say for a long time; probably every waking hour for the last two days I would wager.*

"Aye, that is so, that is so" agreed the Commander softly. But then he asked "So what did you see whilst you were rowing away and where was our training galley and what was it doing when all this was happening?"

"Well them Frenchies was obviously coming to take the training transport as a prize because it and a couple fishing boats and the training galley tied up at the quay were all that were hereabouts at the time. They probably did not know the old cow was so leaky and not at all seaworthy. Whilst we were still in the dinghy rowing we watched whilst the first three French galleys surrounded her and then raised their ladders and began boarding. Slow and stumbling about they was."

"And our training galley, Sergeant? Where was our galley and what was it doing whilst all this was happening?" the Commander asked again very softly.

"Lieutenant Chumley somehow got her cast off from the quay and under way whilst we were rowing for the shallows. She headed straight for the mouth of the river but she was going so terrible slow and wobbly with only a few oars in the water that we thought at first that the French would catch her for sure. But she reached the river before the Frenchies finished boarding my boat and could cast off to go after her. We watched as she kept right on going up the river.

"Actually, it was a close run thing. The two French galleys that came in behind the first three tried to follow the Lieutenant up the river. But they turned around and came back empty-handed about an hour later. Whilst them two were up the river one of the other Frenchies what took my old cow put a line on her and began towing her away. It was all over and the Frenchies were gone and out of sight by the time the sun was overhead."

There was a moment of silence before Commander Boatman pronounced his judgment.

"Well Sergeant Pew," he said with a nod of his head. "You did the right thing. There is no way you could have saved your leaky old boat, but you did save all your men by moving fast. And the boat did not have much in the way of stores aboard it and it already needed to be replaced. So I reckon all we lost that was worth anything were the training swords and shields used by the recruits.

"Besides," the Commander said with a snort and a somewhat satisfied laugh, "the old cow was not seaworthy enough to reach France. That is why she was here in the estuary and only used for training. So she has probably already gone down and taken some Frenchmen with her when she did. A good way for her to go I would think. Eh?"

A much-relieved Sergeant Pew nodded his agreement enthusiastically and so did everyone else. And every man amongst us knew that it was only a matter of time before the Company would put a revenge on the French that would be much more terrible than the Company's loss of an old cog. We had no choice—revenge was required by the Company's articles and had to be done to protect our good name and discourage people from trying to take advantage of us. Besides some of the French transports and their cargos would be quite valuable and make fine prizes.

Our revenge would be much more substantial than merely causing the French to lose a few leaky old cogs. We all understood that. But what would it be and where and when? As you might imagine, most of the talk in the hours that followed was about how and when our revenge against the French would begin and who amongst us would be involved and reap the rewards, both good and bad. It was all very exciting.

What Sergeant Pew also reported, and we all mostly ignored, was something that turned out to be far more important than the French getting away with our leaky old transport. It was that "some knights and a bishop whose name I heard but I forget" had been waiting at the *Red Horse* Tavern for almost a week to talk to the Commander.

What? A bishop in Cornwall other than Cornwall's own? And with knights? It was unheard of. And how did he and the knights get over the River Tamar? We did not make much of it at the time because talking about the inevitable revenge raid on the French was much more interesting, if only because a raid often meant prize money for the men who survived it.

Indeed, to the extent we did talk about the bishop and the knights, which was not all that much, it was to wonder how it was that they were able to get past the outriders based at Okehampton and make their way across the Tamar. That their arrival might result in something significant enough to forever change the Company and England never crossed our minds, at least not mine.

The possibility that a bishop and the knights travelling with him might have been deliberately brought into Cornwall by Commander Boatman's number two, Lieutenant Commander Black who was stationed at Okehampton, also did not occur to us. But it turned out to be true and led to several great events that changed the futures of both me and the royal family.

****** *Lieutenant William Courtenay.*

Sergeant Samuel Pew or Pugh, *the spelling changes from one account to the next*, stayed aboard and came up the river with us. He stood next to me on the roof of the forward deck castle as we slowly and carefully rowed up the River Fowey to Restormel. We did so, rowed up the river that is, in the usual manner with our sailors and archers holding long poles in the bow to test the depth of the water and others standing by on each side to help push us off if we came to close to something that might damage our galley's hull or cause it to get stuck.

The sergeant and I stood off to one side of the Commander and talked as we watched the trees and meadows along the Fowey go slowly past as our galley carefully worked its way upstream. I had to be there because it was my duty station and Sergeant Pew was there because he had where else to go and no one had told him to leave. What I learned about Sergeant Samuel Pew was that he was the son of a former serf who had come to the Company without a family name. He was also not sure whether his name was spelled Pew or Pugh on the roll because he could not read.

What the sergeant did know was that his family name had been assigned to him and entered on the Company roll by the Company clerk who had questioned briefly him for something appropriate to distinguish him from all the other Samuels in the Company. It probably meant he had mentioned something to the clerk that suggested he might have been fathered in a church or birthed or found abandoned on a church pew. Perhaps it was both or that one of the church's not always celibate priests or monks might have gotten his oar in.

How a man's second name came about and ended up being his family name did not matter, just that that he had to have one to serve in the Company. Having a second name was necessary so that everyone would know for sure exactly who was giving an order and who exactly was supposed to carry it out.

Most of the time a man's second name was whatever name was assigned by the clerk who enrolled him based on what little the clerk could find out about the new man in a very short interview. As you might imagine, since every village had at least one smith and many had a miller to grind its grain, it resulted in quite a few men making their marks on the Company roll with family names of Smith and Miller and quite a few men whose names ended in "son" such as Robinson or Richardson or Johnson because they were the sons of Robin or Richard or John.

****** *Lieutenant William Courtenay*

Our hours of carefully rowing up the gently flowing Fowey was a great relief for almost everyone after our long voyage from Cyprus and the brief scare we had enjoyed when we met the French fleet coming toward us in the channel. But it was certainly not a pleasure for me; I had to spend the entire trip up the river on the roof of Ninety-two's forward castle. That was because it was my responsibility as my galley's lieutenant to make sure that we safely moved up the ever-narrowing and constantly twisting river without running aground or getting our hull punctured by a rock or something floating in the river.

As you might imagine, I was intensely alert the whole time and rightly so; it would not do much for my future in the Company if we got stuck on a sandbar or our hull got punctured so that we took on water and sank. Accordingly, I remained on the roof of the forward deck castle throughout the day and spent it talking to Sergeant Pew and watching the green and densely forested countryside pass slowly by except, of course, when I need to run aft and take a quick piss.

We made it even though I had never previously taken a galley up the Fowey, or any other river for that matter. That was only because I had been learnt at the Company school what a captain or lieutenant should do under such circumstances. Accordingly, I gave the order I knew the crew hoped it would hear from a lieutenant who had never before had been responsible for seeing a galley safely move up a river.

"Take us up the river, Sailing Sergeant, and for God's sake be careful not to run us aground!" *I did not become a relatively young lieutenant by being stupid, did I?"*

What I did not add, and did not need to add because it was understood, was the unspoken rest of the sentence "for it will be both our arses if you put us on the strand or our hull gets punctured by a rock or a log floating in the river."

Due to my being learnt at school to rely on the veterans when I did not know what to do, and the sailing sergeant's ability and experience, we had a lovely trip up the Fowey in the warm sunshine, except when we got too close to the riverbank and got besieged by great swarms of the biting bugs that apparently lived along it. What I remember most about going up the river that day was how difficult it was to keep my mouth shut and not fangle whilst the sailing sergeant was giving his orders and how thick and fearful the bugs was that periodically swarmed around me and managed to bite my face and neck and entangle themselves in the hair of my head and beard.

Chapter Three

Another surprise.

We saw Restormel Castle towering above the trees along the river long before we saw its nearby village or the tents and buildings of the Company's training camp that spread out in front of the castle's outermost wall. The sight of the Company's great stronghold in the distance was both welcoming and inspiring.

A few minutes later we came around a bend in the river and there it was with all its power and glory and its nearby village and the Company's training camp for archers—Restormel Castle, the strong and lively beating heart at the very centre of the Company of Archers. It was just as I had remembered it from the many years I had spent at the Company school being filled up to my ears with Latin and summing.

Everyone began cheering and pumping their fists in the air when we came around the bend and saw our Company's great and powerful fortress in front of us, even the Commander, and especially the men who had been away in the east for many years. Many of them had tears in their eyes.

There was no surprise in everyone's response; being overcome with emotion was so was inevitable and so heartfelt amongst those few who had survived years in the east and run the Moorish gauntlet to return that cheering the castle and its camp when they saw it had long ago become a Company tradition. We were celebrating our safe return and rightly so.

In the distance there was a clap of thunder and a great cloud of black smoke rose from beside the outermost of the castle's three curtain walls. It was a sound familiar to every archer and unique to Restormel. We were truly home and the thunder was either a welcome or yet another attempt to make gold out of lead or throw stones out of a ribald, or perhaps both or all three.

Strangely enough, and despite my cheering I felt no real emotion. It was as if I was standing outside my body looking at the castle and everything and everybody in sight including myself.

****** *Lieutenant William Courtenay*

About fifteen minutes after we first sighted Restormel in the distance we slowly and carefully made our way to the only floating wharf along the riverbank that was not in use. The other two wharfs had galleys moored to them. One of the two galleys was obviously the training galley. The other was Company Galley Number Sixty-nine, one of the slightly smaller older-style Moorish-built galleys we had taken out of Algiers as a prize a few years earlier. Both looked to be carefully maintained. So did Ninety-two for that matter; our sail having been re-sewn by our galley's sail maker during the hours it took us to come up the river.

I had no idea why Sixty-nine was here and I knew no one in her crew, but I was not surprised to see it here since I knew we usually had two or three galleys in these waters at any given time during the sailing season. They were here because of there was always a steady stream of Company galleys carrying passengers, cargos, and money orders to and from England and various destinations east of Gibraltar such as Rome, the Holy Land, and Constantinople.

Even so, Sixty-nine's presence was a bit surprising since I had been led to understand that the rise of the Moorish pirates had resulted in only our newer and faster galleys being used on the voyages through the western Mediterranean. Obviously I was wrong; perhaps we still did not yet have enough of the bigger and faster new-builds in service.

Our arrival at the floating wharf was greeted by another round of heartfelt cheering and waving. It was another tradition and this time it came from the people who had turned out to welcome us. A great crowd of people had gathered to greet us and more were hurrying down the well-maintained cart path that ran up to the castle. A few were waving their hands about as they talked to each other but most were silently watching and smiling expectantly—until we bumped up against the wharf; then the crowd exploded into cheers and great welcoming shouts. We had made it home!

It was a typical Restormel welcome for archers returning from the Holy Land and for some reason I think I appreciated it more than ever. It was nothing new for Commander Robertson, of course, because he went east on his annual inspection voyage every year when the leaves began to fall off the trees and returned every year when the buds of the new leaves began to spring out of the winter-deadened branches. But this was only my second return voyage to Restormel since I first went out to the east. That was ten years ago right after I had finished my first four years on active duty with the Company's horse archers at Okehampton on the border between Cornwall and Devon. As you might imagine, I cheered with the best of them and I surely meant it.

And then for a fleeting moment after I finished shouting I remembered the first time I returned with my infant son after Anne, my dear wife who had gone east with me those many years ago had been taken by the plague. She like so many of the archers that went east would never return. Perhaps the Church is right and that her passing was God's Will; I found it hard to believe.

******

My uncle, Thomas Courtenay, the Earl of Cornwall and one of the Company's retired assistant commanders, was in the front row of our greeters on the riverbank. Another white-haired older man I did not recognize, at least not at first, was standing next to him.

Uncle Thomas suddenly recognized me. He smiled and waved cheerfully and shouted "Hoy William; see you soon" as he began moving toward the floating wharf as soon as the boarding plank banged down on it. He was obviously was going to be the first man to come aboard. *And, thank you Jesus, he did not have the sad look on his face that almost certainly would have been there if he was bringing me bad news about my son.*

My uncle hurried across the bobbing and pitching little wharf to the boarding plank as soon as it fell on to the wharf with a loud bang. He quickly ran across the bobbing and pitching wharf and carefully made his way up the wet and slippery boarding plank to the galley's deck.

But instead of coming toward me with a welcoming smile he headed straight for Commander Boatman with a serious look on his face. He must have caught the Commander's eye before coming aboard because the Commander had already come down to the deck from the roof of the forward deck castle and was standing on the deck near the boarding plank waiting for him.

The white-haired older man who looked vaguely familiar had been standing next to Uncle Thomas in the crowd and followed him on to the floating wharf. He staggered across it and almost fell off into the water as he came up the boarding plank right behind my uncle. The wharf's unsteadiness and bobbing and pitching were caused by a large number of surprisingly anxious archers who were jumping down on to it and going in the opposite direction to get to their waiting families and friends. It was a wonder no one fell into the river.

I finally recognized the man with my uncle and I was truly surprised when I did. It was Lieutenant Commander Robert Black, the Commander's soon-to-retire number two who was usually to be found at Okehampton with the Company's horse archers he commanded.

Commander Black had changed markedly since I had last seen him several years earlier on my previous return when I brought my son back to Cornwall to be raised by my uncle's wife. His hair and beard were now as white as snow and his back was bent. But what was truly surprising was that he was *not* wearing an archer's tunic with his lieutenant commander's stripes on its front and back. The absence of his archer's tunic was a great surprise. Something was definitely afoot.

Unfortunately neither I nor anyone else on the castle roof with me had any idea as to what might be in the wind. But we immediately knew it was something significant because the two men pushed their way through the crowd of archers who were waiting to go ashore and hurried up to the Commander—and when they reached him they promptly began excitedly whispering in his ear.

We could tell they were greatly excited because both them had their heads close to the Commander's and were waving their arms about as they spoke. And both of them were so excited that they were both trying to talk at the same time.

The Commander obviously agreed that what they were telling him was important. He was leaning toward them and listening intently, very intently, to whatever it was he was hearing. And from the look on his face it was clear to everyone that whatever he was hearing had surprised him.

"Hmm. Does anyone know what has gotten those two so excited? someone standing behind me on the castle roof asked in a drawling voice full of irony and false boredom. No one answered.

A few moments after Uncle Thomas and Lieutenant Commander Black had begun speaking to him, Commander Boatman jerked his head in surprise, looked about, and then motioned for the two captains standing on the castle roof near me to come down and join him.

They immediately did so and rather quickly since it was obvious that important news had been received. A moment later the Commander began walking to the very front of the galley with the four men following close behind. As he walked he looked up at me over his shoulder and jerked his head with a little "come on" motion whilst twirling his upraised pointing finger in a little circle.

I got the message; I too was to join the Commander. I jumped down to the deck from the castle roof and trotted across it to join him and the captains. As I did I could see that my uncle and the lieutenant commander were still talking and gesturing and Commander Boatman was continuing to listen quite intently. From the way the Commander was standing and the look on his face it was clear that he had an intense interest in what he was hearing. There was no doubt behind my eyes; something important must have happened.

"Say again what you just told me, Lieutenant Commander Black, but make sure only these men can hear you."

Lieutenant Commander Black? Commander Boatman had gone formal and issued a caution at the same time. Whatever it might be, we all instantly knew it was serious.

Chapter Four
England in turmoil.

What we heard was quite astonishing. There were two bishop-led delegations of knights and royal courtiers waiting to see the Commander—and they both wanted something from the Company. One apparently wanted to employ the Company to help King Edward's supporters defend him against his many enemies; the other, or so it seemed, represented the Queen and wanted to employ the Company to help them bring the King down and put his young son and heir, also named Edward, on the throne in his place.

Both possibilities sounded more than a little risky, particularly in the unlikely event we ended up on the losing side, but the leaders of both delegations had implied they had brought a considerable amount of coins with them to pay for the Company's services if an agreement could be reached. Coins and the possibility of a lot of them? There was no doubt in anyone's mind that whatever it was they wanted should at least be considered.

"It was only by the grace of God and some fast-riding outriders that I was able to keep our two groups of visitors apart," said Lieutenant Commander David Black, the Company's elderly number two. "So far as I can tell neither of them knows the other is here and our men do not know the purpose of their visits or their significance."

Lieutenant Commander Black had a smile and a look of personal pride and satisfaction on his face as he waved his hands about and explained what he had done.

"First I told King Edward's men, the Bishop of Coventry and a young man by the name of Hugh Despenser who claims to be the Earl of Winchester, that the Company had always been loyal to the king, and that I was sure you would want to speak to them as soon as you reached Cornwall. I told him your arrival was expected imminently. He agreed to wait for you up at the horse camp when I told him there was plague in Okehampton and Cornwall. Despenser and the Bishop of Coventry have half a dozen knights and sergeants from the King's guards and a couple of priests with them. They also have some servants with them.

"Later that very same day I told the two men leading a much smaller party of Queen's men, a man who named himself as Simon Bereford and said he is the Bishop of Lincoln, and a Sir Hugh Turpington who apparently is commanding the Bishop's guards and servants, just the reverse—that I could not be sure but that I thought it possible that you shared their concerns about the King and his chancellor.

"I also told them that your arrival was imminent and that you liked to hold your important private meetings at the Company-owned *Red Horse* Tavern and courier change station because it was about half way between Restormel and the Company's next courier station and tavern, the *Three Bells*, on the Cornwall side of the River Tamar ford. Meeting important people in such an isolated spot, I told them, is something you like to do because it keeps your meetings and the names of those who attend them away from the ears of the King's spies who infest Cornwall.

"Bishop Bereford and Sir Hugh became quite concerned when they heard that the King had a lot of spies in Cornwall. That is understandable because what they are doing is obviously treason most foul and they will surely be topped if King Edward ever gets his hands on them. Bereford, the Bishop of Lincoln that is, immediately told me that secrecy was also important to him and Sir Hugh and agreed that meeting secretly with you at such an isolated location was probably a good idea under the circumstances.

"As a result, I invited the Queen's bishop and his party off to come across the Tamar and wait for you at the *Red Horse* along with a dozen horse archers to help protect him. He and Sir Hugh accepted the archers with many thanks when I explained that adding some of our men to their party was necessary so that they would have enough men to defend themselves if they were attacked by either the King's men or one of Cornwall's many bands of starving robbers.

"Indeed, I made much of the fact that robbers were everywhere looking for food and coins to buy it because people are always hungry as a result of Cornwall's lands being so poor and the crops having failed again. Then I explained to them why Cornwall's lands being so poor also meant that Cornwall never had many men available for the King's armies—because those that were not working as tin miners for the King either had to join monasteries or go east as archers in order to earn their daily bread.

"I thought telling him about all the problems and dangers might discourage him and cause him to leave empty-handed. But it did not; he said Lord Mortimer had ordered him to come to Cornwall and try to hire men from the Company of Archers as mercenaries and he was determined to do so. In any event, it seems that Bishop

Bereford and Sir Hugh really think the Queen and Mortimer have a chance of winning and putting her son on the throne in place of King Edward."

We all smiled and chuckled when we heard what the Lieutenant Commander told the Queen's men. It was the Company's familiar tall tale about Cornwall and its terrible poverty compared to the rest of England. What the Lieutenant Commander had done and said was immediately understood and appreciated by every man who heard him. That was because the telling of such stories was part of the Company's continuous effort to gull whoever was England's king into not wasting his time by asking Cornwall to pay taxes or provide him with men to fight his wars.

The Company would not risk the loss of its men to fight for either the King or the Queen or pay any taxes, of course, but it was always better never to be asked in the first place. At least that is what we were learnt at the Company school. Even better, the stories that we deliberately spread about Cornwall being so poor also helped discourage nobles and priests from coming into Cornwall to seek their fortunes and then trying to interfere with the Company's operations. It had periodically been a problem in the past but not lately.

Commander Boatman closed his eyes and thought for a few moments about what he had heard. Then he opened them and spoke the words that ended up changing my life.

"You acted wisely, Lieutenant Commander Black. Thank you." ... . "Alright lads, what do you think we should do? You first, Lieutenant Courtenay, being as you are the most junior."

Damn; I knew it. He always starts with the most junior man so he will not be influenced by the thoughts of his betters. It is what we were learnt to do in the Company school, of course, but I did not like having to go first and make a fool of myself.

"Um, I am not sure which side we should support, Commander. It might be best to support neither side in case the other wins or, perhaps even better, we should try to gull them *both* into giving us their coins and then actually do so little for either of them such that the other does not notice and has no reason to get upset with us."

"What is that you say, Lieutenant? Gull them *both* into paying us and then do nothing that would distress the other. How could we do that?" the Commander demanded of me. His eyes were very intent. Later I was willing to swear, only to myself, of course, that his eyes almost glittered like stars in the sky as he rounded on me.

As you might imagine, I did not have a clue as to how we might accomplish what I had just suggested and felt like a fool for having mentioned it. What I should have done, of course, was suggest that the Commander do the safe thing and be called back to Cyprus on an emergency related to the Moors or something to that effect *before* he could make a decision. That is what we had been learnt in school.

To my surprise the idea that we should at least try to simultaneously extract coins from both the king and his enemies without actually helping either of them fight the other turned out to be of great interest to the Commander. He announced his decision after had had listened to everyone's thoughts and concerns.

"Lieutenant Courtenay may well be right that we might be able to lighten both of their coin sacks without taking too many risks. In any event, we have nothing to lose by talking to our visitors to find out what it is they would want the Company to do for them and how much they are willing to pay us to do it."

Everyone, of course, immediately agreed with him.

******

I had just finished visiting my son who was now old enough to be able to walk but did not seem to recognize me or care about me. If it had not been for his flaming red hair being the same colour as my father's I would not have recognized him.

Aunt Eleanor greeted me with a great deal of reserve and barely a peck on my cheek and a perfunctory hug. Her coolness surprised me because she was usually so warm. Everything changed for the better, however, when I told her how grateful I was to know that my son was in her care would always be well taken care of no matter what happened to me in the future. The relief on her face was obvious and I finally understood; she had been afraid I had returned to take my son away with me.

Visiting my son somehow depressed my spirits even though I could see he was loved and well cared for. As a result, I had spent several hours walking around in Restormel's baileys looking at everything and seeing nothing whilst waiting for supper to begin in the castle's great hall. I was very much on edge and quite anxious; but I did not know why.

I was still walking about aimlessly when Captain Robertson's apprentice sergeant found me. He said he had been sent to inform me that I was to accompany Commander Boatman, Lieutenant Commander Black, and Captain Robertson, the Commander's personal aide, to the *Red Horse* in the morning to meet with the people claiming to represent the Queen. From there we would ride on to the Company's horse farm to meet with the King's representatives.

Sergeant Starner's news elated me. I pressed him for the details but the only thing he could tell me was that a fast-riding messenger, one of the Company's outriders, had been sent ahead to tell the Queen's people that Commander Boatman had just reached Restormel and would be riding out to meet with them first thing in the morning as soon as the sun reached us.

According to Sergeant Starner, we would begin riding out to the *Red Horse* in the morning as soon as we finished breaking our overnight fasts. I knew that if we did that and rode steadily with nothing going wrong to delay us we would be able to reach the *Red Horse* before the sun finished passing overhead on its daily voyage around the earth. In other words, we should arrive in time for supper. *I did not say anything about it to the sergeant, of course, but hopefully we will not have to ride in the rain as a wet saddle inevitable turns my arse red and causes it to hurt most fierce.*

What we were learnt later that evening whilst supping in Restormel's great hall was that Queen's men were being offered little in the way of food and drink to buy in order to drive home the idea that Cornwall was so poor. As a result, we would be bringing with us the meat and cheese for our supper and theirs as well as enough for the next day's meals and several skins of French wine.

We were bringing the food and drink with us because we would almost certainly be supping with our visitors who, thanks to Lieutenant Commander Black's quick thinking, were deliberately being fed rather poorly. He had apparently arranged for them to be sparsely provided with inadequate food and drink in order to further support the Company's claim that Cornwall was a land so poor that it could neither pay taxes nor support nobles, knights, and priests like them.

Feeding both the Queen's men and the King's men short rations and watered ale was Lieutenant Commander Black's idea to help further convince our visitors that Cornwall was very poor. It was also his idea to keep both of new arrivals away from our strongholds so they could not see their strengths or the quality of our men and their weapons. As you might imagine, the lieutenant commander was clearly quite proud of himself for having come up with such fine deceptions on short notice and got quite puffed up when Commander Boatman congratulated him for his quick thinking.

More importantly, the effort to gull the Queen's men seemed to be working. If the report that had come in from the archers who were protecting them was correct. They said the Queen's men were worried most fearful that the King's men would come to arrest them and quite unhappy with just about everything else at the *Red Horse*. They were, in a word, impatient to get themselves away to the safety of a fortress with thick walls and were making general nuisances of themselves with their constant complaints about having to wait and the about meagre amounts of food and ale they were being offered and its poor quality

Lieutenant Commander Black had a big smile on his face that evening as he passed on the report about our visitors' fears and shortages and the size of their coin sacks to those of us who were supping with him in the great hall. And, of course, we all laughed when we heard them, even the apprentice sergeant—because we all knew that hell would freeze over before the King's men or anyone else would be able to ride into Cornwall and arrest someone without the Company's permission.

Our Queen-supporting visitors, or so it seemed at the time, were totally ignorant of the true state of affairs in Cornwall or the Company's intentions and abilities. It was all very encouraging and we assured each other that those representing the King were no doubt similarly concerned and misinformed. It was a mistake, of course, but we meant well and had already had too much to drink by the time we began talking about the King and his men.

One thing was certain; eating fresh food and drinking good ale and wine in Restormel's great hall was a welcome relief after so many days at sea. We were able to sup together in the hall that night because earlier, after a long private discussion between Commander Boatman and Lieutenant Commander Black, it had been announced that we would wait until first thing in the morning before setting out to visit the Queen's men at the *Red Horse*.

Commander Boatman also decided that when we did set out for the *Red Horse* in the morning we would carry our own food and drink with us and that our longbows were to be kept out of sight in their leather rain cases. It meant that each of us would only be seen to be armed with a short sword and carrying a galley shield.

The Commander also informed us that we would *not* be bringing any bladed pikes with us, both because there was little chance we would be encountering a force of charging knights in Cornwall and also because we did not the Queen's men to know that we were equipped with modern weapons such as longbows and bladed pikes and knew how to use them.

Captain Robertson explained things even further that night after we finished eating and prepared to settle down and sleep for the night. He waited until after the Commander had left the table to go up the stone stairs to his family's rooms and so had my uncle and my aunt and son. By the time he did Lieutenant Commander Black had already gotten his sleeping skins and retired for the night at the far end of the hall where the candle light did not reach. He looked tired.

"Our being armed with swords and shields to protect ourselves and eating well whilst Cornwall's unarmed commoners starve is what the Queen's men would expect since that is what they would most likely be doing if they were walking in our sandals. So the Commander wants us to behave as they would when he meets with them. Besides, he is not about to eat the slop they are being served if he does not have to do so. Neither am I for that matter."

And then with a big smile and a twinkle in his eye the Commander's senior aide lowered his voice and with a twinkle in his eyes slyly added something new for us to consider and be pleased to know.

"At least the Commander will be able to spend the night with his wife before he rides off to visit with our illustrious visitors, eh? So waiting until morning to set out to visit the Queen's men is truly the right decision for him to have made. A bigger terror than the Moors is what Mistress Alice is when she is ignored."

Chapter Five
An unexpected tragedy.

We slept on the hard stone floor of Restormel's great hall that night and rode out very early the next morning. We mounted our horses and departed immediately after we broke our overnight fasts and thirsts with a couple of bowls of morning ale and all the burnt bread with butter and eggs we could eat. It was the traditional "all you can eat" first meal of the day at the nearby Company school I and the other had attended as boys. As you might imagine, it brought back many pleasant memories and we told each other stories from our school days as we broke our overnight fasts.

The "we" who rode out together in the morning consisted of the Commander, Lieutenant Commander Black, Captain Robertson, me, and two apprentice sergeants, one of whom was newly graduated from the Company school. Four tough-looking outriders came with us to act as our messengers and guards. Our little company was, not to put too fine a point on it, "rank heavy" and strong enough that it was unlikely to be bothered by anyone we might meet on the road. Commander Boatman was our captain because he had the highest rank.

We mounted up and rode out at dawn because the Commander was determined to make it all the way to the *Red Horse* in one day. The night's rain had stopped and the sun was just beginning to arrive as we pissed one last time in the inner bailey's piss pot, and then mounted the horses that the castle's hostlers were holding for us. The horses were waiting on the cobblestones in front of the main door into the castle's citadel and its great hall where I had eaten and spent the night.

My uncle, the Earl, and his wife and the Commander's wife came out to see us off despite the early hour. The Earl lived in his family's rooms on one of the two liveable upper floors of the citadel and the Commander and his family in their rooms on the other floor. My son was holding my aunt's hand and sucking on his thumb.

The only man who had sat with us at the previous night's supping who was not there to see us off was James Thorpe, the Bishop of Cornwall. He was absent due to attending to one his traditional duties associated with the Company school—seeing that the boys were fed as much food as they wanted to eat at each meal because it seemed to help the boys grow bigger just as more food did for calves and colts. Bishop Thorpe had himself attended the school and, although it was not widely known and certainly not at Windsor or in Rome, he held the rank of major captain in the Company after an illustrious career as a Company spy whilst working at Windsor as a cleric in the papal nuncio's household and then in Rome for a Spanish Cardinal.

We had been surprised to learn whilst supping the previous night that both the Earl and the Commander were in the process of building more comfortable places for their families to live outside the castle's walls, meaning something that was significantly less cold, damp, and draughty than their rooms in the castle's citadel. They were both building large walled manors in the Roman style, according to my uncle, except they would have a fireplace in every room and at least two floors so their sleeping rooms would be above the dangerous night airs. We heard all about it because Bishop Thorpe said his wife was jealous and wanted one too.

Living in a nice house outside a castle's walls was a new idea even though it was common in the east. I thought it very interesting, if only because our strongholds always seemed to be so damp and cold and full of windy draughts. If it actually came to pass, it might mean that my son would grow up in a warmer and more comfortable home before he went off to live at the Company school.

Our horses were all good amblers from the Company's horse farm in one of the moors north of Okehampton where the King's men were waiting. Those of us with rank had remounts but did not lead them; the four outriders would lead them along with their own remounts. It was good that we had so many, remounts that is, because we were bringing supplies of food and drink with us and the remounts were also carrying our cased longbows and our quivers. The junior of the two apprentice sergeants also led an extra remount in case one of the horses assigned to his betters unexpectedly broke down.

I was leery about having to ride so far in one day and rightly so; it had been several years since I had boarded a horse and more than ten since I had made my mark on the Company's roll as an apprentice sergeant and served a four year term at Okehampton with the horse archers. On the other hand, I knew as soon as I saw him that the grey gelding I had been given was a good one. Unfortunately I also knew that no matter how good he was my arse was going to be sore and rubbed red by the time the day ended even if it did not rain; if it did rain it would almost certainly be even worse.

Commander Boatman led the way as we rode out of Restormel with Lieutenant Commander Black at his side. The lieutenant commander looked terrible but he was spryly waving his hands about as he spoke with the Commander. I knew he was having problems because he was red-faced and had kept getting up to piss all night long. Sleeping on the stone floor of a great hall instead of on a proper string bed will do that to a man even if he is wrapped in his own sleeping skins and his head is resting on his tunic hood comfy-like.

We rode in a double file at a slow amble through Restormel's three baileys and clattered over the three drawbridges that crossed the moats that each of the castle's great stone curtain walls. Our galley shields were slung over our shoulders and our short swords were in sheathes attached to our belts. Our longbows, quivers full of arrows, sacks of personal food, and our personal sleeping skins were all slung over our horses' backs or lashed on to the saddled remounts which were temporarily being used as supply carriers.

It was early and the sun was barely up. Even so, the castle's three bailies were already full of men and women going about their daily chores and duties. Also, and somewhat of a pain for me to see, there were a surprisingly large number of mothers with children in the outer bailey where many of the archers lived with their families.

Most of the men we saw were wearing archers' tunics. They quickly stopped whatever they were doing and knuckled their heads to salute the Commander as we rode past them. They were not surprised to see us because the word was out; they knew we were riding to the *Red Horse* and on to Okehampton but they did not know why. Rumours of all sorts were undoubtedly flying.

There were great white clouds scattered above us but, thank goodness, rain did not appear to be in the immediate future. On the other hand, it looked to be coming a very warm day such that we would likely be sweating a lot in the hours ahead; and sweat was sometimes even harder on a rider's arse than rain. There was no doubt about it; mine was going to be sore either way. For the first time in a long time I remembered why I had been so pleased years ago when I was promoted to Major Sergeant and was able to transfer from the horse archers to serve as a foot archer on sea duty.

Our ride was not too warm initially even though it was a summer day and there was no rain. In fact, it was quite pleasant for the first few hours. I rode next to Captain Robertson, the Commander's long-time senior aide, and we soon struck up a conversation. Looking back on it I can see that he was questioning me quite closely. I did not, unfortunately, realize it at the time and in response to his questions chattered away about many things including some quite personal such as my ambitions and how I thought the loss of my wife and daughter to the plague several years earlier would affect me.

"Losing most of my family hurt immensely and I would be telling a lie if I said otherwise," I admitted as our horses ambled along the road. "I miss them greatly. On the other hand, my son is particularly well-cared for and my being alone in the world does give me more freedom to go places and do things that I might otherwise not do and to take chances I might not otherwise take."

Without knowing it at the time, I had once again opened my mouth and put my foot in it.

******

The Company-owned *Red Horse* tavern and the couriers' way station attached to it were about half way between Restormel and the next Company-owned tavern and couriers' way station, the *Three Bells* at the Tamar ford. The road between them was in good shape despite the constant rains and the streams that ran across it. And that day it was frequently crowded with walkers and wagons going in both directions.

Despite the crowded road we made good time and were usually able to ride two-abreast and talk as our horses ambled. It was neither raining nor was I sweating, both which I knew from my past experiences and schooling was a good thing; wet tunics and saddles, for some reason, cause a rider's arse to rub harder and turn red and sore even faster than when the weather is dry and cold.

One reason we were able to move so fast was because we were able to almost constantly keep our horses in a comfortable mile-eating easy amble. Another was that most of the time, except when the road ran through heavily forested areas, we could move a few paces off the road and out into the fields and pastures along it to ride around the wagons and carts we encountered.

What was encouraging as we rode, at least to me and I think to the others, was the response of the people we met along the way; it was inevitably friendly and cheerful. In addition to the travellers, the fields were full of franklins and their women and children ploughing and harvesting.

It was an interesting ride. Several times we had to ride around large gaggles of geese with nobbled wings being herded down the road by young boys and girls with herding sticks, and once we were slowed to a walk by a great flock of sheep that filled a stretch of the road where we could not ride out and around them.

I mentioned the people's apparent good will and friendliness to Captain Robertson and he agreed. He also agreed with my observation that it was good thing the Queen's men had travelled in the rain and only gone as far as the *Red Horse*; if they had gone farther into Cornwall's countryside when the weather was as nice as it is today they would have known we were misleading them with lies about Cornwall's poverty and might have wondered why.

All in all it was an easy ride. We talked as we rode and I periodically practiced bringing my wrist knives out and every hour or so we stopped to take a quick piss or shite. Usually we did so when there was a stream running across the road so we could water our horses and our arses at the same time. Our other breaks happened when the Commander stopped to chat with people we met along the way. According to Captain Robertson, stopping to talk with people on the road was something the Commander routinely did in his travels in order to get a feel for the people and their problems.

The Cornish people we encountered and saw in the fields had been quite friendly to the Company for as long as anyone could remember and today was no exception. It probably helped their good spirits that the sun was out. In any event, they mostly waved and smiled and sometimes ran over to the road when they recognized the Commander and wanted to talk to him.

When they did talk they mostly talked about the weather and their crops and, more than a few times about a son who was serving in the Company's ranks or had once done so and was gone. Once we stopped briefly in a little village of three or four families whilst the Commander settled a minor dispute over the use of its common pasture.

Our amblers made good time despite our brief stops and it soon became clear we would reach the *Red Horse* before the sun finished moving west and disappeared over the horizon. That was good news because there is nothing worse than having to sleep outside in the rain that would inevitably sooner or later begin falling since we were in Cornwall, especially when you are travelling without a wagon to sleep in or under.

Overall, our ride was mostly pleasant even though I could feel my arse began to turn red and bother me despite my tunic and saddle not being wet. I could not see that it had turned red, of course, but I could feel it and knew what was happening. As a result I spent most of the last three hours of our ride standing in my stirrups whenever possible.

And I was not the only one standing in his stirrups and getting worn down by it. By the time we reached the *Red Horse* just about everyone had a sore arse and was standing in their saddles. The four outriders were the exception; they had hard arses from constantly riding and were clearly amused at our discomfort and trying hard not to show it.

******

We caught sight of the *Red Horse* as soon as we came out of a little stand of trees. It was a welcome sight and the steady stream of smoke pouring out of its chimney instead of drifting up through its thatched roof was somehow quite comforting. I was more than ready to call it a day and have a bowl of ale and something more to eat to go with the cheese and bread we had been periodically taking from our saddle sacks and nibbling on as we rode. Not having to eat it in a smoke-filled room was a bonus and greatly appreciated. It was early in September in the year 1326 and it had not rained all day.

A long line of horses were moored to the skinny tethering log that ran along in front of the *Red Horse.* That was to be expected since our visitors were all on horseback and there were a dozen or so horse archers there to protect them. Also tied to the log were the two fresh horses that were always saddled and moored there as remounts for the next courier. They were always at the hitching post saddled and ready for the courier to climb aboard one of them and ride off leading the other.

Everything always happened quickly when one or both of the two fresh horses were needed: The arriving courier would inevitably leap off his tired horse, piss while he was gulping down a hastily fetched bowl of ale, and then gallop off riding one of the fresh horses and leading the other as a remount in case the horse he was riding faltered. Even better, at least so far as the couriers were concerned, sometimes there would be a fresh rider available and waiting. Then the arriving courier would gallop up, hand off his courier's pouch to the waiting fresh rider who would gallop off even before the new arrival dismounted.

Our arrival must have been noted because men lounging about outside the building got to their feet and others began coming out of the *Red Horse.* Many of them, but certainly not all, were wearing archers' tunics. Most of the archers were wearing the two stripes of chosen men or the three stripes of sergeants. The horse archers had either sent some of their steadiest long-serving veterans to "protect" our visitors from Cornwall's dangers and any of the King's men who might be lurking about or, and even more likely under the circumstances, they had used their seniority to get away from their wives and Okehampton for a few days.

It happened just as we were dismounting in front of the *Red Horse*. Lieutenant Commander Black just tipped over to starboard and fell out of his saddle. Even before he hit the ground everyone who saw him go down knew it was serious.

Just about everyone who saw it happen rushed to him and the lieutenant commander was soon surrounded by a rapidly growing crowd. The first men to reach him tried to raise him up. One of them slapped his face in a vain effort to wake him; another shook him. Then they shook their heads and climbed to their feet; they knew he was gone because his eyes were open and unseeing.

"Dead before he hit the ground, the poor old sod," said one of the sergeants mournfully. It was a bit strange to hear the sorrow in his voice since the Lieutenant Commander had a reputation as hard taskmaster who was feared more than he was loved. But it was no surprise; being around someone who has just died always seems to change how he was viewed by those who knew him.

"My uncle was the same," another man said as the men gathered around the Lieutenant Commander. "One minute he was in his field cutting hay with a scythe and the next minute he was on the ground dead as a door nail."

A man still in the process of donning a bishop's robe and putting a mitre on his head hurried out of tavern's door with a partially armoured knight right behind him. It was uncommonly warm to be wearing heavy robes and armour so it was likely they heard the sound of our arrival and quickly began putting them on in order to make sure Commander Boatman would be appropriately impressed by their ranks and importance.

The man wearing the bishop's robe and mitre hurried toward the fallen man whilst making the sign of the cross. He obviously recognized the dead man because he then made a mistake that subsequently cost him dearly—by callously inquiring about something he considered more important than a dead archer.

"Did he bring the archers' commander?"

Commander Boatman meanwhile had dismounted and pushed his way through the crowd to see for himself what had happened. The men wearing hats and caps were already removing them as he did. Everyone was just standing about helplessly and talking to each other quietly with a bit of excitement in their voices as is usually the case in such a sad situation.

The Commander himself had been wearing a crude farmworker's hat woven out of straw to keep the sun out of his eyes and off the bald spot on the top of his head. He stood for a few moments shaking his head whilst looking down at the fallen man. Then he took it off his hat slowly and dropped it at his feet whilst shaking his head sadly— then he raised both hands and began praying loudly in Latin as all the men gathered around the body, except the bishop, dropped to their knees.

As the Commander prayed the bishop began making his way through the now-kneeling men to join him; and was promptly and summarily ordered by a hard look and a motion of the Commander's open hand to step back and keep his mouth shut.

When the Commander finished his prayer in Latin and everyone sorrowfully joined him is saying "Amen," Commander Boatman looked around and said all that needed to be said.

"He was a fine archer and a good friend; we will miss him."

By then the Bishop of Lincoln was nowhere to be seen; he and Sir Hugh had gone back inside the tavern to wait for the Commander to join them.

******

Everyone including the alewife waited outside the *Red Horse* whilst the Commander and Captain Robertson met privately with the Bishop of Lincoln and the knight who was riding with him. The meeting began immediately whilst the food we had brought with us was taken to the tavern's kitchen to be cooked.

The kitchen was immediately behind the tavern and the cooking was done by the tavern keeper and his wife who had been summoned to do so from the nearby village. They had been temporarily exiled whilst the Queen's men occupied the tavern and the archers with them slept in the stable. It seemed as if the burning of the chicken meat we had brought with us in our saddle sacks took forever because we were so hungry, at least I was; but it was actually not very long before the delicious odours of baking bread and burning meat filled the air.

Everyone except the four men in the meeting were gathered around the kitchen by the time the first flatbreads began coming off the beaten iron plate that the tavern keeper's wife had laid across the top of the kitchen's fire. They were subsequently joined by French loaves and strips of burned chicken and sheep.

The distribution of the food was interesting to watch because everyone was on their best behaviour—without a single order being given we all got in a single long line regardless of our ranks and were handed food as soon as it was ready. And then we took it and moved to the end of the line and ate it whilst we waited to reach the front of the line to get some more. There was no ale because the alewife's barrel with the ready in it was in the tavern where our betters were meeting and no one was brave enough to interrupt the Commander long enough to put a lid on the barrel and roll it out of the tavern.

The day was coming dark and many men were still eating when the Commander's initial meeting with the Queen's representatives broke up. We first knew the meeting had ended when Commander Boatman came out and began looking around for someone—and then, God forbid, he saw me and gestured with a nod of his head that I should join him as he walked away from the crowd of men who were yarning with each other in little groups in front of the *Red Horse* whilst they ate and waited for the ale that the alewife had begun fetching.

Commander Boatman got right to the point.

"Lieutenant, I have just informed Bishop Bereford and Sir Hugh Turpington that the Company would *not* be able to provide any men for the Queen to employ as mercenaries in her coming war with the King and his supporters. I told them that we would *like* to support the Queen and assist her but, unfortunately, we could not no matter how many coins the Company was offered because we have so few men stationed in Cornwall.

"I also lied a bit and claimed that even if we did have men available I could not *order* any of them to serve the Queen despite my great willingness to help her in any way I could. The men could not be ordered to do so, I told them, because it was in the contract on which the men of the Company made their marks that they would only be stationed in Cornwall or in the east in order to fight the Moors and assist pilgrims.

Then with a brief hint of a satisfied smile Command Boatman told me the outcome of the meeting.

"The Bishop of Lincoln, however, has agreed with my suggestion that a small company of about thirty English volunteers with a dependable captain might be recruited from the men who are willing to *leave* the Company to help guard the Queen's son, Prince Edward, from the undependable foreigners from the lowlands around Anvers who apparently make up the bulk of her army.

"I am also pleased to report that Bishop Bereford accepted my suggestion despite the large number of coins that would be immediately required to pay for the volunteers' services and compensate the Company for their loss. He did so when I pointed out that the Queen would, as a result of employing the volunteers, be safe so long as she stayed with her son and that her personal guards would then be freed up to fight in her army's ranks.

"I am happy to tell you that the Bishop of Lincoln and I have made our marks on a contract for one year for thirty men's services and that the payment for the entire year is being made as we speak. There will also be a substantial bonus of "success coins" if the prince is still alive at the end of the year.

"It had been my intention to send Captain Robertson to command the young Prince's English guards. But the death today of Lieutenant Commander Black changes everything. As a result of that sad tragedy I have promoted Captain Robertson to the rank of Major Captain to replace Lieutenant Commander Black at Okehampton Castle. Effectively immediately he will assume command of the Company's horse archers and be responsible for defending the approaches to Cornwall and keeping Cornwall free of robbers and troublemakers.

"Whoever is appointed to be the captain of the Prince's thirty guards will report to Major Captain Robertson. You will be interested to know that he has recommended you for that position and I have agreed subject to your acceptance of the appointment. It would mean an increase in your rank to that of captain. So do you want to accept the appointment and wear another stripe when you return to the Company or do you want to stay at Restormel with your son?"

I was astonished. *Captain!* There was nothing I could do but reply with what I knew to be the truth.

"My son is in good hands, much better than mine, Commander. So of course I will accept the appointment. I would be honoured to do so. And thank you to you and to Major Captain Robertson for giving me the opportunity. I will not let you down; you can count on it. *What else could I say, eh? Talk about being in the right place at the right time. Maybe my luck was changing.*

Chapter Six
My life is changed.

Everyone turned out less than an hour later to bid farewell to the Lieutenant Commander. His body had been hurriedly wrapped in his sleeping skins and was being sent to Okehampton in a wagon with a driver who knew the road and an escort of four horse archers. It would of necessity be a fast trip. It was already turning dark but they would leave immediately and travel at night whenever there was enough light from the moon and stars.

Normally an archer was buried where he fell so he would be remembered by his mates as he was before the body he left behind began to go foul. But in this case the Lieutenant Commander's home and family were close enough that if his escorts left immediately and travelled fast, including that night whenever there was enough light from the moon and stars, they would make it in time despite the warm weather.

I was still so excited by the news of my unexpected promotion that I barely heard the rest of what I was told— that the rest of us would leave the next morning, ride hard all day, and make it to Okehampton in time to be present for the burial prayers. That, at least, was the plan.

But then, upon seeing the preparations being made for the immediate departure of the body, Bishop Bereford and Sir Hugh requested another meeting with the Commander

and everything changed. Suddenly, a few minutes later, I could see the men accompanying the Bishop and Sir Hugh also begin preparing to leave immediately even though night had already fallen.
'

I was watching their preparations in the moonlight and wondering what was happening when Captain Robertson came out and walked over to where I was feeding my horse. I could see in the moonlight that the Captain had a strange, almost pleased look on his face. I assumed it meant he was coming to tell me that we would leaving as soon as possible, possibly tonight and certainly no later than in the morning and ride hard in order to be at Okehampton for the funeral service and burial.

But that was not it; the new major captain just gave me a funny look and told me why he had sought me out.

"The Commander wants to talk to you again, William. There has been a change in our plans. You are to report to him immediately. Follow me."

Oh my God; has he changed his mind about promoting me? Did the Queen's men change their minds about employing English guards for young Prince Edward? My mind was whirling like a drunken Scot.

******

I followed Major Captain Robertson as he walked rapidly into the tavern. He seemed to be in a hurry. The Commander was standing by a table holding a lighted candle lantern when we entered. There was a parchment on the table.

"The parchment is the Company's contract with the Queen's men for the releasing of thirty volunteers to guard young Prince Edward, Captain Courtenay. I want you to sit down and read it. And try to remember what you read."

I had been given a formal order so, as was required of me, I replied by repeating it back to prove I understood it.

"Aye Commander, I will sit down and read it and try to remember what it says," I said as I sat down on one of the stools that were placed around the table. As I did I moved the candle lantern closer so I could see what had been scribed on the parchment.

The contract was short and to the point and quite readable even though I had to squint and put my head close to the parchment because the letters in the words that had been scribed on it were so small that they were hard to read in the flickering light. When I finished I stood up and reported "I have read it, Commander and I believe I understand it."

It basically said that in return for a very large amount of coins thirty men would be allowed to resign from the Company and become the Prince's guards for one year. It also said that under no condition would they be expected to fight against the King or be under the orders of those who did. It also said that the Company would be paid a success bonus if Prince Edward was alive at the end of the twelve months. It also said that the Company would receive half the bonus coins immediately and return them if the Prince was either dead or captured.

Commander Robertson rolled up the parchment and tucked it under his arm as soon as I stood up. As he did he began giving me orders and explaining them.

"Bishop Bereford and Sir Hugh have heard about Lieutenant Commander Black's body being sent immediately back to Okehampton so he can be buried tomorrow with his wife present. They are now saying that if the body can leave immediately and travel at night, so can they and their men. Accordingly, they have informed me that they are going to leave immediately because they have so far to go and need to get there as soon as possible to prepare for the arrival of the Queen and her army."

Then he smiled and added an additional explanation.

"The real reason they want to leave immediately, of course, even though they do not want to admit it, is that they think Cornwall is dangerous because we told them about all the outlaws and the King's men who might be lurking about. They are particularly afraid of travelling by day for fear of being seen by some of the King's men and being captured or killed. In any event, they have decided to abandon the bishop's wagon and leave immediately with Bishop Bereford and his servants on horseback. And that means you must leave with them.

"Initially Bishop Bereford and Sir Hugh refused to tell me their destination, saying only that they were going where they expect to meet the Queen, Prince Edward, and Lord Mortimer who commands the Queen's army. But they relented and admitted they expected to meet them at the mouth of the river Orwell in Suffolk. They did so when I pointed out that the thirty English volunteers who they had just employed needed to know where to find you and Prince Edward so they could assume their duties.

"In any event, Suffolk is where the Bishop and Sir Hugh now say they are headed and expect the Queen's army to come ashore along with the Queen and Prince Edward. I want you to stay with them at least until they are out of Cornwall and past Okehampton. After that you and your men can go on to Suffolk alone although it might improve your subsequent relations with the Queen's supporters if you stay with the Queen's men and help them reach the Queen and her army.

"Bishop Bereford and his men will be leaving in a few minutes and you are to ride with them and assist them at least until they get past Okehampton and on to the London Road. You can take young Thomas Corn, the new apprentice sergeant, with you as your assistant and also two of the outriders. I have already sent someone to notify them to get ready and report to you immediately. Each of you is to take fresh horses from the stable and leave your tired ones behind.

"Thomas and the outriders should be fetching the horses as we speak, one for each of you to ride and a second to be your remounts. They have also been told to fetch a sack of oats for your horses and some bread and cheese so you will have something to eat until you reach the Company's *Three Bells* tavern and courier station at the Tamar ford.

"But what is really important is that you and your three men should take on board all the food and oats you can carry away from the *Three Bells* so, if necessary, you can get all the way to Suffolk with stopping to buy supplies. Hopefully, of course, you will be able to stop along the way and buy whatever you need. But these are strange times so you must not count on being able to do so."

At that point Commander Boatman paused for a moment to gather his thoughts, and then he told me about the men who would be in my company.

"When Major Captain Robertson and I get to Okehampton we will select the thirty archers who will volunteer to serve in your company and also a lieutenant to be your number two. We will do the selecting ourselves since you will need men who are proficient with galley swords and shields in addition to being good with their horses and longbows.

The volunteers will either catch up with you on the road or join you in Suffolk at the village of Ipswich at the mouth of the River Orwell. They will be bringing extra arrows with them; they will *not* be bringing pikes, however, because we do not want the knights on either side to know we have them and know how to use them.

"And, of course, you will need coins to pay your men and cover their expenses in the months ahead," the Commander said as he handed me two pouches heavy with silver and gold coins.

"You are," he told me, "to carry one of the coin pouches and keep it with you at all times. Your lieutenant is to carry the other pouch in case yours is somehow gets lost or taken. Thomas can it carry it for you until your lieutenant hooks up with you." More coins, Commander Boatman hastened to assure me, would be forthcoming if they were required.

Then, with Major Captain Robertson listening intently, the Commander gave me several orders that turned out to be important.

"I want you to keep me and Major Captain Robertson closely informed as to the plans of the Queen and, to the greatest extent possible about the plans and location of her army and Lord Mortimer. But only send the information verbally using one of your archers so there is never any evidence that the Company is involved.

"Also, and this is important, I want you to take off your stripes and always pretend to have permanently left the Company in order to guard the crown prince. The men I send to you will all be ordered to do and say the same.

"If you and your men are asked why you volunteered to protect the prince, and you almost certainly will be asked, you are always to say that you have heard many good things about the Queen's son and were tired of being in a company of miserly merchants, and also that you wanted to the captain of your own company so that you would be paid more and eat better."

"In other words, William, we want both the King and the Queen and their men to believe that you and the thirty archers we will be sending to you are totally out of the Company of Archers and are now in a free company of sword carrying mercenaries, some of whom you were able to recruit because they previously served with you in the Company.

"What you must remember at all times, and this is important, William, is that you and your men are *only* employed to protect the Queen's son, *not* to fight in her army. We do not want the Company to be named as traitors and thrown out of London if everything turns to shite and the King wins.

"Under the terms of the contract you are only responsible for the safety of Prince Edward. That means that no one, not even the Queen, can give you orders. No one, mind you, and certainly not Lord Mortimer or the Queen's courtiers.

"And always remember that you are only responsible for the Prince's safety; just the Prince. So take the Prince with you if you have to run, and his mother too if she is with the Prince. What you must never do is fight in the Queen's ranks against the King and never surrender to the King's men so they can question you and learn of the Company's involvement. Do you understand what I am telling you, William?"

"I think I do understand, Commander, and you can count on me to do everything possible to keep the prince safe and the Company's involvement a secret. I will be on my horse and ready to leave whenever the Bishop and Sir Hugh are ready."

"Good man, Captain, and may God keep you safe." And with that Commander Robertson turned around and started toward the tavern's door. But then he stopped and gave me one final order.

"Oh, and William, it might be best if you kept your wrist knives under your tunic and out of sight for a while. There is no need for the Queen's men to ever know you are carrying them—unless, of course, you need to use them. Also please do your best to get Bishop Bereford and Sir Hugh as far past

Okehampton as possible before you ride off and leave them. We would not want them to meet the King's men who are waiting at the horse farm would we?

My God. Is he warning me about the Queen's men? It set me on edge. Was there something I was not being told?

****

The Queen's men were still getting ready to ride and, in doing so, they were beginning to worry me. They appeared to be slow and uncertain about what they were doing. Horsemen with a competent sergeant or captain they were not. It meant we could be in big trouble if we run into some of the King's men. But then I realized that my men and I had not agreed to defend them, only the Queen's son. That brightened my thoughts considerably.

"Sod them all," was my somewhat cheerful initial thought. "We will leave them and run for Suffolk if there is any trouble on the road."

But then I got to worrying that the bishop and his men might be moving so slow that the King's men would finish their negotiations with the Commander and ride fast enough to catch up with us. I was also worrying that if we rode away from the Queen's men whilst they were being attacked the survivors would bad mouth us in the Queen's camp and we would not be trusted to guard the Prince. It was enough to make my head hurt.

My new *and first* apprentice sergeant, Thomas Corn, was standing behind me in the moonlight holding our riding horses and remounts whilst we waited the Queen's men to finish their preparations. About the only thing I knew for sure as we waited was that our new horses were fresh amblers from the stable whereas the ones we had ridden in on were still a bit tired as a result of having been ridden all day. So was I for that matter.

The two outriders who would be continuing on with me as "volunteers to help guard Prince Edward and his entourage" were standing near Thomas with our horses and saddled remounts. They were not completely happy about exchanging their personal horses for fresh ones. But they understood that the horses they rode in on were too tired to immediately start another long ride and had grudging moved their saddles and saddle sacks to their new horses.

It was a warm and balmy Cornwall night; in other words, fairly rare. The sky was relatively clear, there was a three-quarters moon, and my arse still hurt from the day's ride. I had slept in the saddle when I was with the horse archers but never whilst standing in the stirrups. Was it even possible? I had a feeling I was about to find out.

A man left the little knot of men where the Queen's horses were being assembled and began walking toward where we were waiting. In the moonlight I saw the glint of the breastplate he was wearing over the embroidered tunic that covered his chain shirt and knew it must be Sir Hugh; he was the only knight in the Queen's party and the only man I had seen wearing armour.

Actually, truth be told, it had been a warm day and I was somewhat surprised Sir Hugh had continued to wear his armour after he hurriedly put it on in an effort to impress the Commander. Did he really think that the King's men might be coming and we could be riding off to fight at night? Perhaps he had no supply horse to carry it. So far as I knew he and I were the only ones wearing chain shirts. I, however, was not wearing a breastplate.

"Your name is William Courtenay?" he said as he walked up to me. "I am told you have extensive experience fighting the Moors and have left the Company of archers to become the captain of the men who have been employed to guard the Queen's son? Why are you willing to do that?"

We were standing in the moonlight and Sir Hugh was clearly suspicious of me and trying to put me into what he considered to be a commoner's proper place somewhere far below him. In the background I could see more of the horses of the Queen's men being saddled.

Truth be told, I was more than a little taken aback and surprised by Sir Hugh's words and the concerns they implied. In any event, they seemed a more than a little late since Bishop Bereford had already signed the contract and handed over the required coins.

"I could tell you it was because I get sea-poxed when I am at sea and my arse gets saddle sore when on land because of all the riding that is required, Sir Knight, but those are not the reasons why I agreed to leave the Company of Archers. The truth is that I want my own company and to be paid more than I am now earning and eat better." *It was not the truth, of course, but it was the story I was told to tell.*

"But you are not knight, are you? So I will have to appoint a knight to guide you, eh?"

"No, I am not a knight, Sir Hugh." I said very emphatically with a touch of hardness in my voice as I leaned forward and deliberately put my face close to his in the moonlit darkness. "And according to the contract the Bishop of Lincoln just signed on behalf of the Queen, I answer only to her about matters concerning her son and my men and I fight only to defend her son. That means that neither you nor any other knight will be giving me orders, only the Queen and only when it has to do with her son.

"But you need not worry about the abilities of me and my men to guard Prince Edward, Sir Knight." I said quietly and ominously as I put my face even closer to his and explained.

"*We* know much more about fighting than men who are naive enough to think that having a king tap a sword on their shoulders and being able to joust in tournaments and wear armour means they know how to lead men and win battles. They do not; my men and I do.

"Moreover, now that a contract has been signed that obliges my men and I to protect the Queen's son; I will be ordering my men to immediately kill any knight or lord or anyone else who tries to kill or capture Prince Edward or causes him injury or distress during the next twelve months. So be warned—that includes *you* if you ever decide to change sides or do anything to distress or endanger the Queen's son whilst my men and I are under contract to protect him."

I leaned forward said it very softly and with great deal of menace in my voice.

Sir Hugh had stepped back quickly when I put my face close to his. It was not at all the response he expected. "We will see," he said, "We will see," he said as he turned and walked away. His breathe smelled quite foul as if he had been eating garlic to ward off a pox.

The knight faded off into the moonlit darkness and a few minutes later we mounted our horses and got underway. It had been an interesting confrontation. But I was not at all sure I should have been so threatening or put him down so thoroughly.

******

There was a surprising amount of cheerful talking and much too much unnecessary noise from the Queen's men as we rode out on to the nearby road in the moonlight and began riding east towards Suffolk. It surprised me; I had not been aware that they had been so anxious to leave. It was probably the food.

Sam Atkins and Jack Frodesham, the two outriders who had been "volunteered" to come with me, were at the very front of our little column. Both were two-stripe chosen men who had ridden over the road between the Restormel and Okehampton so many times previously that they could "do it in the dark" which, of course, was exactly why they were up front and leading the way.

Thomas Corn, my new apprentice sergeant, and I rode at the front of the Queen's little column immediately behind the two outriders. According to what I had been told by Bishop Bereford and Sir Hugh, our immediate destination was the Company's *Three Bells* tavern and couriers' horse-changing station at the Tamar ford. They knew about it because they had stopped there for the night whilst on their way to meet with Commander Boatman.

After a brief pause at the *Three Bells* we would splash our way across the Tamar ford and continue eastward past the cart path that led up to Okehampton until we reached the old Roman Road that ran between London and Exeter. Then we would head east on the London road to Suffolk so as to be there when the Queen and her son and her army came ashore. At least that is what was supposed to happen.

Within minutes my arse was so sore I thought I was sitting on a cooking fire.

Chapter Seven
On the road.

Avoiding the King's men so as not to have to fight them or be forced to abandon the Queen's men seemed like a reasonable idea to me. Men can get hurt when there is fighting even if they are on the winning side.

On the other hand, there was doubt in my mind that no matter what the recent contract said, the Queen's men were likely to be pissed if we rode off and abandoned them to their enemies. Then whatever the survivors who reached Suffolk said about our deserting them would almost certainly undermine us in the eyes of the Queen and her supporters. They would more likely kill us or send us away than let us guard the prince. Besides, if we rode off and abandoned some of her followers when danger threatened the Queen would almost certainly fear we do would do the same when her son was in danger.

I was not concerned about the next few hours or even the next day or two. That was because I knew Commander Boatman intended to delay the departure of the King's men from the horse farm by dragging out his talks with them. If he was successful in delaying them it was unlikely the King's men would be on the road travelling back to Windsor in time to catch up with us. But what should I do if the Queen's men moved so slowly that the King's men *were* able to catch up with us; or if we met with other King's men along the way?

There was no good answer because if I told the Queen's men that I knew for sure that the King had men in Cornwall they would know the Company had been also talking to the King's men and fear that we might betray them or even try to assassinate the Queen or Prince Edward. My men and I would not last long in the Queen's camp if her supporters found out about the forthcoming meeting at the horse camp.

All I could do under the circumstances, I decided, was to do my best to keep Bishop Bereford and Sir Hugh from learning that representatives of the King were meeting with Commander Boatman. In other words, I needed to keep the Queen's men moving east towards Suffolk as fast as possible so the King's men meeting with the Commander would not catch up with us. I also resolved not to pull my wrist knives out unless I meant to use them.

In the end, all I ended up actually doing that night, at least at first, was ride in the darkness beside my new apprentice sergeant, Thomas Corn, and try to find out more about him such as where he was born and how his family name had been selected by the school clerk. In other words, we talked about the usual kind of things archers talk about in the middle of a dark night on a long and boring ride when they had sore arses.

Thomas started to answer my first question in Latin, probably to show me that he could use it, but I quickly rounded on him such that he stopped in mid-sentence.

"Careful, Thomas," I cautioned my apprentice sergeant softly so that no one else could hear me. "Speak only English or French whenever possible. We do not want the Queen's clerics to know we will be able to understand them when they gab to each other in Latin do we?"

Thomas immediately changed to crusader French. Crusader French being the way of gabbing and gobbling many were beginning to call English now that the crusades were over and the crusaders were mostly either buried in the Holy Land or had returned to whatever was left, if anything, of their lands and families.

Hour after hour we rode in the moonlit darkness. We made progress in the sense that we were moving ever closer to the River Tamar which was the border between Cornwall and Devon. It was slow going because we dared not allow our horses to go faster than a walk because it was so dark.

In fact it was periodically so dark when clouds cut off the light from the moon and stars that we had to stop. There was some talking at first but after a while it was also deathly quiet such we could only hear the clip clop of our horse's shoes and the periodic plop of horseshit. Even the initial murmur of the men's voices behind us faded away after the first hour or so.

I was half asleep and nodding off in the saddle when I suddenly realized I had forgotten something. A cold chill suddenly descended on me when I remembered it and jerked awake with a moment of panic. But after I thought about it for a while I realized it would have to wait until the morning. *And in the morning I had forgotten what it was.*

Several times the outriders leading the way were forced to stop when clouds covered the moonlight and stars such that you could not see your hand in front of your face. When that happened Sam or Jack would quietly say "we have to stop" or something like that. As soon as I heard that I would turn in the saddle loudly shout "Everybody halt!" at the column of Queen's men riding behind me.

I shouted loudly because the first time we stopped I had passed the word too softly. As a result the bishop and his men riding behind us just kept coming in the dark and got all tangled up such that at least one of them fell off his horse. I was no exception; the horse of someone riding behind me rode into mine after I had gotten off to take a piss. My horse, in turn, bumped into me and caused me to wet my own leg—which, as you well might imagine, made me quite angry.

The worst part about it was I had no one to angry at except myself. That did not stop me, however, from swearing many curses at the rider whose horse had bumped mine. He said not a word and I never did learn whose horse did it.

******

The arrival of the first faint light of the coming day found us on the road about ten miles west of the River Tamar and strung out in a long and totally disorganized column. It would not have surprised me at all to learn that some of the Queen's men had dropped out during the night and would never be seen again. But at least now we could see enough to begin moving faster. *And it is a damn good thing that there are no King's men on this side of the Tamar; this lot could not fight off a band of castle cooks.*

We four archers nudged our horses in the ribs to get them moving faster and they began ambling down the road. That lasted until I looked back a few minutes later and saw what our increased speed was doing to the riders in the column behind us.

The Queen's men were trying to keep up, I will give them that. But it was not to be because none of them were aboard amblers and most of them were not experienced horsemen. They were aboard a diverse group of rounceys and had them trotting as fast as possible in an effort to keep up with us.

Anyone who has ever been on a horse knows how painful a prolonged fast trot can be on the arse and on backs of inexperienced riders such as the bishop, the priest who was his cleric, and their servants. Already some of the Queen's men were pulling out of the column to rest their backs and arses. It could not continue. I slowed my horse to a walk and began giving new orders.

"Sam, you told me you knew the *Three Bells* tavern keeper quite well from your previous visits when you were a Company courier. So I want you to take Jack with you and ride on ahead to the Company's *Three Bells* tavern at the ford. Take my supply sack and the sergeant's with you.

"As soon as you get to the *Three Bells* I want you to fill all of our supply sacks with as much bread, cheese, and other food as you can get into them. Get French loaves if possible because they will last longer than flatbreads. Get some meat into the sacks as well if there is any to be had, even if it is uncooked. We can burn it later. Also oats for our horses if any are available; an entire sack or even two."

Then I explained my order.

"It is going to be a very long ride from here to the Suffolk coast and we do not know what dangers we will find along the way from the supporters of the King or who we will find in the Queen's camp when we get there. So we may well need all the food we can carry away from the *Three Bells*.

"I hope I am wrong, of course, but I do not want to put us in danger by being forced to look for food in unfriendly places or starving because there is no food available when we arrive in Suffolk or wherever it is that we are finally able to meet Prince Edward.

"Mind you, it is not that I think we can make it all the way to Suffolk with the food we can carry away from the *Three Bells*. But having as much as possible with the four of us at all times will let us bypass towns and taverns where visiting might be dangerous.

"Also you might want to tell whoever is running the *Three Bells* these days that a convoy of very rich pilgrims on horseback will be there in a few hours and will want to buy additional bread and cheese to eat on the road in the days ahead and oats for their horses. But do not mention a word about the pilgrims coming and what they might buy until *after* our food sacks are full and we have enough oats for our own horses."

The outriders both knuckled their heads to acknowledge the order and Sam repeated it back to me. A moment later they kicked their horses in the ribs and began ambling down the road heading east towards the *Three Bells* and the Tamar ford.

I did not know anything about the two outriders but my confidence in them was growing; it was obvious from the looks on their faces that they both understood what I wanted them to do and they agreed with it. Their agreement was no surprise; it is always better to eat without having to fight for your food or share it with others such that you end up going hungry.

Thomas Corn and I then dismounted and waited for the Queen's men to catch up with us. The wind had picked up; it felt as if it would soon be starting to rain again.

******

We met a good number of people on the road that day. Most of them were on foot but some were in wagons. We also saw many farmers and their families working in their fields. That lasted until the rain started. Then most of them somehow seemed to disappear. We did not have the luxury of taking shelter and continued riding in the rain towards the east and Suffolk.

Indeed, the only thing of note that happened as we continued riding eastward was a fast moving Company courier who came galloping past us in the rain. He was obviously on his way to Okehampton or, perhaps, to one of the Company's other strongholds along the Cornwall marches such as the castles at Launceston or Plimpton. He waved as he and his remount came galloping past but did not stop.

Five hours later our slow moving column finally sighted the racks of antlers that hung all along the front of the Company's *Three Bells* roadside tavern and courier horse changing station. The River Tamar ford lay just beyond it. I was soaking wet and more than ready to take a break with a bowl of ale and so was my apprentice sergeant. Hopefully the fireplace in the public room would be lit so I could stand in front of it for a few minutes to dry my clothes whilst quaffing a bowl of ale and munching on fresh bread.

Our Queen-supporting travelling companions were also ready for a break, or so I hoped—because right after dawn arrived, I had briefly stopped our little column and gathered its dismounted members around me for what we in the Company call a "come to Jesus" meeting when we are trying to get everyone to do something. Sir Hugh attended even though he glowered at me the whole time and Bishop Bereford just stood there and acted bored. Everyone else, however, paid rapt attention and nodded their agreement when I finished.

"You are all supporters of the Queen," I told them. "But not everyone agrees with you; many men still support the King. That is why my men and I are concerned about riding with you. We are fearful that we will come to the notice of the King's supporters who abound in the lands on the eastern side of the River Tamar, the lands which we will reach later today when we cross the river.

"What worries me and my men is that the King's supporters will hear about your efforts to support the Queen and either chase after us or lay an ambush for us to ride into. If either happens we all almost certainly have a good chance of getting ourselves killed most painful.

"That is why it is important that all of us, every single man including me, must *always* pretend to be pilgrims accompanying the Bishop of Bristol, Bristol *not* Lincoln, on a pilgrimage to Winchester. And you must *never* ever admit to anyone on the road or when we stop for food or a dry place to sleep that you are supporters of the Queen or that my men and I are contracted to protect her son, Prince Edward.

"We are pilgrims and their guards and only pilgrims and their guards until we reach our destination. Do you understand?"

It was not at all true, of course; I had no idea if the people on the other side of the river cared who England's king was so long as he and his armies and taxes stayed far away. But I was attempting to put a frightener on the Queen's men so they would do what I wanted them to do— keep their damn mouths shut when we met people on the road and when we stopped along the way for food and drink and someplace dry to sleep.

Chapter Eight
Crossing the Tamar.

We rode into the yard of the *Three Bells* and used our reins to tie up our horses to the horse-mooring posts that stretched across the front of the tavern. The craggy faced ox-driver of an overloaded hay wain coming towards us on the road smiled and raised his hand in a friendly greeting as we did. I lifted mine and nodded to acknowledge him.

There were still puddles of water on the ground in front of the tavern from an earlier rain but the sun was out and shining. We were wearing our sun-dried archers' tunics and the shutters on the *Three Bells'* wall opening had been thrown open so we could see into its public room and whoever was in the tavern could see out.

Sam Atkins and Jack Frodesham came out of the door with ale bowls in their hands and watched as we dismounted, pissed next to the nearest mooring post, and tied up our horses to it. I was more than a little stiff as I did. But I was encouraged because the first thing Sam did was give a little smile and a discreet thumbs up. *We had our sacks of food.* I gave him a smile and nodded my understanding and appreciation. It was a good start.

"Any problems?" I quietly asked Sam as I walked toward the entrance door. He seemed to be the leader of the two outriders even though they had the same number of stripes on their tunics.

"None at all, Captain. I explained to Mistress Green, the alewife, about the pilgrims we are convoying and she is all aboard and ready feed them as soon as they come inside. She is also preparing bread loaves and some cheese wheels for them to take with them when they leave. She has no meat ready for the Bishop and his men to take with them and eat I am sorry to say, but one of our sacks has a couple of previously burnt chickens in it.

"And how was your ride, Captain? Any problems along the way? You were so long in coming that me and Tom was starting to get a bit worried until a Company courier came in to change horses. He told he us had ridden past you an hour or so earlier and you was going really slow. Jim Reynolds it was. Him whose pa was lost when the Company raided Tunis when Jim was a tyke."

"Aye, so he did. I thought it was Jim. I remembered him from my time at Okehampton. But he did not stop or even slow down so I was not sure. He just waved most friendly and kept on going. It is doubtful he was carrying a message that we should know about or else he would have stopped."

******

The *Three Bells* was empty when we arrived and there was no fire laid in the hearth. That was no surprise; the travellers were on the road taking advantage of there being no rain and the franklins were back in their fields with their families making hay whilst the sun shined. *And better them than me as everyone knows who has spent an entire sunny day cutting grass or grain with a scythe.*

Thomas Corn and I followed the smiling alewife to a corner table with Sam and Jack following close behind. The bishop and Sir Hugh came in a minute or so later, and were made much of by the alewife which pleased them.

Sam must have said something to her earlier because she led them to a table on the other side of the room. By the time she had them seated Thomas and I already taking our first sips of her ale. *Not bad; a little fruity. Maybe she threw in a couple of apples.*

"What did you tell the alewife?" I leaned toward Sam and asked quietly.

"I told her they were rich pilgrims who had been visiting the monastery at Bodmin with some arsehole bishop who was after their coins. And then I explained that because they did not know Cornwall they had asked for the Company's protection for fear of robbers on the road between here and London."

"Good man. It is such a fine story that I think we should keep using it as long as we are travelling east towards London. We can say we are going somewhere else when we get to the turnoff to Suffolk."

More and more of the Queen's men came in and sat themselves as we were talking; they looked as exhausted from riding all night and most of the next day as I felt. The bishop and Sir Hugh had gotten bowls from the alewife and seemed to be watching us. Out of the corner of my eye I saw them put their heads together and begin an animated conversation. After a while Sir Hugh stopped waving his hands about, got up, and walked over to where we were sitting. He had a complaint.

"Did your men tell the alewife that Bishop Bereford would pay for everyone's food and drink and then tell her our men could order whatever they wanted?" he asked somewhat belligerently.

"Aye, they told her because I told them to tell her. It is the custom in Cornwall for the senior man to pay and I knew he ranked you because he is the one who signed the contract for our services. Besides, I did not want to embarrass him and have his being stingy call the alewife's attention to himself and his men." *There was no such custom, of course, but there should be and that was close enough. Besides it was a good story and quite believable.*

"Well, you should not have done so without asking him first," he said with a touch of anger in his voice.

"You are wrong, Sir Hugh," I said. "If I had not done so both the alewife and the travellers visiting the tavern might have noticed and said something to the King's supporters about outsiders being in Cornwall. Even worse, they might have asked your men why they were paying and wanted to know the name of the miserly bishop. Then the King's men would have learnt you were here for sure. *It was all ox-shite of course but I did not like the sanctimonious bastard.*

"Am I wrong in thinking that Bishop Bereford is already known to be a supporter of the Queen" I asked with as much wide-eyed innocence as I could muster. "I thought he was trying to prevent it from becoming known that he has been in Cornwall because it might endanger both him and you on the road ahead. Is that not so?"

"There is something else," Sir Hugh said. "It is already late in the afternoon and everyone is tired after riding all last night and all day today. The Bishop wants to stay here tonight and rest. He and I will share the bed that is available and everyone else can sleep here on the tavern floor. We can leave in the morning."

"That is not a good idea," I told him as I vigorously shook my head to emphasize how much I disagreed.

"We need to push on to the London Road as soon as possible. Every minute we delay makes it more likely that the King's men will learn about you and Bishop Bereford being on the road and have time to put a force together to intercept us."

What I did *not* tell Sir Hugh was that I wanted the Queen's men to continue riding east because the Commander told us he intended to ride to Okehampton today, spend tonight there, and then ride up to the horse farm in the morning to meet with King's men. In other words, if we stay here tonight the Commander is more likely to catch up with us. *My God, what if the Commander decides to spend the night here; they might renegotiate the agreement and then where will I be?*

But then I reconsidered. What harm would there be if the Commander shows up later this afternoon on his way to Okehampton? We already have the bishop's payment for our services.

Actually, I decided, it might be good thing if the Commander did arrive and find the Queen's men still here— because then he would see how slow the bishop's party is going and know to lengthen the delay before the King's men get on the road behind us.

"Alright," I finally agreed after taking another sip from my bowl and pretending to think more about it. "But we will have to leave first thing in the morning. I am not going to risk *my* men by waiting any longer than that. If you and *your* men are not ready when the sun comes up my lads and I are going to ride off and leave you to find your own way to Suffolk."

Sir Hugh gave me a hard look in response to my threat. Then he turned and went back to the table where the bishop was finishing his meal. A few minutes later he and the bishop got up from their table and retired to the room they had hired. Their men immediately began ordering more food and ale and I began giving orders.

"Sam, I want you and Jack to ride a ways back down the road and wait for the Commander. He will be along sooner or later and will need to know that the Queen's men are spending the night at the *Three Bells*. He will know what to do when he is learnt about them." *I hope.*

The two outriders left immediately. About five minutes later a horse-riding traveller wearing some sort of a monk's robe came in for a bowl of ale and something to eat. He spoke most friendly to some of the Queen's men and the alewife, finished his meal, and rode off.

******

It was less than an hour before Sam returned.

"The Commander will be here soon, Captain; and he wants to talk to you *before* he arrives."

I put down the piece of cheese I had been about to bite into and jumped to my feet.

"Stay here and keep your eyes open, Sam. Sergeant Corn and I are going to ride out to see the Commander."

And with that I headed to the door with Thomas following close behind. We unmoored our somewhat rested horses from their tethering pole and began ambling back down the road towards Restormel.

Less than half an hour later I was riding next to the Commander and Major Captain Robertson and telling them all I had learned about the Bishop of Lincoln and Sir Hugh, which was not very much except that the bishop and his men were slow movers and complained a lot.

"I feared as much," Commander Boatman said when I finished my report. Then he made a decision which made me and Major Captain Robertson smile and nod our heads in agreement.

"It is almost dark. So we are going to stop up by that little flow going across the road up ahead of us to water our horses and eat some of the bread and cheese we are carrying. Then, as soon as it gets dark, we are going to ride right on past the *Three Bells* and continue on to Okehampton.

"I do not fancy crossing the Tamar ford in the darkness, but I understand from the travellers we have been meeting that the water level of the river is not high so it should be doable. I will send a galloper on ahead to tell Okehampton we are coming and to have a late supper waiting.

Then he smiled and added.

"Based on what I heard from you, William, I suspect I will be quite tired in the morning and decide to sleep in. And then, of course, I will have to do what is expected of me and inspect the castle to make sure its siege supplies are adequate. That will take at least another day and perhaps even two if I find anything that needs to be set right.

"So it is likely to be two or three days before I will be able to spend a day riding up to the horse farm to see what the King wants of us and how much he is willing to pay to get it. Do you agree, Edward?"

"Oh yes," replied the new Major Captain with a smile. "It will take several days at least and likely more."

Chapter Nine
Unexpected Trouble.

We rode out of the *Three Bells* yard an hour or so
after daybreak. My men and I had risen before dawn,
broken our fasts, turned our tunics inside out so we would
not be recognized as Company archers after we left
Cornwall, and saddled our riding horses and remounts. Our
supply sacks were stuffed with food and we were ready to
ride when the sun arrived. It was all for nought; the Queen's
men were not close to being ready to ride.

Fortunately, the resulting wait for the Queen's men to
finish their preparations was not an entire waste. Sir Hugh
emerged from the bed he shared with Bishop Bereford in
somewhat of a good mood and was willing to talk about
how our little band should react to some of the various
types of attacks and problems we might suffer in the days
ahead.

It was known to me that both Sir Hugh and Bishop
Bereford were each accompanied by a servant who was
some kind of ex-soldier and supposedly knew how to use
the sword he was carrying. If it was true, and Sam and Jack
had been talking to the two men and thought it was. If so,
there were seven of us including Sir Hugh who might be
capable of using the weapons we were carrying and six men
who were unarmed and would be useless in a fight.

The problem was that Sir Hugh did not have a clue as to how we should respond in the event we were attacked— and worse he thought he should be in command if we were. I disagreed. He was a crusty old bastard so I did so as gently as possible under the circumstances with a smile and an inquiry.

"As I told you before, Sir Hugh, I am neither willing nor required to put my archers under your command. Not now and not ever. *But* if I were to agree, what orders would you be giving this morning to get us ready to fight off an attack?"

Sir Hugh obviously had never thought about it and did not have a clue other than "keep our eyes open and our weapons close."

I motioned for him to continue and asked for more. "And what do we do if there is a sudden attack from our port side or we see a roadblock up ahead?" I asked. "How should we deploy the seven of us who can fight and what does the bishop and the others do? And when should we run and to where?"

The knight started to speak several times and then, after taking another sip of his breakfast ale, shook his head. How the seven of us with weapons should respond to an attack was obviously something he had never considered. Finally, he looked up and asked "what do *you* think we should do?"

******

We splashed across the nearby Tamar ford less than an hour later and rode steadily eastward. By late afternoon we had moved past the entrance to the cart path leading up to Okehampton Castle and were on the main road running between London and the west of England. We turned to the left on the old Roman road and began slowly moving easterly towards London and Suffolk. Had we turned right we would have ended up in Exeter and Plymouth.

My three archers and I rode at the head of our little column with one of my three men always riding several miles ahead to scout for trouble. He was to come galloping back to sound the warning if he saw anything ahead of us that might be dangerous. One of the bishop's former soldiers was riding several miles behind us for the same purpose. Bishop Bereford and Sir Hugh and their clerics rode together with one of their servants leading the four horses that were carrying their tents and supplies.

Suffolk is in the east of England beyond London. To get to the Suffolk coast where the Queen and Mortimer and their army were expected to land with their mercenary army meant we would have to ride all the way across England from Cornwall in the west to the coast of Suffolk in the far east. It would be a long trip.

The problem of course was that almost of the main roads in England led to London. And London was thought to be strongly for King Edward because he and his men held the Tower which overlooked the main road we would be travelling on. So a major question was whether we should we stay on the main road and risk riding through London or should we go around London even though it would mean using secondary roads and would add at least several additional days to our journey. And how far out from London should we go if we decided to ride around it?

Three days later we were approaching Salisbury and I was once again thinking about the route we should take to get to the Suffolk coast when Sam Atkins all of a sudden said "oh shite."

I looked up and could see Jack Frodesham riding hard toward us and holding his bow over his head. The fact that Jack was coming back fast and had already pulled his longbow out of its leather shoulder carrier was more than enough for me. My bow was slung over my shoulder and encased in its leather rain protector. I instantly pulled my bow's rain protector around so it was in front of me and pulled my bow out. Thomas and Sam were already doing the same.

Without a word being spoken all three of us immediately leaned out of our saddles and pushed one end of our bow against the ground to bend it enough to string it. Retrieving our bows from their rain-protecting wraps and stringing them whilst on horseback was something each of us had done many times before, even young Thomas. *Thank God it was not raining to wet our bowstrings. We all had several spares in our pouches but they would not last long in a heavy rain.*

Jack was riding hard to re-join us and appeared be lashing his horse to get it to move even faster. Behind him on the road we could see a group of men coming around a bend in the road. Many were on foot but at least seven or eight were on horses—and they appeared to be chasing after Jack.

I immediately kicked my horse in the ribs and rode forward and off the road and up into the sheep pasture on my right. Sam and Thomas followed me and so, rather slowly, did the young man from the Bishop's party who claimed to know how to ride and was leading our remounts.

Jack veered towards us as soon as we began galloping into the pasture. He knew what we would be doing and was on a course to intercept us.

As I jumped my horse over the little drainage ditch that ran alongside the road I turned in the saddle and roared "turn around and begin falling back" at the Queen's men who had been riding behind us on the road. Jack had seen us gallop into the pasture and had already come off the road and was galloping to intercept us. It was the move he had expected us to make.

We were riding amongst the sheep that had been grazing on the grass and brush on the side of the gentle hill on both sides of the road. Those in front of us scattered in all directions as we came off the road charged up the gentle grass-covered hill that was their pasture.

As the three of us came off the road I pointed towards the top of the little hill which was about a mile behind us and shouted "Wait up there" to the Bishop's servant who was acting as our horse holder. He seemed to be riding well and moving as fast as could be expected for someone leading a string of four horses. At least he did not fall off his horse a few moments later when his horse and the remounts he was leading jumped over the little ditch and moved into the pasture.

We had ridden at a gallop for less than a minute. Even so, I was breathing hard from the excitement of it all when we pulled up on the hillside above the road. The sheep that had been grazing there were still moving away. I also felt amazingly clear-headed.

When we stopped we were facing Jack who was galloping toward us and the horsemen riding behind him. At that moment we were about six or seven hundred paces off the road and up the hill to our right and about four hundred paces in front of where we had been on the road when we first saw Jack coming to sound the alarm. My horse and those of my men were skittish and moving about excitedly but not at all winded or tired. We all had arrows out and ready to be nocked.

In effect, by moving well off to the side of the road and slightly forward we were forcing the riders coming toward us to declare their intentions *before* they reached us. At least that was my initial plan and, unfortunately, the whole of it. What we would do next would be determined by what the horsemen did next and the intentions signalled by their behaviour.

If the horsemen following Jack continued riding on toward the little column of Queen's men on the road we would ride down and try to take them in the flank and rear; if they came toward us we would wait and see if their intentions were peaceful. The only thing certain at this point was that we would not let them surround us or get near enough to use their swords and spears. If they tried to get closer than shouting distance we would move further forward and further up the hill.

It was all very exciting and very strange: I knew everything was happening very fast and yet everything also *seemed* to be happening very slowly at the same time. It was almost as if I was outside my body watching myself and what was happening.

******

To my surprise the leader of the riders chasing Jack acted as if he knew my plan. Just as Jack reached us and pulled up his winded and blowing horse four of the riders pursuing Jack came off the road and headed up the hill and towards us. The other five or six horsemen kept going towards the Queen's men and the baggage horses that had turned around and were now hurrying down the road to get away from them. The great mass of men on foot, twenty or thirty of them, were still on the road and moving down it towards the bishop and Sir Hugh. And we still did not have a clue as to who they were or what they wanted.

"Were there any knights amongst them?" I shouted out to Jack who was breathing hard as he pulled his somewhat winded but still very useful horse around and came to a halt next to me. I still was not sure who the on-coming men were, only that they appeared to be hostile. Jack was wide-eyed with excitement. His horse was sweating from its exertions and so was he.

"Maybe one man who appeared to be wearing armour, Captain," he gasped. "But I am not sure. Once they started coming after me I did not wait around long enough to find out."

The four riders who had been chasing after Jack were riding straight for us and all four were riding with drawn swords. Their course was taking them mostly parallel to the road but they were also climbing higher and higher on the hill as they came towards us.

"Follow me in a line astern," I shouted as I put my heels into my horse's side and leaned forward to shout "hiya" into his ear. He shot forward and was instantly at a fast amble.

We did *not* ride straight at the riders who were still about half a mile out and lower down on the sheep-covered hill. That would have caused us to move slowly but surely down the hill. Instead we rode around the hill on a slightly *upward* course that would keep Jack's pursuers both below us and off to our left.

The four riders who had continued after Jack were soon spread out in their own line astern as our line of riders, riding further up the gentle hill, crossed above and in front of the thruster who was their leading rider. We began pushing out arrows as soon as we got in range. At least two of our arrows hit the first rider and I saw another take his horse squarely in its chest. The second rider was also hit.

We were all pushing out arrows as my line of riders crossed in front of them and I led my line of men in great looping half circle to come around below the remaining two of the four enemy riders who had come up the hill after us. They both pulled up in confusion and began turning their horses to face us as we swept back towards then still in a single line astern file. This time when our line crossed their line we were slightly below them on the hill.

Once we each again got off multiple arrows as we rode past them at about forty feet. The tail-end enemy rider, the one closest to us, was quickly wounded and hanging on to his horse's neck to avoid falling by the time the four of us finished riding past him. Beyond him, further up the hill, I could see the first rider on the ground with his fallen horse struggling to get to its feet and the second horse running off with its saddle empty.

The one remaining mounted horseman escaped either because he was very lucky or because he understood what we were doing; he had begun riding straight *up* the hill when he saw us make our great sweeping turn to come back to cross just below the tail-end of our line of pursuers.

We totally ignored the escaper. Instead my little company of line astern riders continued straight ahead at a hard gallop in an effort to catch up with the enemy riders who had stayed on the road and were about to reach our now-abandoned pack horses. The host of enemy foot were still at least a mile down the road behind us and seemed to coming down the road at a fast walk. So far so good.

Sir Hugh and the unarmed and totally terrified bishop and most of his men had already abandoned their pack horses and fled on their horses in all directions just as they had been ordered to do in the event of an attack. *And probably would have done anyway even if that had not been the plan.*

In front of me as I pounded down the road I could see the enemy horsemen who had stayed on the road. They were going for our baggage horses instead of chasing after the fleeing men. *That is good news* was my thought as I nocked another arrow and my galloping horse brought me within arrow range of the first of them; it means they are robbers going after our goods, not King's men going after traitors.

I ignored the only man who had dismounted and was trying to grab the reins of one of the pack horses. Instead I pushed an arrow at a rider who was leaning out of his saddle in an attempt to catch the halter of another of the pack horses. I missed.

Thomas who had been galloping close behind me did not miss.

The rider's horse screamed when Thomas's arrow hit it and went down sideways, and then rolled over its still-saddled rider as we thundered past them at fairly close range whilst pushing out arrows and then turned around to make another run past them.

Several of the enemy riders had seen us coming and had immediately begun riding away in an effort to escape; several others were still galloping after our baggage horses which had become excited and begun running away. There was a lot of confusion and shouting.

It is hard to push arrows accurately out of a longbow when you are astride a galloping or fast-ambling horse unless you are reasonably close to your intended victim. But the third time was the charm as I wheeled my horse around to make yet another run past what was left of our baggage train.

This time I got the dismounted man as he was desperately trying to climb back aboard his horse. As I did, I turned in the saddle and saw Thomas wheeling his horse around to come back and help me and that both Jack and Sam were going after the enemy riders who had been chasing after the bishop's now scattered and running pack horses.

There was a fifth rider but he had seen the fate of his mates and was riding hard to reach the relative safety of his mates in the mob of men coming down the road on foot.

Chapter Ten
The Commander and the King's men.

Commander Boatman decided that it was time for him to ride up to the Company's horse farm and meet with the King's emissaries. He had completed the two days of required inspections at Okehampton and a courier coming in from the Company's London shipping post had brought back word that he had passed Captain Courtenay and the Queen's men as they were approaching Salisbury. That was far enough towards London to convince the Commander that the King's men would not be able to catch up with slow-moving Queen's men even if they left almost immediately and rode hard.

The Commander was increasingly looking forward to meeting the King's men waiting at the horse farm. He had learned from the archers who had accompanied them to the horse farm that the Bishop of Coventry and the Earl of Winchester had been riding through western England doing the very same thing that the Queen's men, the Bishop of Lincoln and Sir Hugh Turpington, had been doing— attempting to hire mercenaries and, at the same time, going all out with promises and threats to recruit nobles and their knights and levies to the King's cause.

He had also learned that the King's men's visit to recruit men from the Company of Archers in isolated Cornwall in the far west of England was last stop on their recruiting effort just as it had been the final stop for the Queen's men. According to the handful of archers at the horse farm, the servants of the King's men said they had been told they would be riding straight back to Windsor after the meeting.

Even more importantly, the archers at the horse farm reported that the King's men appeared to still have two full horse-loads of coin sacks. It was likely, therefore, that those coins were all they had left to buy the services of the archers as mercenaries just as all of what was left of the Queen's coins had been available to buy their services.

It was believable that the King's representatives had arrived at Okehampton with many more coins than the Queen's men had brought to Cornwall. The King was far richer than the Queen such that his men had undoubtedly started their search for mercenaries and knights to hire with more coins than the Queen's men who had been doing the same thing. *Or was it that the King's men found fewer takers for some reason? Hmm.*

The Commander also learned from the archers who had remained at the horse camp that King Edward's men seemed to be greatly worried about something and had been talking in whispers about it ever since they arrived. Perhaps they thought they were being delayed so they could be betrayed and captured? A reliable sergeant had been sent to the horse farm to try to befriend them and find out more.

What was known was that the King's men were led by the Bishop of Coventry and Hugh Despenser, the Earl of Winchester and the father of King Edward's lover who was also named Hugh Despenser. It was a large and impressive party as befit the importance of the King they represented. In addition to its two distinguished leaders, there were five knights, a couple of clerics, more than a dozen of the King's guards, and another dozen or so of servants to do their cooking, erect their tents when they could find no place to sleep inside, and to see to their horses and weapons. It was a mini-army.

"It costs more to be a King," Major Captain Robertson had observed wryly that evening as he raised his bowl to toast the Commander's comments about the size of the King's party compared to the Queen's. "Probably because if you think you are an important king you also think you have to send your courtiers out with bigger retinues in order to impress your lords and their vassals."

The Commander laughed and lifted his bowl to acknowledge the Major Captain's thought and added something to it.

"And let us pray that the King also sent them out with more coins such that they arrived here with even more coins than the Queen's men brought to the table when we met them at the *Red Horse*."

What the Commander did not do was tell anyone at the table what he had decided to propose to the Bishop and the Earl of Winchester after he rejected their offer to hire the Company to fight for the King as mercenaries. He certainly had smiled to himself when he thought about it. But would the King's men fall for it?

******

Major Captain Robertson accompanied the Commander to the meeting and was introduced to the King's men as Captain Alfred Ginger.

The meeting was held in the horse camp's empty tavern. It was initially quite cordial and cautious with each side on its best behaviour and feeling out the other. It started well with everyone exchanging the traditional meaningless pleasantries with everyone else.

Commander Robertson began by apologizing for the ill-winds that caused his galley's tardy arrival and the rough accommodations wherein the Earl and the Bishop slept in the tavern keeper's bed and the rest of King's people on the tavern's floor and in some of the farm's horse stalls.

It did not take long for the purpose of the visit to be revealed; the Bishop of Coventry and the Earl of Winchester wanted the Company's archers to fight for the king and, even worse, they did not want to pay for their services. The Commander told them he had expected as much because he had received a message saying they would be visiting here for that purpose.

"Good," said the bishop. "Then you know you are required to provide yourself and your archers for the King's service because you and everyone else in England are the King's vassals. It is God's will that you do so," the bishop explained.

"Of course it is God's will," the Commander replied, "and we would be pleased to send every available man to support the King. But we have no archers available to send. They are almost all in the east helping pilgrims at the request of the Pope. And there are no knights and levies in Cornwall and in the lands along the border marches because the land is too poor to support lords and their vassals due to all the tin in it.

"As things stand today, the men here at the Company's horse farm are all that are available other than the handful older men at Okehampton Castle and the men who came with me on the galley that brought me back to England. Indeed, the reason I returned was to recruit young lads who are willing to go for an archer," he cheerfully explained. "We need them in the east to replace our recent losses.

"The Earl and I were told in Windsor that you had hundreds of men," said the bishop with a questioning and accusative tone in his voice.

"That was two years ago when we had a particularly big intake of men willing to go for an archer because there was plague in their villages. Unfortunately, those that survived the plague were all sent east at the beginning of summer to replace the men who had gone down in storms or fallen to the Moors and the plague.

"I know that for a fact because I sailed out to Cyprus with them. And even if they were here I could not *order* them to join the King's army because of the terms of the Company articles on which they made their marks."

Then the Commander leaned forward and confided very softly. "But there may be a way to get some very experienced fighting men into the King's service if you have enough coins."

It was exactly what the Earl and the Bishop wanted to hear. The expressions on their faces improved and they instinctively leaned forward to hear more.

"This man right sitting here with me is Edward Robertson, the former captain of a mercenary company. Edward has experience using guile and gulling to get men into enemy camps, and then used those men to rescue captives that were being held as prisoners. It takes daring and courage and the men commanded by this man have it. If you have enough coins you could employ Edward and his mercenaries to protect the young prince until he can be delivered to King Edward.

"Edward, of course, is a great supporter of the King and has already volunteered to risk his life to protect the King's son and restore him to the King. He will not have to be paid. His men, however, are another matter. Thirty of them came back to England with him a few years ago and made their marks to join the Company of Archers when Edward decided to retire to Cornwall where he was birthed.

"As it stands, any order for Edward's men to risk their lives on behalf of anyone outside the Company automatically releases them from their contract to accept their captain's orders. *Such nonsense; they do it all the time to protect our cargos and passengers. But it was a good story and the earl and the bishop looked to be eating it up.*

"Moreover, the men would have to agree both to serve the King by rescuing and protecting the Prince and to buy their way out of the Company so their mates would see them as free to go off and do so. *More lies but acceptable under the circumstances.*

"The problems caused by the Company's charter exist to prevent a captain from misusing his men or putting them needlessly at risk. But the problems can be overcome; *if* the archers Captain will need to employ to help him protect Prince Edward are paid enough coins. Only then will they be able to buy their way out of the Company and be willing to join the dangerous efforts need to protect the Prince and get him away from the Queen.

"I must warn you, however, that knowing Edward's men as I do, I know they will have to be paid a great deal of coins to risk their lives and the coins would have to be paid in advance so they can buy themselves out of the company and because of the great dangers they will face if they go into the Queen's camp and protect Prince Edward until they can deliver him to the King. *And also because everyone knows the King's payment is not likely to ever be made no matter what he promises.*

"On the other hand, I am sure the King has many men searching for the Prince who would be able to re-join the King's army and make if more powerful if Captain Robertson and his archers take up the task of protecting the Prince until the King can do it himself.

"So let me ask you this—how badly do you want to protect the Prince and do you have enough coins to pay some archers to leave the Company and join Captain Robertson in an attempt to rescue him? And what kind of bonuses will the archers and the Company receive from the King if they do successfully rescue and protect him."

Of course the King and his men want Prince Edward found and protected. If the Queen was unable to put her son on the throne in place of King Edward her supporters would disappear like rain puddles after the sun comes out.

******

The negotiations that followed were at times intense, especially when they dealt with the important question of how the surviving archers would get their substantial bonuses of "success coins" if they protected Prince Edward until he could be safely delivered to the King.

In the end, the King's men agreed to deposit the archers' rather large success bonus with the Company and let the Company pay it to them. They did so when Commander Boatman agreed that he himself would be personally be responsible for returning the volunteers' "success coins" to the King if Prince Edward was not successfully protected until he was in King Edward's hands.

A contract was drafted and signed. The Company immediately received the required coins both to release the archers and to pre-pay the archers for their efforts and to reward them substantially if they protected the prince successful and returned him to his father. By an amazing coincidence the amount of coins which the King's men handed over to Commander Boatman turned out to be almost all the King's men were carrying with them.

Early the next morning the King's men mounted up and were led down the cart path to Okehampton—and then were sent on their way to report their successful efforts to King Edward who was mustering his forces at Windsor Castle. The Commander and the coins left the horse farm an hour or so later after the Commander finished his annual inspection.

"Look at it this way, Eddy," the Commander said to the new Major Captain as they rode back to Okehampton. "If the Queen wins we will keep the King's coins no matter what happens to the boy because the King and his supporters will not be around to claim them. On the other hand, if the King wins we will claim that you and your archers protected the prince and keep them."

"But what do we do if the boy dies or the Queen flees back to France and takes the boy with her?"

"That is a good question for which I have no immediate answer. Hopefully Captain Courtenay and his men will be able to protect the boy and not let that happen. On the other hand, the Company will already have the coins and their possession is almost as important to England's noble justiciars as the coins for their personal purses that affect their decisions. So I am sure someone will think of some reason or another why we can keep them if the time ever comes."

Commander Boatman smiled at thought the Company would keep the coins no matter who won the war. He felt very content even though it smelled like rain.

Chapter Eleven
On the road again.

Thomas and I nocked our arrows as our horses ambled up the road towards the robbers who were coming down the road towards us on foot. They were still coming. Perhaps they thought we were some of their mates coming to fetch them to help carry the loot. Behind us the bishop and Sir Hugh and their men were beginning to ride back to what was left of their convoy.

Everything suddenly changed before we reached the men who were walking towards us. Perhaps they had gotten close enough to see what had happened to some of their horsemen. Or perhaps they were alerted by one of the men on horseback who had escaped us. It did not matter. What did matter was that all at once they stopped coming towards us.

A moment later they turned around and began scattering in all directions. It was every man for himself and most of them seemed to be headed toward a thick forest about a mile off the road on our port side.

The road was deserted by the time we reached the place on the road where the robbers on foot had begun to run. We rode up to where they had been before they scattered and found a large number abandoned clubs and spears, several swords, and a number of empty sacks.

Almost certainly we had seen off a band of would-be robbers.

Sam and Jack had finished off the horsemen they were chasing and rode up just as Thomas started to charge off after the fleeing men. My apprentice wanted to ride the fleeing men down before they reached the safety of the forest.

"Come back, Thomas. Come back, damnit." I shouted loudly. A moment later Thomas pulled his horse to a stop and turned around to start back.

"He's a good lad," I said quietly to Sam as he pulled his hard-breathing horse to a halt next to mine and we watched Thomas turn his horse to ride back and join us. "And he will be a good sergeant someday if he lasts long enough for us to bring him along."

"Where were you going and what were you going to do when you got there, Thomas?" I demanded of my excited apprentice sergeant when he got back. Jack had ridden up and joined us by the time he did. I was so angry at Thomas that I shouted at him.

"I was trying to catch them before they reached the trees. Should I not have done?" Thomas said with a sheepish look on his face a few moments later. He obviously already knew the answer.

"Of course you should *not* have chased after them," I snapped. "It is one thing to risk getting yourself and your men killed or wounded to do what must be done; it is something else again to risk anyone's life for no good reason, including yours.

"Saving the Queen's men was necessary. We had to make the effort so we would be welcome in the Queen's camp; ridding Wiltshire of one of its bands of robbers is not something the Company has been paid to do. What if you had caught up with some of the runners who had not thrown their weapons away and they had turned on you and got you; we would have lost your services if you had been hurt or killed, eh?"

A seriously chastened apprentice sergeant said not a word as we rode back to re-join the Queen's men who were once again gathering on the road. Jack and Sam had fallen back and were riding behind us, probably to hide their smiles.

******

All was not well when we reached what was left of our little column. Supplies were scattered all around that had come loose from at least one of the pack horses and another horse carrying one of our two tents had somehow managed to run off and disappear.

The biggest loss, however, was the unarmed young priest who had been serving as the bishop's cleric; he had stayed with the supply horses for some reason and taken a sword chop from one of the riders. Now he was white-faced and clearly dying from having most of his arm cut off and bleeding too much.

Bishop Bereford was on his knees next to the white-faced lad and beside himself with anger and grief even though he had ridden off and left the lad in order to save himself.

"You should have been here to fight them off and save him," the bishop shouted up to me as I leaned over my horse's neck to look down at the bishop and the dying priest. He was clearly upset.

But blaming me and my men after we had just saved his life even though we had no obligation to do so? I was having none of it and angrily replied.

"No Eminence, it was *you* who left him; *you* should have made sure he was mounted and with you when you began running. If my men and I had been here waiting for the attackers to fall on our little convoy we would have all been killed including *you* and *all* of your men. There were other men on horses who had to be killed or driven off in addition to the swordsman who did for your priest. And that is what my men and I did."

"Besides," I said angrily as I pointed to the man on the ground, "he should have done what I told him to do and ridden away when you and the others did. If he had listened and done what he had been told to do he would have saved himself despite you abandoning him. He is dying of being a fool and that is the long and the short of it. Sir Hugh can probably explain it to you."

Actually, when I thought about later I realised that Sir Hugh probably could not explain why we fought as we did because he thinks like most knights that fighting means man against man to show how brave you are instead of fighting as an army to win. But I felt I had to say something in reply before I said "paugh" and rode away after a dismissive "be gone" wave of my hand.

******

The next hour was a busy time. The priest spent it dying with the bishop and the rest of the Queen's men gathered around him to pray and wring their hands; my men and I spent it checking out the robbers who were dead or wounded and recovering their weapons and saddles and whatever else of value they might have been carrying or wearing. It was not much.

Several of the robbers were still alive even after we finished retrieving our arrows by pulling them out or pushing them on through from wherever they were stuck. As you might imagine we did not knock the wounded robbers on the head so they would not jump around whilst we were retrieving our arrows until *after* we had finished questioning them.

What we learned from the wounded robbers was that they were members of a band of road robbers from Salisbury. We also learned from the weapons and valuables they were carrying that they were not as poor as church mice but close enough. Neither the King nor the Queen were ever mentioned. Our attackers were obviously road robbers pure and simple—and damn unlucky and poorly informed because they attacked a party that included men who knew how to fight them off.

Travellers on the road had begun reaching us from both directions before the priest finished his dying and we were ready to leave. As they passed him they made the sign of the cross to help send him on his way and we told them the story of the attempted robbery and got their heartfelt thanks:

"A band of robbers based in Salisbury somehow learned that a Welsh bishop was carrying a valuable gold cross on his pilgrimage to pray at the shrines of various saints. They attacked him and his fellow pilgrims in an effort to rob him or his cross and his coins. Fortunately the Welshmen the bishop had employed as guards had driven them off; unfortunately one of the bishop's party, a fine young priest, had been killed. We also could not find the baggage horse that had bolted with the bishop's tent and other of his personal supplies." *It was a good story and had the fine merit of being at least partially true.*

Sam and Jack helped the King's men lash the dead priest's body onto one of the remaining baggage horses and we set off once again for Salisbury. The priest would be buried in the graveyard of the city's great cathedral according to Bishop Bereford. We could also, or so Bishop Bereford claimed, safely spend the coming night sheltering at the cathedral as the guests of the Salisbury's Bishop Martival and his priests.

Bishop Bereford said he knew it was possible for us to shelter there for the night because he and the Queen's men had stayed there for several days whilst they were moving westward toward Cornwall in search of supporters and mercenaries for the Queen to employ. Moreover, Bereford said, we would receive a particularly warm welcome because he was a personal friend of Salisbury's Bishop Martival from their days together as priests in Lincoln.

It seemed like a reasonable thing to do and I did not think as much about it as I should have done.

******

The tall spire of the Salisbury's great cathedral could be seen for several hours before we actually reached the city gate and rode through it and into the city. It was late in the afternoon. I did not particularly like the idea of spending the night in the cell-like rooms the cathedral provided for pilgrims and other paying visitors but reluctantly agreed to do so when we were hit with a heavy rain just as we entered the city.

Dry is always better than wet—but agreeing to spend the night at the cathedral turned out to be a mistake, a very big one.

Our visit started off well enough. The Bishop of Salisbury himself came hurrying out to greet us and then waited patiently whilst we dismounted and pissed. After a few words of arm waving explanation from the Bishop of Lincoln he promptly set the cathedral's grave diggers to work preparing a place for the dead priest to be buried in the morning. He also invited Bishop Bereford and Sir Hugh to take their suppers with him and promised to find a suitable place for them to spend the night.

Everyone else was treated as well as the Church and its bishops always treated commoners; in other words, we were treated like dirt. We were sent off to ride in the rain to a nearby stable in the city to board our horses for the night after being informed by one of the archbishop's officious priests that someone would be along in a while to fetch us to our rooms.

Our horses had been unsaddled we and the bishop's men were feeding them when a rather arrogant priest showed up and, without saying a word, jerked his thumb toward the cathedral as a signal for us to follow him.

The priest led us along a cobblestoned street, through a little gate, and into a dark stone building next to the huge cathedral. Once again the people on the street and watching down from the wall openings in the building along it looked at us with curiosity in their eyes as we passed in the rain. They had done the same when we rode past them on our way to the stable. And once again none of them said anything or waved a greeting. At the time I attributed it to the rain and the fact that we were hurrying with our hoods up to get out of it. *Only later did I come to believe it might have been that they knew something we did not.*

We followed the priest through a side door into the building and immediately found ourselves in a dark and narrow stone corridor that had little cells for the cathedral's monks and priest opening into it. It was where we four archers were to spend the night with the four of us squeezed together into one of the austere and dimly lit little rooms. The servants of the bishop and Sir Hugh were similarly squeezed into a similar room near to ours in the same hallway.

After we looked at the stone-walled cell assigned to us I sent Sam back to the stable to stay with our horses and look after our equipment and supplies. He was glad to go and said as much. "You lot are welcome to sleep here; I will take the good clean straw of a stable any time.

But there was problem; a big problem: We were without our weapons because the officious priest who had been ordered by the cathedral's bishop to show us to our rooms refused to let us take our weapons with us when we left the stable.

"No weapons in God's house," he had announced with a shrug of his shoulders and a tight smile. "You must leave them in the stable with your horses."

"At least we will be dry when we eat the food we brought with us," Jack quipped when we began putting our sleeping skins down in the place where we three were expected to spend the night. I, of course, took the little bed, and rightly so, because rank has its privileges even when the privileges are quite small. Thomas and Jack would have to sleep on the stone floor next to my bed.

Jack was right about the stable being the preferable place to sleep; the cell was dry even if our clothes were not. It was also small and dingy and dark with a narrow string bed and a low stool on which a man could kneel and pray to the wooden cross that was leaning against one of the walls. Two very narrow wall openings with wooden shutters were all that lit the cell and there was no way to bar its short and narrow door. From the looks of it the room had not been occupied for some time.

"They are all like this," Thomas said a moment later after he returned from the piss pot that stood at the end of the corridor. "The Queen's lads are in a room a couple of doors down," he added. "But where are all the monks and priests?"

Yes, where are the cathedral's monks and priests? They were probably at their interminable prayers. Even so, something did not feel right.

"Jack I want you to quietly go back to the stable and help Sam saddle and load our horses so we can leave on a moment's notice. Take your sleeping skin with you. When you finish getting the horses ready I want you wrap our swords, bows, and quivers in your skin and bring them back with you. Bring our shields too and tell Sam I said he was to sleep with his bow strung, his sandals on, and his sword unsheathed."

"What about the horses of the Queen's men, Captain?"

"Leave them be. And do not say a word to whoever is watching them. If anyone asks why you are saddling them, tell him you were ordered to get the horses ready to leave at first light and are afraid you will not wake up in time.

Chapter Twelve
We are betrayed.

Roger Martival, the bishop of Salisbury, was a good host and lived well. His well-appointed rooms and his private dining hall were in an annex directly attached to the rear of the great cathedral. His rooms had their own outside entrances, of course, but the fastest and driest way to get to them from the front of the cathedral was by walking through the cathedral itself. The annex also contained a section of cell-like rooms where the monks slept, a second and similar section that was used to house visiting pilgrims, and a third for the cathedral's servants. They each had their own eating halls and their own doors into the rear of the cathedral.

The Bishop of Salisbury led Bishop Bereford and Sir Hugh through the cathedral to his rooms. And he did so whilst chattering away despite the presence of parishioners quietly arriving for the next prayer service and a long line of chanting monks and priests being led into the cathedral at one of the far corners of the great building.

As he led them through the cathedral the Bishop of Salisbury was in the middle of explaining that he now had enough coins to start the final phase of building the cathedral, but suddenly stopped talking when he saw Bishop Bereford's and Sir Hugh's eyes widen as a line chanting priests and monks walked down an adjoining aisle and were led to their chapel by a priest holding a bible over his head and another holding up a cross. What had surprised both men were the red crosses on the white tunics they were wearing over their priestly habits.

"They look like Templars?" Bishop Bereford said incredulously as he stopped to stare. There was a question in his voice.

"Most of them were at one time, yes," Bishop Martival replied. "But now with the suppression of their order by King Phillip and its dissolution by the Pope many of the survivors who escaped to England have become Cistercians. And they are very fine priests and monks. Indeed, they have transferred many of the Templar lands in this part of England to the cathedral so as to support themselves and the Church whilst they are here.

"The last time you and Sir Hugh were here most of our priests and monks were away to attend their order's annual retreat at Royston and initiate new members. As you may have heard, most of the Templars who survived the French king became either Cistercians or Hospitalers when the Templars' order was dissolved by the Pope. I myself am just a poor Franciscan and not so strict," he would later say as he belched and stood to refill his bowl from the silver pitcher on the table.

"And that brings up something rather important that we need to talk about and rather quickly—but only in private."

******

Bishop Bereford and Sir Hugh were wide-eyed and anxious about ten minutes later as the Bishop of Salisbury told them about their fates unless they acted quickly. They had put their bowls of wine down and were staring at him in disbelief with their mouths agape in astonishment by the time he finished explaining the danger they faced from the cathedral's Cistercian priests and monks.

"They hate France's King Phillip for torturing their friends and brother Templars to force them to make false confessions, and then executing them based on their confessions to escape from having to pay back the money the Templars loaned to him so he could pay for his wars.

As I am sure you, they support King Edward against the Queen. One reason they are doing so is because King Edward gave shelter to those of their order who were able to escape from France. Another reason is because the Queen is the sister of the French king who is actively supporting her efforts to have the Queen's son replace her husband on England's throne.

"What you need to understand is that there are many former Templars amongst the Cistercian priests and monks. They fear that if the Queen and Mortimer take power in England they will do what the Queen's brother did in France—hunt them down and torture them to find out where they hid their coins and to whom they transferred their lands. They also know that *you* have been actively encouraging the barons to support the Queen and have been hiring mercenaries to fight for her—and they are angry with you two for doing so.

"They hate the Queen and fear what she and Mortimer will do if they oust King Edward. As a result, they are sworn to do everything they can to stop her. That includes killing her supporters wherever they find them. And being experienced fighting men they certainly know how to do it. You two only escaped their wrath and revenge when you stayed here last month because the Cistercians were off to their order's annual conclave at Royston.

"And you, Roger; where do you stand?" a now-worried aghast Bishop Bereford demanded anxiously. He had known there would be problems if he supported the King but he had not realized they were so close at hand.

"I serve only the Church, of course, as I am sure you know, Henry. But much of the cathedral's lands came from the Templars and perhaps their ownership was not always transferred as properly as might have been done. Those lands today are providing a good portion of the cathedral's revenues. I need them to finish building the cathedral and I certainly would not like them to be seized by the Crown in order to pay for its wars."

"So you stand with King Edward?"

"No, I do not. I stand only with the Church and my only interest is the cathedral's completion and prosperity. My priests know that and appreciate it. I am in no danger from the Cistercians because I want what they want. But you two certainly are because you are working to bring the Queen to power and my priests and monks know it; and most of them hate and fear you for it. So you must save yourselves by fleeing from Salisbury as soon as possible.

"They knew you would be coming back and almost certainly they have made a plan to murder you later tonight. So you two must very quietly slip out of here and ride away from the city whilst they are at their evening prayers.

"Act as you would always act in front of the servants. But do not alert your men or they may give your plans away—and use the city's east gate when you leave Salisbury as it is well known that its guards will open it at night for a couple of copper pennies."

****** *Captain William Courtenay*

Our sleeping arrangements were more comfortable than I would have expected. Perhaps because we had brought our own sleeping skins and did not have to use those that were in the monk's cell. They were unbelievably foul, probably because Jesus was a God and never had to wash or wipe his arse. As a result many monks and priests trying to live like him also never did so. But their sleeping skins were useful despite their foul smell—we threw them in a corner and hid our weapons under them.

We were asleep when suddenly there was a great commotion in the corridor and the door to our cell was thrown open and three sword-wielding men rushed in. They were each carrying a candle lantern in one hand and a sword in the other. There were more men in the corridor and a moment later we could shouts and screams from the Queen's men in the nearby cell.

As the first Cistercian through the door raised his sword to cut down Thomas, I shouted "Stop. You will not see God's face if you kill a priest."

I do not know what possessed me to shout out the warning to the swordsman. It was all I could think to do as Thomas instinctively raised his arm in a futile effort to block the blow.

"Stop," I said again. "He is an Angelovian priest. We all are. You will burn in purgatory forever if you kill us." I shouted it out in Latin.

The swordsman stopped and looked over at me in surprise in the dim and flickering light. "Quid Est?"

"You are Angelovian priests? the second man into the cell said with suspicion in his voice as he held a sword to my throat. "What are you doing here?" he asked in crusader French with a heavy French accent. The man who was about to chop down on Thomas listened intently.

"We are Angelovians in the Company of Archers and contracted with the King to be the guards of Prince Edward.

We are on our way to take up our duties," I answered. *My God; he is wearing a Templar's tunic. Are they back?*

"You lie. You are supporters of the French whore that wants to replace King Edward with her son so she and Mortimer can rule England."

"No. No." I replied in Latin. "We are Angelovian priests in the Order of Poor Landless Sailors. And we do not support the Queen in any way. We have been ordered by our order's commander to be the guards of King Edward's son, his heir and England's crown prince, because it is God's will that his son be the next king of England.

"I swear it in the name of God and Jesus," I said in Latin as I made the sign of the cross and nodded my head emphatically to agree with the truth of what I was saying.

I suddenly realized who our assailants were—they were Cistercians who wore white tunics with a red cross instead of the plain brown priestly cassocks of the Franciscans. Most of them *or was it all of them?* were wearing red crosses on their tunics to show that they had once been Templars. Was it possible?

More importantly, they were supporters of King Edward because he had allowed the French Templars to seek refuge in England even though he too owed money to the order and could have done what the French king had done—killed them and seized their lands to avoid having to repay his loans to their order.

"We are Angelovian priests serving in the Company of Archers and you are Templars serving as Cistercians," I said once again in Latin. "You know us. Our company and our order are the friends of the Templars and Cistercians and certainly wish them no harm."

I followed that up by issuing a warning of my own.

"King Edward will surely consider you and your order to be amongst his greatest enemies and seek revenge if you put his son at risk by killing his son's guards."

Out of the corner of my eye I saw Jack slide his hand under the pile of foul sleeping skins. I shook my head "no."

But then from out of nowhere a thought found its way behind my eyes and I let it out without thinking.

"The Company of Archers is well known for honouring its contracts as I am sure you know if you have ever been a Templar. And we have no agreement or reason to defend or assist the Queen, only to protect her son because it is God's Will and that of King Edward that his son become England's next king.

"But as you can see there are only four of us. So instead of trying to kill us, why not *help* King Edward stay on the throne by making a carta with the Company of Archers to provide more men to help defend the King's son. We could also provide you whatever information we can uncover about the Queen's plans for the men who used to be Templars and the Templar properties?

"It could even specify that the men of the Company would never lift a weapon to defend the evil Queen or to hurt good King Edward. I am a captain in the Company and can make my mark on such a carta to commit the Company. And you know I can because you can see the four stripes on the front and back of the tunic I am wearing." *If I turn it inside out again.*

And then I had another thought as I put my feet on the stone floor so I could stand up.

"You can pay us with some of the cathedral's prayer offerings and the rents the cathedral has collected from its lands. Thirty good archers sounds about right to find Prince Edward and protect him. And that will require about three thousand pounds of silver coins if we are to get the Company's very best men. We will need it in advance, of course, to pay the necessary bribes to get enough men to leave the Company and take the additional risks."

Chapter Thirteen
On the road again.

It took more than a little talking and negotiations to convince the Cistercians that we would be able to employ more archers to help guard the King's son. And then it took even longer to reach a satisfactory agreement with them as to the price that they would have to pay up front.

Without a doubt it helped that Thomas and I had both been ordained as Angelovian priests when we graduated from the Company school because it meant our talks could be conducted in Latin. And then it took a while to scribe a mutually acceptable carta and even longer to pry the necessary coins out of the cathedral's treasury room.

Everything took time, particularly as the Cistercians periodically had to go off to chant and pray. And each time they did they returned with new questions and concerns. As a result, it was not until the next afternoon that we were able to saddle up and ride out of Salisbury with our saddlebags and supply horses carrying the coins and enough food to get us all the way to Suffolk—a destination I had *not* shared with the Cistercians for fear they would inform King Edward's men as to where the Queen and his son might be landing.

Instead I implied that we expected to be informed where we were to meet the Prince and take up our duties when we reached London. I also told them that it was in

London where we would get the additional archers from our shipping post and galleys.

What I did not tell the Cistercians, of course, was that I already knew that as many as thirty additional archers were already on their way to join us in Suffolk to help guard the young prince and that the Queen's men had already paid for their services. *I also did not tell the Cistercians, because I did not know at the time, that the King's men had also paid for thirty archers to help guard the Prince.*

The Bishop of Lincoln and Sir Hugh were long gone by the time my talks with the Cistercians were successfully concluded. They had apparently been warned in time to escape the fate that befallen their men when they abandoned them without trying to alert them to the danger they faced in time to escape. Unfortunately their servants and vassals had tried to save themselves by claiming to be Queen's men and were promptly slaughtered. I know because I heard them being killed and saw their bodies.

When we first went to the stable whilst the Cistercians were off to pray Sam reported that the two leaders of the Queen's men had hurried into the stable on the night of our arrival, saddled their horses, and rode off in such a hurry that they left the horses and equipment of their soon-to-be-butchered men behind.

It was right then and there that I decided that we when we rode off we would take whatever was left of the bishop's and Sir Hugh's horses and equipment with us as well. They were, I told myself, and later told my men, prizes due to us for saving the Queen's poor sods the first time they were attacked. We would sell them in London.

We also took with us one of the Cistercian monks who had agreed to make his mark on the Company's roll and temporarily become an archer and adhere to the Company's rules. Taking him with us was part of our contract to protect Prince Edward and spy for the former crusaders who were now Cistercians. It seems the former Templars trusted us because of the Company's of Archers' well-known and richly deserved reputation for honouring its contracts, but not completely. And that was not all bad if the man they sent to keep an eye on us was as handy with a sword as his brother monks claimed.

The man they sent with us to help protect the Prince and send back any information we uncovered was an Englishman, Brother Peter, the son of a miller and a one-time Templar from Lancaster and now a Cistercian monk. Peter must have had enough to eat as a lad because was almost as tall as Thomas and me. According to his fellow Cistercians Peter had a good reputation for being a man to have by your side during a fight and he knew how to ride. *What I later learnt by talking to Peter was that he had been stationed at several Templar strongholds in the east and had returned to England just in time to help some of his Templar brothers in France escape to England.*

Peter's betters had initially wanted to send one of their knights with us but, fortunately, they did not press the point when I adamantly refused to even consider the possibility. That was probably because several of the Templar veterans amongst the Cistercians knew that knights and their sons were not allowed to make their marks on the Company of Archer's roll. So we managed to dodge that arrow and move on to finalize the carta setting out our agreement.

******

The five of us rode out of Salisbury on the London road with Jack and Sam each leading a string of five baggage and remount horses. The coins the Cistercians "obtained" from the cathedral's bishop to cover our expenses and pay for the additional archers were divided amongst our saddle bags.

My initial thought was that we would camp along the road in the tent abandoned by Bishop Bereford and bring the prize horses and equipment over to the Company's London shipping post to sell. Jack and Sam were already talking about the prize coins they hoped to receive from the sale of the horses and Sir Hugh's armour and how they might spend some of them on London's women without getting poxed. Wearing a couple of garlic bulbs and rapidly saying ten "Hail Marys", they assured each other, usually worked.

We splashed our way across the Thames at the ox ford a few days later to avoid paying a toll to use the bridge, spent the night camping in a little woods east of Oxford village, and started out early the next day to ride to the stables of our London shipping post. I thought about swimming the horses across the Thames closer to London in order to get there sooner, but decided against it because it is hard for a rider to swim a horse across whilst leading a string of other horses, particularly if he is worried about falling off the horse he is riding because he does not know how to swim.

Besides, truth be told, only Sam and Jack were known to me as truly competent horsemen and only Thomas and I knew how to swim as a result of our days in the Company school. In addition, although I never mentioned it, some time had passed since my last swim and I was concerned that I might have forgotten how to do so whilst wearing a chain shirt and sandals.

A small disaster struck late on the second morning after we crossed at the ford: one of the prize horses, I think it was Sir Hugh's spare riding horse, threw a shoe. It was a fine mare and much too valuable to abandon. So we camped off the road somewhere between Beaconsfield and Windsor and continued on the next day after digging a pebble out of its hoof and getting a new shoe put on it by the smith in a nearby village.

Peter and I talked a lot and exchanged stories about our lives and experiences as we rode. Amongst other things, he confided that he had been pleased to have been chosen to accompany us because he had been getting a bit bored doing nothing but praying and chanting. Interestingly enough, he knew very little about Cornwall despite having been birthed in England. I found his ignorance about Cornwall very encouraging and promptly began telling him how poor Cornwall's land and people had become in case he ever talked to others about his time with the Company.

The road was crowded with travellers and there was an unexpected roadblock of King's Guards on the outskirts of Windsor. They did not say why they were there or what they were looking for. All they did was ask who we were and why we were on the road.

I forthrightly explained that we were archers from the Company of Archers on our way to London to pick up horses for use in Cornwall because the horses of Cornwall grew up too small from not eating enough due to Cornwall's weak land.

Fortunately the Guardsmen knew even less than Peter about Cornwall and the Company of Archers and did not bother to ask why we were not wearing Company tunics with the telltale stripes of our ranks. What the King's Guards did know and commented on, and it surprised me to my bones, was that a large force of the Company's archers, about thirty they said, had passed through a couple of hours earlier on the King's business. *On the King's business?*

I was expecting thirty archers from Okehampton to join me in Suffolk. And we had experienced several delays en route so I was not surprised that they might have passed us on the road and gotten ahead of us. But thirty Company archers on the King's business? Could this be true or was that merely the story the archers told the King's men at the roadblock to gull them into letting them through? Or had Commander Boatman decided that the Company should support the King after all?

******

We rode along the city of London side of the Thames and reached the outskirts of the city in mid-afternoon on a beautiful summer day in early September. In other words, it was damn warm riding in the sun. An hour or so later we were riding past the city's great wall and then past the Tower itself. My four companions were gawking at everything. They had never been to London before. The bridge across the Thames particularly impressed them; Jack wondered aloud if it was safe to cross and how often people got overbalanced and fell off it into the river to drown.

The main entrance door and the wall openings of Company's shipping post looked out on to the river road and the Thames flowing along next to it. We rode right past it, however, because our destination was the Company's stable. That was where the Company's new horses and new recruits were housed in its stalls until they could be sent west either on foot in the case of the horses or via a westward bound Company galley or transport for the men.

Our stable was a short three or four minute walk down the river from the Company's shipping post and two narrow streets in from the road along the river. The stable's entrance was on a side street and the stable itself took up the entire centre of the block on which it stood. It was a fine location and I remembered hearing my uncle say that various and sundry merchants constantly inquired about buying our rights to the land on which it stood.

We rode into the stable yard and were surprised to find it filled with archers including a four-stripe captain, George Wainwright, who turned out to be the captain of our shipping post. But what truly astonished me was that standing with George and enthusiastically greeting our arrival was Major Captain Robertson. *What is he doing here? He is supposed to be commanding Okehampton and the approaches to Cornwall?*

I quickly learned why the major captain was so pleased to see me: He jovially announced that he had expected to have to ride all the way to Suffolk to explain what had happened *after* my men and I had ridden out of Cornwall and give me my revised orders. *Revised orders?* I must have looked greatly confused as to why he was anxious to talk with me.

A cheerful Major Captain Robertson smiled at my confusion and immediately took me by the arm and led me off to a nearby tavern so he could explain the changed situation without our being overhead by our men and the stable's hostlers.

We walked to the nearby *The Ship* tavern. When we got there and were seated in a quiet corner by the alewife he began explaining what had happened as a result of Commander Boatman meeting the King's representatives—that the King had *also* hired the Company to protect Prince Edward. It was important, he leaned forward and said in a low voice after the alewife placed our bowls on the table and walked away, that neither the King nor the Queen ever found out about the other also paying the Company to protect the prince.

He had come all that way, he said, so he could warn me and explain to me that things had changed because *both* the King *and* the Queen had hired the Company to protect the Prince even though each did not know the other had done so. It changed everything, he said, and was so important that instead of scribing a message that might be intercepted he had come himself to explain things to me and make sure I understood and could properly explain them to my men and to the Queen's supporters—"because sure as God made green apples they will find out sooner or later."

What it meant, he said, is that there would have to be an important change in how my men and I were to present ourselves when we reached the Queen's camp. We were still to claim to be a free company but we were now to wear our distinctive Company tunics with our rank stripes. If asked, every man was to say "I am one of the archers employed to guard the prince."

"On the other hand, what our men must *never* do is say *who* it was that had employed them to guard the prince. If a man was asked he was always to say "I do not know" and report the inquiry immediately.

"You must let every man know in no uncertain terms that he will lose his stripes and never get them back if even hints at who had hired him and his mates to protect the prince."

I, of course, nodded enthusiastically and responded by telling major captain about our fight with the road robbers and about the Cistercians also paying us to protect Prince Edward "for the king" and also to try to find out the Queen's intentions toward them and the many Templars who were now in their ranks. I also told him how bitterly the former Templars seemed to hate her and were loyal to King Edward.

He smiled and gave me a playful poke in the shoulder when he heard that I had signed a carta and the Company had been paid for a third time to do the same thing—protect the young prince. He also gave a start and whistled when I told him how much the former Templars had paid.

"I did not know they had been able to save so much of their order's treasure. Hmm. They really must be worried that their friend, the King, will lose if he does not have the boy and that the Queen and the French will come to power if they have him. I wonder why? Do you suppose they know something we do not?"

Then he smiled and nodded his satisfaction at what I had done. Although he had narrowed his eyes at first when I described saving the Queen's men and the loss of the priest—and started to admonish me for risking my men until I explained that I felt the need to do so in order to be welcome in the Queen's camp.

"Aye, you were right," the major captain said slowly after he thought about it for a bit. "And it was good thinking of you to winkle the Templars' coins out of the Cistercians instead of getting chopped," he added with a pleased smile as he motioned to the alewife to refill our bowls.

"It was a good day's work you did in Salisbury, William, and no mistake. It will not be forgotten. And, of course, your bringing in so many of the Templar coins to London changes everything for me. It seems as though I will have to stay in London until the next Company galley arrives so I can take them with me when I return to Cornwall.

"I had planned to ride back to Okehampton with a couple of men as escorts. But that would not be enough to guard so many coins since we might have to ride fast and switch to our remounts to escape from road robbers or the prying eyes of the King's men. But if we ever had to do that we would almost certainly be forced to ride off and abandon the remounts and baggage horses carrying the coins. And there is no sense in taking chance on losing them, eh?"

My response was properly obsequious.

"Your command of the marches along the border of Cornwall is more important than anything else, even the Templar's coins, Major Captain. I could wait here with my men to help guard the coins and send them on the next galley. Or you could entrust them to the captain of our London shipping post to see to their shipment. Either way you could ride back immediately. Or you could take the coins with you and ride back to Okehampton with some or all of the men I am taking to Suffolk to help guard them."

"No William. Those are possibilities that will not do at all, not at all. You must get to Suffolk as soon as possible with all the men we have contracted to provide to guard the prince. It will be noted and there will be trouble if you do not. So I am going to sail with the coins to Okehampton and send them on to Restormel myself."

He laughed uproariously at the thought and leaned forward to confide in me.

"Those coins you brought in and the many our shipping post has taken in during the past few weeks are a good excuse for me to travel most of the way on a galley instead of rubbing my arse raw on a horse. I have not been on a horse for years and I am already so saddle sore that it hurts to sit down. It will also be a much safer way to transport the coins since a galley can get almost all the way up the Tamar at this time of year.

"Besides, if I stay here with Captain Wainwright and take the coins back to Okehampton on the next Company galley that arrives *all* the archers I brought with me can accompany you to the Queen's camp. And you may well need every one of them to fight your way clear if anyone who paid us finds out we have also been paid others to do the same thing and gets pissed about being gulled."

Chapter Fourteen
The worried Lord Mayor.

George Wainwright, the affable captain of the Company's London shipping post, was waiting for me on the street in front of the shipping post when I walked there from the tavern after my private talk with Captain Courtenay. George was a roly poly man with a big smile and an even bigger beard. He was a son of the Company in that his father had been a ship's carpenter on one of our transports and then settled in Cyprus to help the Company build wains and galleys. George's apprentice sergeant was waiting with him. *I never did learn the name of the young apprentice sergeant who was accompanying him, probably because he fell a few weeks later in the London riots that occurred due to the fighting between the supporters of the King and the Queen.*

"Hoy, Major Captain," George Wainwright said with a big smile as he bustled out into the street in front of our shipping post to greet me I walked towards it. His eager and sadly-fated young apprentice sergeant came out with him. I was alone because Captain Courtenay had returned to the stable to gather his men and begin his long ride to Suffolk. *George has been waiting for me. How did he know? I must have told him I would be coming here after my meeting with William.*

"We have an important visitor waiting to see you. In addition, the Bishop of London, Bishop Gravesend, has sent a messenger asking for meeting with you as soon as possible. I am not sure how they found out you were in London; they probably had spies watching our stables, eh?"

"Spies, George?" I said as I stopped in the street in front of our shipping post and cocked my head. "Why in the world would our stables be watched by spies? Someone probably saw us ride in on the Thames Road and knew I would be visiting you here sooner or later."

"London is like that these days, Major. Everyone knows Mortimer and his mercenaries are coming and they are bringing the Queen and Prince Edward with them. Upset and worried is what London is these days and there are spies everywhere. There have been fights and riots between the supporters of the King and those who favour the Queen almost every day for the past week or so."

"And who, pray tell, is the important visitor that has come to see me?"

"It is the Lord Mayor himself, Sir Hamo de Chigwell, the head of the Fishmongers Guild. He has come to you wearing his mayor's chain and badge so it must be very important. Those men over there are his guards from the city's night watch."

I was incredulous in addition to being slightly tipsy from The Ship's juniper-flavoured clear ale.

"The Lord Mayor is a fishmonger? The city's guilds elected a fishmonger to represent them as the city's mayor?"

"Oh aye, Major; so they did. Very rich he is I am sure. There are good coins in fish these days."

"And he is really a lord and a knight?" *That sounds unlikely.*

"Oh aye he is. That way he can talk directly to the King when the King needs something from the city. It has been a tradition for some years now although I am not sure those are permanent titles for the man who holds them; I think they may only good for so long as he is the mayor."

"Well then, George, we best go find out what His Lordship the Mayor wants of us, aye?"

******

Sir Hamo might be a questionable noble and knight but he was indeed a prosperous man if his fine clothes and their lack of a strong fishy odour were any indication of his wealth—at least they did not smell at all like old fish which is what I had expected when I advanced to meet him in the post's very small front reception room. On the other hand, they also did not smell like my clothes which after so many days in the saddle reeked of good old-fashioned horse and people sweat.

London's lord mayor was altogether full of smiles and goodwill.

"Ah, it is good of you to meet me on such short notice, Major Captain, good of you indeed. Thank you so much. Thank you indeed"

He knows my rank? George must have told him.

The Lord Mayor bowed most respectful as he spoke and held out his open hand to show he had no weapon in it. I, of course, was very much on guard being as he had been elected by his fellow guild masters and was no doubt quite devious. But I reciprocated warily and we clasped hands and shook them up and down most cordial.

I did so, clasped his open hand that is, because it was, or so I had been told by travellers and heard in the east, the coming greeting amongst today's modern men. Sir Hamo was not as tall as I me and his beard and hair were well trimmed. He appeared to be about my age, somewhere in his late thirties or early forties.

"It is an honour to meet you, Lord Mayor," I said with a little bow of my head as we shook our clasped hands up and down in the latest fashion. "You have obviously gone out of your way to visit our Company's humble shipping post; is there something you or the city needs or any way my men and I might be of service to you?"

"Yes there is, Major Captain. It is why I am here. It is a delicate matter. Fish do not travel well, of course, so I have never done business with your shipping post. But I am aware from my fellow merchants that the men of the Company of Archers are quite dependable and can be trusted to keep a secret and honour a properly signed carta. Is it true?"

"I believe it is true, Lord Mayor. Yes it is. We go out of our way to honour our contracts and agreements. We do so because we know it will be bad for attracting customers to our galleys and transports in the years ahead if we do not do so and that our custom will grow if we do."

"So I have been told; so I have been told," the Lord Mayor said. He was eyeing me warily as he acknowledged my words. He was agreeing but he was obviously more than a little concerned and uncertain.

"Well then, Lord Mayor, it sounds as though you have something in your mind that we might find it profitable to talk about."

And with that I made a gesture with my hand to invite him to precede me into our post's middle room where our shipping post captain and his men met with the Company's would-be shippers and those who had come to claim their cargos and money. It was immediately behind the reception room that opened on to the street.

I followed the Lord Mayor in to the post's meeting room. George held the door open and bowed us in. Then he came in himself and joined us. His apprentice came in silently behind him and stood next to the door.

A few moments later the three of us were each seated on one of the stools next to the little table on which the post's contracts and agreements were scribed and coins were counted. The room was lit both from openings in the room's outside wall and from the door to the entrance room which had been left open. There was a candle lantern on the table but it was not lit.

"Captain Wainwright and I are honoured by your visit to our Company's shipping post, Lord Mayor. Can you tell us the reason for it?"

"Well yes. I am here, you see, because there is talk in the city about the Queen returning to England with her son and an army to fight with the King and try to put her son on the throne to replace him.

"Already there has been fighting in the city between the King's supporters and the Queen's. And today an army of two or three dozen heavily armed archers wearing your Company's tunics turned inside out was seen riding into the city. It is rumoured amongst my fellow merchants that they are headed eastward towards the Suffolk coast where it is thought the Queen and her army will land."

The Mayor sighed, took a deep breath, and looked at me intently whilst he began telling me the reason for his visit.

"To put it bluntly, Major Captain, there is chaos and rioting in London and my friends and I do not know what to do to stop it or whose side to take. The people in the city seem to be supporting the Queen but the King is strong in the city because he has the Church's support and because he holds the Tower and its garrison appears to be loyal to him. In a word, we are afraid of backing the wrong horse and paying dearly for it."

Then he adjusted his tunic, looked at the door, and sighed.

"So will you please tell me who the Company is supporting and what you think will happen?"

It was an interesting question, and also very much what I was hoping to hear. Even so, I delayed answering it for a few moments to gather my thoughts and add gravitas to my response.

"Cornwall is far away, Lord Mayor, and very poor as I am sure you know. It has no knights and levies to provide men for either side. That is because most of Cornwall's men and boys are in the east earning their daily bread helping the

Company of Archers move cargos and passengers from port to port. Accordingly, we have no dog in this fight.

"We have, it is true, scraped together a small company of volunteers who at this very moment are riding eastward out of London in search of the Queen and her army—but *not* to join her men or to fight against them. The volunteers from the Company are under contract to do only one thing—to protect the young prince who is with her from the French lords who want to kill him so they can put a French noble on England's throne when King Edward goes to heaven.

"As you might imagine, both the King *and* the Queen have been quite pleased to learn of the Company's commitment to protecting their son. That is because, despite their quarrel, they both want Prince Edward protected so he can take the throne whenever God decides to call King Edward to join him in heaven. We have become, it seems, everyone's friend.

"Unfortunately, the prince is still at great risk because their majesties' supporters who reached out to us on his behalf are not rich men. They could not come up with enough coins to pay for the archers' food for more than a few weeks. But guarding the prince and keeping him safe and alive for a short time is better than not at all, eh?"

There were no flies on the Lord Mayor. He sat up straight and his eyes opened wide as my answer and its implications reached him.

"How long do you think the prince will need to be protected," he asked.

I waited inside our shipping post until the Lord Mayor and his guards were out of sight. He, the Lord Mayor that is, had one copy of the carta we had hastily scribed and I had the other. It provided for city of London to pay for thirty archers to find and guard Prince Edward for the lesser of twenty-four months or the resolution of the dispute between the King and the Queen. "Resolution" meaning that there had been an end to the dispute such as would occur if one or another of the parties defeated the other.

"It was very astute of you," I had assured the Lord Mayor as he got up to leave, "to come up with idea of using all of the city's available coins to pay us to protect the young prince. It means that the city will not be able to help either the winner or the loser of the coming war and, in so doing, piss off the winner if you had chosen wrong."

It had been my idea, of course but I was telling him that he could claim credit for it with his fellow merchants. Of course I did; it might help him to win their votes when the time comes and he will owe us a debt of gratitude. Every little bit helps, eh?

"Aye Major Captain, it will empty the city's chests but that is certainly preferable to having our heads chopped off or our necks stretched or our taxes increased because we backed the loser and pissed off the winner," the Lord Mayor had commented as we once again shook hands and he got up to leave.

"Aye, Your Lordship. And I believe truer and smarter words were never spoken. As you yourself just said, you can now truthfully say that the city spent every penny it had to protect Prince Edward such that it has nothing left to give to either of the royals."

The Lord Mayor looked at me and smiled as he went out into the street. But then he turned and said something that chilled my bones.

"You know, I hope, that the city has likely escaped the winner's wrath by finding an excuse to spend all its coins on a cause acceptable to everyone. But the archers you have arranged to guard the Prince will not escape it if Prince Edward is lost whilst they are guarding him?"

"Yes, I know," I responded. "They will be in grave danger if the Prince goes down. Thankfully none of them are on the Company's rolls." *What else could I say, eh?*

I also knew that in an hour or so George Wainwright's wife and the post's wives would bar the shipping post's outer and inner doors and George and all but one of his post's archers would go heavily armed to the Company stable to obtain a wagon and then proceed on to the guild hall to collect the coins. I, however, would not be present; I would already be off to Saint Paul's Cathedral to visit the Bishop of London as he urgently requested. The post's one remaining archer knew the city and would be my guide.

Chapter Fifteen
We accept the bishop's coins.

We travelled in a horse cart because it is quite a long walk from the Company's shipping post on the Thames Road to the Bishop's palace on Ludgate Hill next to London's recently completed Saint Paul's cathedral. We were going there because it was the home of the Bishop of London. The archer riding with me in the cart was a long-serving chosen man by the name of Thomas Meadows. We were both fully armed with longbows, galley shields, and short swords.

Stephen of Gravesend was the bishop we were going to visit. His request for a visit "as soon as possible" had been delivered to our shipping post by a young priest and addressed to "whoever is the senior man of the Order of Poor Landless Sailors now in London." That was obviously me because all the men who make their marks on the Company's roll are automatically also enrolled in the Order.

And it certainly was a surprise to receive Bishop Gravesend's message because very few people in England know about the Order since its main function has always been to provide the "prayer coins of the ocean travellers" to the Pope for his personal purse each year. They contributed them for his prayers for their save arrivals.

The Company did so, shared *some* of the coins we collected for the Holy Father's prayers with him, in exchange for being able to name an Angelovian priest as the Bishop of Cornwall whenever there was a vacancy and for being able to claim we were under the Holy Father's personal protection and following his orders whenever we found it helpful when dealing with overly religious princes and Christian zealots. So far as I know it has always been a win-win arrangement for everyone except the passengers we lost despite their paying for the Pope's prayers for their safety. *"The Pope did not pray hard enough" the hard-bitten archers would say when one of our galleys or transports was reported lost.*

According to what I had been learnt at the Company school, the Order of Poor Landless Sailors had been formed right after the Company's handful of surviving crusaders had gotten into the cargo and passenger carrying trade when its then-captain somehow got his hands on a galley that could be used to carry the Company's survivors back to England—and discovered that it could also be used to earn coins by carrying pilgrims and refugees to safety.

It is uncertain how the Poor Sailors order came into being soon thereafter to ostensibly do at sea what the Hospitallers and Templars were doing on land—assist pilgrims and crusaders to safely get to wherever they were going. But it was certainly different from its land-oriented counterparts. For one, it certainly did not loan out the coins it received from its passengers and had not evolved into being a major money lender and property owner as the Templars did with the coins it received for allowing its piece of the true cross to be kissed—and caused the Templars to get so rich that when they became moneylenders and the King of France suppressed them so he could seize their lands and would not have to pay back the huge sums he had borrowed from them to pay for his wars.

So far as I knew the only priests in the Order of Poor Sailors were Angelovians and the only Angelovians were men like me who had been ordained when they passed out of the Company school so they could earn their daily bread as priests and clerics if they were not up to serving in the Company as archers. Ordaining us was easy for the Bishop of Cornwall to do since he was one of the Company's major captains and we students were learnt to scribe and gobble in Latin so we could scribe messages and contracts whilst we were in the Company's service.

******

My ride from the Company's shipping post to the bishop's palace at the top of Ludgate Hill was eye-opening and somewhat surprising—because we rode through cobblestoned streets that were bustling and peaceful. Based on what the Lord Mayor had told me earlier I had been expecting to find riots and trouble. In fact, I found nothing of the kind and remarked on it to my London-based companion.

Thomas explained why that was as we rode briskly past Londoners and the carts and stalls of small merchants carrying out their normal day's activities of buying, selling, and pissing in the streets. People were everywhere and we rated barely a glance from most of them.

"The rioting and looting is mostly happening in and around the cathedral and in the Westminster area where the city's criminals and street women live in order to be near their best customers, the priests, the King's justiciars and clerics, and the members of parliament when one is being held. The market is also nearby and most of the merchants live near it—so they and the priests and clerics think the whole city is in trouble because that is all they see."

Saint Paul's looked impressive and so did the palace of the bishop that was adjacent to it. Both buildings and a rather large cemetery were inside a low wall. We entered through an un-gated opening in the wall and walked through the memory stones and wooden crosses of the cemetery to reach the main entrance door into the bishop's palace. A small flock of sheep were grazing between the tombstones and crosses.

Our approach must have been seen because the door opened and a man armed with a short spear came out to welcome us. He just stood there waiting silently on the door step until we reached him.

"Hello," I said as I lifted my hand in greeting. "I am Major Captain Edward Robertson, a priest in the Order of Poor Landless Sailors. I am here at the request of the Bishop of London to meet with him. Is he available?"

The man at the door said not a word; he merely stepped back inside the door and closed it in our faces. We waited. Several minutes later the door opened again and beardless young priest with somewhat of a smirk on his face made the sign of the cross to bless us and bowed us into an unfurnished entry room dimly lit by wall opening running along its front wall. The entry room's dirt floor suggested the poverty and piety of its priestly residents.

Everything changed when we followed the young priest into the reception room beyond the entry room. It was quite elegant with carpets on the floor and an elevated throne-like chair at the end of the room. A splendidly robed and mitred bishop and three older priests entered the room from another door as we did. The well-dressed bishop was obviously Stephen of Gravesend, the Bishop of London. He gracefully held out his ring to be kissed as we approached each other. I promptly kissed his ring as soon as his hand was within reach.

"It is kind of you to come so quickly, Father Edward," he said as he made the sign of the cross to bless me. *Father Edward? He knows I am an archer and he is reminding me that I have also been ordained as a priest; why is that?*

Stephen of Gravesend, the Bishop of London, was a tall, lean, grey- bearded man who waved his hands about as he spoke with a high voice and very feminine gestures. It was soon clear that he spent most of his time at the Kings' court and was a strong supporter and personal friend of King Edward. He proudly spoke ordering all the priests in his diocese to remind their parishioners that it was Edward who God had chosen to rule England, not the Queen or Lord Mortimer.

"The Church," he said rather primly, "supports the King because God chose him to rule over England and his lands in France."

I nodded without saying a word. *Not in agreement, mind you; just to acknowledge that I had heard him.*

"We have summoned you here because God has set a task for you." *We? Summoned? A task?*

"And what task might that be, Your Eminence?"

"God wants you to summon the men of your order to help defend King Edward whom God has placed on the throne of England." *Oh oh.* "He is being threatened as I am sure you know by mercenaries hired by the French whore he married and her lover."

"I am sure you are right, Eminence. Of course you are. Unfortunately there are a number of problems no matter how much the Commander and men of our order might agree with you and would like to assist King Edward.

"One problem, as I am sure you know, Eminence, is that we are very few in number here in England because Cornwall is so poor that most of the members of our order must be in the Holy Land and in the waters around it to earn their bread.

"Another is that our order is virtually penniless at this time because we just sent this year's "prayer coins" to the Holy Father in Rome. *Well, a few of them.*

There is a third problem, which I do not think I will mention at this time—that we do not take orders from anyone in the Church except the Pope, and then only when it suits us. And a fourth that we are not stupid enough to risk supporting the loser in the coming war such that the winner becomes seriously pissed at us.

"Having said all that, Eminence, I am happy to report that we have been able to gather up a few coins from our supporters and have used them to employ a company of mercenaries to guard the King's son so that someone chosen by God will reign in England in the event King Edward should fall.

"The mercenaries are already on their way to Eastern England to take up their duties as soon as Prince Edward comes ashore. Hopefully they will get there in time to save the prince because there are strong rumours that the French are planning to kill him as soon as he reaches England. It is said they plan to do so in order that a French prince or noble can take the throne when both King Edward and his son are gone.

"Unfortunately, our supporters are not rich and we have so far only been able to put together enough coins to employ the mercenaries for a few weeks. But every little bit helps and knowing his son will be protected for the next few weeks will no doubt comfort the King, eh? And best of all, of course, it will please God for it means someone God has chosen will sit on England's throne *if* the dispute between the King and the Queen is settled quickly." *In other words, we are only going to guard the Prince and will not be taking a side in this dispute no matter how much you might want us to do so.*

"Protecting the Prince from the French you say? The Prince will be protected from them so that God's Will can be carried out when King Edward passes? Hmm. Yes, I can see that both God and the King would be pleased if his son is protected so that he can succeed to the throne when the time comes.

And there is no doubt about it, the Holy Father will be pleased when I inform him of your order's efforts and take credit for them when I do.

There were similarly no flies on Stephen of Gravesend— he was as quick as the Lord Mayor and instantly understood what I was telling him. As a result, he too immediately asked the question I hoped he would ask.

"I may know some barons who support the King and might want to help protect his son, Father Edward, and perhaps there are some coins of the Church also available for such a good cause. How long do you think Prince Edward will need protection from the French and what do you think it would cost to keep the mercenaries in place?"

Chapter Sixteen
William encounters a problem.

We rode out of London and headed for Suffolk the next morning. There were thirty-one of us, a virtual army, and we were riding with the stripes on our tunics showing us to be Company archers and carrying our bows and swords in plain sight. My lieutenant, Thomas, and our sergeant major knew where we were going and why; but no one else did. They would be told when they needed to know.

Every man except me was leading a saddled remount carrying a food and water sack, additional quivers, and his sleeping skins. My remount was being led by a young archer assigned to lead mine in addition to his own. We even had three spare remounts in case one of our horses unexpectedly broke down and two of them were carrying rain tents.

My lieutenant was a veteran archer sergeant major, Harold Goodman, newly promoted from his previous posting as Okehampton's sergeant major. My number three was a newly promoted and relatively young sergeant major, Arthur Donaldson, from the Company's Horse Archers. Arthur had attended the Company school just as I had done years earlier. Jack and Sam stayed with me to carry my messages and run my errands.

Lieutenant Goodman was a grizzled Company veteran who had just been promoted to a rank higher than he had ever expected to reach—and was obviously quite keen to show that his promotion was not a mistake. I assigned Thomas to him as his apprentice sergeant because the new lieutenant did not know how to read, sum, or scribe.

Thomas's assignment to be Lieutenant Goodman's apprentice sergeant was a recognition of the importance of my new lieutenant's responsibilities since apprentice sergeants were usually assigned to archers with the rank of Captain or higher. As you might imagine, the newly promoted lieutenant was as pleased to have an apprentice sergeant of his own as I had been only a few weeks earlier when I had unexpectedly been promoted to captain and Thomas had been assigned to me.

"The lad is a good one, Lieutenant, but still a bit young and excitable. If he survives he will be important to the Company in the years ahead when you and I are retired and gone. It is up to us to bring him along. So please keep him informed as to the reason for your decisions and assign a couple of steady veterans to stay close to him to make sure he does not get himself needlessly killed if there is fighting. They can be his assistants and messengers.

What I did not tell Lieutenant Goodman was that what I said to him was word for word what I had been told by Commander Boatman only a few weeks earlier when he assigned Thomas to be my apprentice and I assigned Jack and Sam to watch over him and try to keep him out of trouble.

******

Our ride out of London towards Suffolk was uneventful until we reached Colchester. I amused myself by practicing with my wrist knives and we made good time despite the crowded road. There was no surprise in the good distances we covered each day because every man was an experienced rider who was mounted on one of the Company's amblers and leading another in case he needed a fresh horse.

The travellers we encountered seemed wary of us and understandably so. They inevitably saw a large group of heavily armed and fast-moving mounted men as a potential danger. Some responded by hurrying off the road in order to avoid us but others pressed on, probably because they could see we were not harming the travellers we were riding past. As you might imagine, the archers riding in our column were repeatedly asked who we were and where we were headed and why.

As you might also imagine, rumours had spread amongst the archers as to the reason for our march and our destination. As a result, they gave all kinds of well-meaning answers to the inquiries they received. That would never do because it might implicate the Company if things turned to shite. Accordingly, as dark approached on our first night out of London I led my little army off the road to a relatively isolated place along a river where we could camp without being overheard.

When we dismounted I gathered the men around me and told them what they needed to know and how they must always respond if they were ever asked what they were doing.

"Lads, people are going to be constantly asking who we are and what we are doing. What is important is that we all give the same answers in order to protect the Company from being blamed in case everything turns to shite.

"What we want everyone who questions us to believe is that we are a free company of mercenaries who have been employed to protect an English prince from being killed. We do not yet know the name of the prince we are to protect; we do not yet know where the prince is located; and only our captain knows who hired us.

"So you must never mention Cornwall or the Company of Archers and the only acceptable answer no matter how the question is put to you is this," I shouted:

"We are a free company of mercenaries who have been hired to protect some prince."

I had the men repeat it together out loud over and over again, and then I had each man shout it out individually so the others could hear. It was, I told them, the approved answer and the only one allowed.

In the days that followed, Lieutenant Goodman and the Sergeant Major paid close attention to what the men said to outsiders and came down hard on even the slightest deviation from the approved story. Whether it fooled or misled anyone by pulling their thinking away from the Company and Cornwall I do not know.

******

Everything changed about the time Colchester Castle came in view. One of the two archers who had been riding a couple miles ahead of us as scouts came galloping back to report that a large armed host was moving into position to block the road in front of us.

"Several hundred of them I would guess and maybe more, and some of them are wearing armour." Our scout had, of course, and rightly so, not stopped to count them. His mate, the second scout, would do the counting if he had enough time before he too had to gallop back.

"There may be trouble ahead, Lieutenant Goodman," I immediately said to Lieutenant Goodman who had been riding next to me at the head of our little army of princely guards along with his new apprentice, Thomas Corn.

"There is no way to know if there will be a problem but it is always better to be safe than sorry. So please ride down the column and make sure each of our men are mounted on his freshest horse and they all have their weapons ready to use on a moment's notice. But tell the men not to string their bows just yet."

My order was a formal order so my new lieutenant repeated it back to me with alacrity and rode back along the column to carry it out. Thomas Corn, of course, dutifully followed along behind him to help in whatever way he could.

I continued to lead my men on down the road toward the unknown host; but now at walk to rest the horses instead of at an amble. There was a sudden burst of bustling movement amongst the men riding behind me as Lieutenant Goodman and Thomas rode down the column. Some of the men were switching horses and others were repositioning their weapons to get them ready.

Lieutenant Goodman rejoined me about five minutes later and reported that our archers were fully ready to either ride away or fight. "Every man is ready in case there is a fight" he said with a great deal of determined satisfaction in his voice.

* * * * * *

We continued moving down the road and soon saw a great host of disorganized men waiting in front of us. They filled the roadway and spilled over into the fields on either side of the road. It was usual disorganized mob-like battle formation of an English lord who was unprepared for a battle and thought he was.

As we got closer I could see that there were two or three hundred men in the mob-like host with a dozen or more mounted knights out in front of them on the great ponderous destriers that were needed to carry knights wearing heavy armour. Immediately behind the knights stood a small group of priests. They were there to bless the men and assure them that God was on their side and would protect them, especially if they bought a few last minute indulgences for their sins. It was either the personal army of one of England's great lords or the combined village levies and knights of several smaller ones.

I raised my hand to stop the column of archers who were now walking their horses behind me. Once I was sure the column was stopped I put my heels into the ribs of my horse and ambled on down the road with Lieutenant Goodman and Thomas Corn following close behind. Sam and Tom waited at the front of the column for my return.

Sergeant Major Donaldson also stayed behind and waited at the head of the column. He would lead the men if I waved a signal at him to turn them around or move them off the road. Hopefully I would not have to do anything.

Four horsemen detached themselves from the waiting host and rode forward to meet us. We stopped and waited for them just out of crossbow range. I did not see anyone in front of me with a crossbow but it is always better to be safe than sorry when you are not sure if anyone has one; just ask old King Richard.

"Who are you and what are you doing here?" the well-dressed young man leading them demanded rather arrogantly as he rode up to us.

Our questioner was wearing a very expensive suit of armour and riding the biggest horse I had ever seen. The men who had come forward with him were two knights wearing armour of a lesser quality and riding horses that were almost as large. They were accompanied by a white-haired priest riding a mule. Neither knight was wearing a cross on his tunic to indicate he had been a crusader and might know something about fighting other than man to man.

"We are a free company of mercenaries who have been employed to guard the Crown Prince of England. And who be you and why are you and your men blocking the road?" I replied.

The arrogant young man looked down from his high horse and rather proudly thumped on his chest and identified himself as the Earl of Essex.

As soon as the Earl named himself I knew he was almost certainly a staunch supporter of the Queen. It was well known that the Despensers had dispossessed the Earl's now-dead father from his lands in Essex and Suffolk as a result of his father's alleged participation in the murder of Piers Gaveston. If his son was here with his knights and their levies it would be to fight for the Queen in the hope that she would reward him by returning his family lands.

In response I patted my chest and identified myself as William Archer, the captain of a free company of archers who were mostly from the midlands and Wales. I did so even though we were wearing our Company tunics with their telltale hoods and rank stripes.

I did not mention that my real family name is Courtenay because I did not want to start a feud with his family if I had to kill him. Instead, I did my best to placate him.

"It is good to know that you are the Earl of Essex because we have been employed to protect the Queen's son, the crown prince. Surely your family has not turned against the Queen and is now supporting King Edward?" I said the words with a question in my voice. What I did *not* say was who had employed us.

My effort to distract the Earl from asking questions about our employers was successful.

"Of course we support the Queen, you fool, but what would you have done if we had been the King's men instead of the Queen's?" He asked the question in a dismissive and insulting way as if he already knew the answer.

Fool? I had to bite my tongue to avoid doing something stupid such as provoking an unnecessary fight and killing him when his family and vassals would know it was an archer who had done it.

I ignored the insult; it was all I could do under the circumstances. But it grated on me and affected my thinking.

"Our only commitment is to protect the crown prince, Your Lordship. There is a rumour that certain of the French nobles will try to have him killed when he reaches England. They apparently want him dead so there will be no one for the English to rally around in the years ahead after King Edward is gone." *Whether that was true or not about the French I did not know. But it was a good excuse for me being there with my men. Commander Goodman had suggested it.*

And then I challenged the earl to see if I could make sure of his intentions and loyalties—and in so-doing convince him that we were not threat.

"So be you and your men for France and want Prince Edward dead or for England and want him alive?" I leaned forward in my saddle and asked my question with an edge to my voice.

The Earl seemed surprised at my question; it had apparently raised a possible French threat to his lands and title that he had not previously considered.

"Why England, of course."

I already knew that would be his answer because if the French really did come and put a French prince on the English throne they would more likely than not take all of his family's lands for themselves and their supporters, not just those they had already lost in Essex and Suffolk.

"That is good to hear, Your Lordship. So to answer your initial question as to what we would have done if you had tried to stop us from reaching Prince Edward and taking up our duties to protect him: The answer is that we would have considered you and your men to be supporters of the

French nobles who want Prince Edward dead and immediately killed you and your knights and dispersed your army."

There was no such rumour about some of the French nobles wanting the Prince dead, at least not that I knew of, but it was a good story and would probably be true if something happened to end the life of the young prince. Commander Goodman had suggested I use it to deflect questions away from having to say who had paid us.

The eyes of the Earl and his men and their priest widened at the implications of my words. It was not the answer they expected since they greatly outnumbered us. The younger of the two knights could not contain himself. He was, I later discovered, the Earl's younger brother and he scoffed at my words in a most insulting manner.

"*You* and your company would destroy *us*? I do not think so, *Captain*." He said it incredulously with a scoffing sneer and spoke the word "captain" as if it were a meaningless title.

I was having none of it and did not like the tone of his voice. So I replied with a sharp combination of derision and condescension of my own.

"Of course my men and I would destroy your army, Sir Knight. You and your fellow knights are on lumbering slow horses that could never catch ours and most of your poorly armed men are on foot with nothing to hide behind except their homemade shields. So we would just ride in a great circle around and around and around you and push out our arrows until your horses and men were all either dead or wounded on the ground with arrows sticking out of them or hopelessly scattered and running for home.

Then I leaned forward in my saddle and explained the facts of life in a very intense and patronizing voice.

"In the real world, Sir Knight, wars and the guarding of someone or something are *not* at all like one of your tournaments where it is man against man and there are rules of engagement. You and your knighted friends might want to pretend that war is up close and man against man. War may have once been that way in years gone by but it is almost *never* that way in today's modern world."

The Earl and the men with him listened intently and seemed surprised at what they were hearing and the intensity and tone of my voice. I was hoping it would convince them that we were serious about guarding the Prince and would be able to do so better than anyone else. And, of course, I failed. It was also a great mistake on my part because it made an enemy out of the embarrassed young knight.

As we rode out into the countryside and around the Essex men I suddenly realized that I had just done something incredibly stupid—I had not only made an enemy, I had just told men whose army the Company might have to do battle with someday how we were likely fight them. Now all I could do was hope that they were not open-minded enough to understand what I had just foolishly revealed.

Chapter Seventeen
The camp of the Queen's supporters.

We took no chances; we rode around Essex's host instead of through it. Three days later my men and I could see the coastal village of Ipswich in the distance—and my thinking about the outcome of the coming war had begun to change.

It had changed, my thinking that is, because somewhere along the way I realized that I had learned something important from my meeting with the Earl of Essex and his host: It was that whomever was making the decisions for the Queen's supporters might be a competent military commander instead of the usual hereditary bungling oaf chosen by God and the Pope.

Why had I begun to think that might be the case? Because I had come to realize that despite all *his* personal shortcomings the Earl of Essex's host had been perfectly placed to delay or even prevent the similar hosts of King Edward's supporters from reaching Ipswich in time to prevent the Queen and her army from coming ashore.

More specifically, what I realized was that whoever was making the Queen's military decisions had either been extremely lucky or had carefully looked at a map of England and arranged for an army loyal to the Queen to sit astride the eastern road at exactly where it would be the most effective in blocking the road to Suffolk.

In essence, *if* Essex's host had been deliberately placed it was quite likely that the King might be in for the fight of his life, a fight which he might well lose if he was not as proficient as the Queen's commander in leading his supporters into battle—which King Edward was not if his past efforts as a military commander and decision maker in his wars with Scotland were any guide.

In other words, I was beginning to think for the very first time that the Queen and her supporters might have a very real chance of winning the coming war and being able to put her young son on the throne in place of King Edward—the young son who was the prince we were supposed to guard.

On the other hand my thoughts as to who might win did not matter: my men and I had been ordered to remain neutral and we would do our best to do so until our orders were changed. Neutrality and staying away was the Company's traditional position when it came to fighting in England's wars.

Staying neutral was important, as I had been learnt in the Company school, because the wars were inevitably meaningless except for the king and the handful of great nobles who were for him or against him—all they did was shuffle around the ownership of their lands and titles in England and France based on their wars' outcomes. The Company had better things to do with its men and treasure than use them up in such zero-sum games.

******

There was an encampment of another and much larger army of armed men and camp followers on both sides of the road as we approached Ipswich. A good part of the host turned out to be the men and followers of the Earl of Suffolk, one of the Queen's relatives and a strong supporter.

It was haphazardly encamped on both side of the London road on the outskirts of the village.

I knew it was the Suffolk host because immediately next to the road on its starboard side there was a group of several dozen or more tents including a relatively large linen tent of many colours flying the pennant of the Earl of Suffolk. On the other side of the road across from the Earl's tents was a much larger and even more haphazard collection of smaller tents, wagons, and makeshift shelters of all kinds. There were many men, and quite a few women and children, standing and sitting around them.

As soon as I saw the tent flying the Suffolk pennant I halted my little army and gathered my men around me. Some of the people in the camp had begun standing up to get a better look at us; others were ignoring us or eyeing us out of the corners of their eyes as they went about chores. It was the typical response of a military encampment when something new occurs to break its long hours of boredom.

"There are only three things to remember before we ride into the camp of the Queen's supporters, lads," I told my assembled men as they stood in a half circle in front of me holding their horses. And you must remember them or you will be lucky to lose only your stripes.

"The first is that each of you left Cornwall to go for a mercenary because Cornwall is so poor that its Company of Archers was not able to pay you or provide you and your families with enough food.

"The second is that you must always tell everyone who asks that you greatly respect the Queen but you are only here because the free company you joined has a contract to provide protection for the Queen's young son who is some kind of prince."

"The third is that you have no idea who is paying your free company to help guard the prince.

With that I pulled my horse around and began ambling slowly down the road toward the big tent with my men following along behind me in a long column of twos. When I got closer to the largest tent I motioned for my men to stop and continued on down the road alone.

"Hoy," I said to the handful of spear-carrying men who appeared to be standing guard at the entrance to the big tent. I did so as I pulled up in front of them and dismounted. "I be William the Archer. Please tell whoever is your commander that I have come from London with the men of my free company to take up our contract to guard the Queen's son."

The only man carrying a sword instead of a spear immediately disappeared into the tent; the other two just stood there and looked at me. I was definitely the curiosity of the day. A moment later a finely dressed man wearing a fine embroidered tunic came out of the tent to greet me. He was almost certainly a knight and possibly the Earl of Suffolk himself. Several other well-dressed men and a couple of priests came out behind him.

"Who be you and why are you here," the man demanded.

"Captain William Archer is my name, Sir Knight," I said as I deliberately misnamed myself and bowed just as I had been learnt to do at school. "I have come from London with the men of my free company to take up our duties to guard the Queen's son."

I bowed again when I finished introducing myself and held out a rolled up copy of our contract.

My greeter instinctively held out his hand and took it.

What followed was a serious questioning of me as to who I was and who had sent me whilst one of the priests read the contract that had been scribed on the parchment. The names of Sir Hugh Turpington and Simon Bereford, the Bishop of Lincoln, on the parchment apparently carried significant weight. The priest whispered into the man's ear after he finished reading it and the man immediately nodded his head in agreement.

"You and your men are well come to the Queen's camp, Captain Archer," the finely-dressed man said with a strange smile.

"I am Thomas of Brotherton, the Earl of Norfolk. My cousin, the Queen, and her princely son will be arriving with Lord Mortimer and the rest of the Queen's army in the next few days. Please make your camp wherever you can find room."

I bowed my acceptance of his offer and led my horse back towards my waiting men. My head was in a whirl as I walked because I had just realized that the Queen's position might be much stronger than I had been led to believe—and mine infinitely more dangerous.

It was whirling because as I stood there listening to the Earl of Norfolk's welcome I had realized that he was much more than a distant cousin of the Queen; he was the half-brother of the much older King Edward.

In other words, I had just met the man who might well be England's king if something bad happened to the young prince my men and I were supposed to guard.

******

We spent the next three days at the encampment of Queen's supporters who were awaiting her arrival. It stretched out between the banks of the River Orwell and the London Road on the outskirts of Ipswich. It was muddy, foul, and disorganized. It was also constantly growing with the periodic arrival of the armies of additional noble supporters and additional camp followers of all types and varieties including sutlers, women and children, prostitutes, and thieves. In other words, it was a typical English army encampment.

My men and I found a place and erected the four small tents we had brought with us. We could squeeze into them with our weapons if we carefully arranged ourselves and at all times left at least three or four men outside in the rain or dark to watch over our nearby horses.

There was no shortage of food to be had in the camp if a man had coins. It was available from the camp's sutlers and from the enterprising farmers and fishermen's wives who had begun bringing in their fish, sheep and cattle for sale to anyone who would pay their price. A constant stream of men and women walked to the river to get water and the sound of axes cutting wood for the cooking fires in the nearby stands of trees was constant from dawn to dark.

Each day I walked to the Earl's tent to see if there was any news of the Prince's arrival. Inevitably there was not. What there was, however, was a growing sense of anticipation. By the third day I realized that there was a degree of organization within the camp that had initially appeared to be so chaotic. The tents of the lords, knights, and clerics were on the starboard side of the Ipswich road along with their horses and wagons. Their servants were on the other side of the road in smaller tents and their levies were beyond the servants and further off the road in various tents and makeshift shelters.

It bothered me greatly that I had not been invited to camp with the knights and nobles on the starboard side of the road. I would not have done so in order to stay with my men, of course, but it grated on me that my men and I had not been considered important enough for me to be invited.

In the middle of the fifth day there a great stirring suddenly swept through the camp. Within minutes everyone knew that a large fleet of boats had begun entering the Orwell's estuary. The Queen and her son and her army of mercenaries had begun arriving from the lowlands.

Chapter Eighteen
Dangerous moments.

It was not until the day after she came ashore that my men and I finally were allowed to meet the Queen and her son and take up our duties as the Prince's guards. And it almost did not happen because of my poor judgement when I was summoned by the Earl of Norfolk.

As I followed the Earl's messenger back to the Earl's tent next to the road I saw that several additional large tents had been erected next to the Earl's. The pennant of England with its three gold lions on a red field was flying over two of them. *Ah, so this is where the Queen and her son will be residing and are to be guarded.* I was excited at the thought of finally seeing the young prince my men and I were supposed to guard from the French.

Two of the sides of the Earl's large tent had been rolled up to improve the light and there were a half dozen or so of well dressed men standing around a table on which a large leather map had been unrolled. Several smaller groups of men were standing by themselves outside the tent near the rolled up sides so they could be seen. They looked to be clerics or knights and nobles waiting to talk to the men in the tent or to run their errands and laugh at their jokes.

One of the men standing outside the tent spoke loudly with a sneering tone in his voice as I walked toward them and the Earl's tent. He was standing with two other men. They appeared to be French Knights.

"Ah, here comes the mercenary who thinks he can do a better job of guarding the England's prince than you, Sir Giles." One of the three said sarcastically to the man standing beside him. He spoke in French and loud enough for me and the men standing around him and in the tent to hear.

It was the wrong thing to say about me with the insulting tone of voice in which it was said. I was already in a bad mood because I was not considered as important enough to be offered a place in the camp with the nobles and knights. Also, truth be told, I may have been a bit edgy because I had been feeling rather horny of late and not sleeping well, probably because I had not been with a woman since my wife and daughter fell to the plague. It was either that or some bad cheese.

The well-dressed men standing around the table in the tent heard the comment as the speaker no doubt intended. Several of them looked up from the map spread out on the table to see what it was all about.

"Ah yes. Captain Archer is it?" One of the men standing at the map looked up and said. It was the Earl of Norfolk. "Well then, Captain Archer, it appears your services will not be needed as some French knights have volunteered to guard the Queen and her son. You may report to my cleric, Father Joseph, and he will assign you and your men to a place in one of my companies." He gestured dismissively towards one of the priests standing outside the tent.

I did not agree.

"No my lord Earl; unfortunately I cannot agree even though it would be a great honour to serve you and fight under your banner. Fighting under your command is *not* why my men and I are here. We are a free company and we have been employed by the Queen's representatives to guard the crown prince and that is the whole of it. Guarding Prince Edward is why we are here and the only thing we have been contracted to do."

The Frenchman with the sneering voice spoke up loudly once again.

"Does someone who is too cowardly to fight alongside an English earl think he is up to guarding the English prince? I for one do not think so. What would he do if fighting men like my friends and I decided to attack the prince? Plead with us? Show us a parchment?"

I could not let that pass. His insults were too much. Besides, he was French and I never had liked them. So instead of entering into the tent to confront the Earl and explain myself I stopped in front of the three Frenchmen and threw out an insult and threat of my own.

"I would do neither, you fool. I never plead and I doubt you could read if I showed you a parchment—I would just kill you three myself and be done with you."

The three Frenchmen initially just smiled at my reply, pleased to have drawn the attention of the Earl and the other men in the tent. Their lack of response pissed me off even more so I added to my insulting threat.

"If I thought you lot were even thinking about harming England's prince I would kill off the three of you right here and now. And rightly so under the terms of my company's contract with the Queen to protect her son." *I emphasized the words 'with the Queen'.*

The French knight who had started the exchange could not stop himself.

"Should we shake and shudder?" he said loudly with a sneer. His friends looked amused.

By then I had stopped in front of the three French knights and all the men in the tent had stopped looking at the map and were looking at us. So was everyone else in the surrounding area including a group of men and women who had started coming out of one of the nearby royal tents to see what was causing all the commotion.

"Yes, you are confronting an Englishman so shaking and shuddering is exactly what you should do," I said. "Particularly if you intend to harm the Prince so a Frenchman can seize the throne when King Edward goes home to God."

The loudmouth pretended to tremble his hands with a nasty smile on his face, and then he began shaking them in my face and kept shaking them. A moment later his two friends joined him and all three shook their hands as if they too were all atremble. They thought their response was funny; I did not.

"This is intolerable," I said as I turned my head away from looking at their shaking hands in front of my face and spoke to the Earl and the men standing around the map.

"These three Frenchmen just threatened an English prince," I said loudly. "A prince they no doubt wish dead so a Frenchman can take the throne." *They had not actually done so but it was close enough and I was in a bad mood.*

"Do I have your permission to eliminate them even though it means fouling your camp with their blood?" I asked the Earl.

I doubt the Earl of Norfolk even thought about it before he nodded and made a casual "go ahead" gesture with both of his hands.

By now I was intense and ready.

As I turned back to face my three taunters my left hand wrist knife came out of the sleeve of my tunic and into my left hand. Its point swept up under the hands of the leftmost of the three men that were still being shaken in my face; it went in under his chin and up almost to its hilt into his mouth and head.

At the same instant my right hand wrist knife came out and with a great backhanded sweeping motion I whipped it across the neck of the middle man and continued on with it to my right until I pushed it into the stomach of the third Frenchman. It went in up to its hilt and then I ripped it upward with a great grunt.

It all happened in the blink of an eye and it was a good thing that the third Frenchman was not wearing a chain shirt like mine.

There was a moment of stunned silence and then more than a few shouts and gasps and at least one woman screamed in surprise somewhere in back of me.

All three men stumbled over backwards and fell down on the ground. Two of them were clutching at the blood spurting from their gaping wounds and trying to get to their feet. The third was flat on his back with his arms spread out and his feet already trembling.

There was a moment of silence and then a great deal of noise and commotion.

"Did you see that?" .... "My God." ..... "What happened?"

Everyone was stunned, including me, for a second or two. I just held a knife in each hand and looked down at the Frenchmen. It was if I was standing back and watching everyone else including myself. *It worked; my God, it worked. I had only used them for real one time before and that was in a tavern brawl.*

People were shouting and seemed to be running towards us from everywhere in the camp to see what was happening.

And then everyone began talking at once and the Earl and the men standing with him around the map were staring at me in disbelief with their mouths gaped open in surprise.

At first the man whose belly I had opened so completely just sat there on the ground and looked up at me with disbelief in his eyes. Then the pain hit and he began screaming and trying to get to his feet and hold his stomach together all at the same time. So I leaned over and cut his throat to silence him.

The other two Frenchmen could not talk but the man in the middle with his throat cut, the one whose insults started it, jumped around for a while holding his throat and making all kinds of strange gurgling sounds. But then he stopped and fell back.

I tried to be nonchalant.

"Do any of you know of someone else who might be a threat to the English prince on whom all of our futures depend?" I inquired of the men around the table with a polite and somewhat conversational edge to my voice as I wiped my knives off on one of the Frenchmen's clothes and gave them a little bow to the earl.

As I asked my question I realized that a well-dressed young woman had emerged from one of the nearby tents and was standing behind me. What I noticed most about her was that her eyes were shining with excitement. It was probably the first time she ever seen violence done beyond the swatting of a fly.

The men all stopped talking and began bowing most respectful. It was the Queen. I, of course, began bowing also. I had never realized she was so young. She had seen everything.

******

"You killed the French knights King Charles sent to guard his sister, Captain. My God you killed all three of them and the Queen saw you do it."

That was what the Earl of Norfolk said to me a few minutes after the still-excited Queen had returned to her tent along on the arm of one of the men at the map table who turned out to be Lord Mortimer. His Lordship was still having trouble believing what he had seen.

"Of course I killed them, Your Lordship. It is what the Queen's representatives contracted for me and my men to do. I did so because they threatened a prince of England, the prince who must be kept alive if you and your friends are to overthrow King Edward in his name. *It was not, as everyone now knows, the only reason I killed them. But it was good enough and the only explanation I could think of at the time.*

Chapter Nineteen
I meet the Queen.

The question of what would happen to me and my company as a result of my killing the three Frenchmen was soon answered. Lord Mortimer brought the answer with him when he returned to the Earl's tent a few minutes after escorting the Queen and her attendants back to the Queen's tent.

"Her Majesty wants Captain Archer's mercenaries to be Prince Edward's guards. She said she had never trusted the French knights to guard her son even though they claimed her brother had sent them to do so. She told me she feared they would harm the Prince and was glad to see them gone.

"She also wants to talk to Captain Archer and for him and for his men to immediately take up their duties as Prince Edward's guards."

Lord Mortimer gave me a mysterious little grin and nodded for me to leave as he reported the Queen's desires to the nobles assembled in the Earl's tent. As you might imagine, I respectfully bowed my understanding and acceptance of the Queen's wishes and backed out of the tent. I needed to go get my men and walk to the river to wash the blood off my hands before I met with her.

****** *The Queen's wishes*

I had never before spoken to a noble lady let alone a queen surrounded by three of them. But that did not last long—I was still down on one knee bowing and trying to be obsequious when she fluttered her hand in some kind of "go away" signal to send her attendants out of the tent "so we can speak privately with our son's guardian." *We? Our?*

"Tell me about yourself, Captain Archer," the Queen said as her ladies were leaving. It was about then that I realized that she was dressed in black.

"My name is actually William Courtenay, Your Majesty. Your lords have been correct in naming me as Captain Archer because I was a captain in the Company of Archers until my men and I volunteered to guard your son.

"I am a soldier and experienced with the weapons that will be needed to defend your son. I have been stationed in Cyprus for the past six years and most recently have been serving as the lieutenant of one of the Company's war galleys. Before that I attended the Company of Archer's school at Restormel Castle and then served four years at Okehampton as a sergeant in the Company's horse archers and then as sergeant major."

"And your family? Do you have a family, William?"

"I am a widower your Majesty and I have a young son who is being raised by my aunt at Restormel Castle. My wife and daughter were taken by the plague several years ago."

"A widower! Well that is a surprise. I consider myself a widow as you know. My first and only husband, King Edward, is now dead to me because of his sins and his abandonment of me when he ran from the Scots and left me behind. That is why I consider myself a widow and always wear black."

"I see. You are a widow. I am sorry to hear of it. Please accept my condolences." *No I really did not see since I knew she was married to the King and he was alive. But what else could I say, eh?*

"For a time I had high hopes for Lord Mortimer as I am surely you will sooner or later be told. But he is married and already has so many children that he is no longer interested in trying to make any more. All he wants now is to put my son on the throne and be the chancellor.

"How about you, Captain. Do you want to get married again and make more children? Perhaps with one of my ladies if she and God are willing?"

"Oh .. ah .. well .. it is .. um .. yes, .. er...um .. no .. of course, Your Majesty; someday perhaps. .. but."

Good Grief. What should I say?

****** *Captain William Courtenay*

My next few days were quite hectic. More and more lords brought in their knights and levies and camp followers to join the Queen's army. As a result the camp continued to grow until it totally surrounded the tents of the Queen and her son. It was then that I made an important decision and implemented it: I moved the Queen and her ladies into a new and somewhat more isolated tent camp to get them away from the stench and Queen-gawking of the main camp.

On the very next day Lord Mortimer led his army out of their camp to begin marching against the King's army which was forming up around King Edward at Windsor. Mortimer led his men north toward Lancaster to join up with the supporters of the Queen who were assembling there. They would then, Mortimer had told the queen and she told me, march south to join with the Queen's supporters who were mustering at Northampton.

Queen Isabella seemed particularly pleased with her new living arrangements. She had always had her own tent but tents of Prince Edward and her ladies had been so close that she could hear everything that was said in the other tents and everyone could hear what was happening in hers. Now they were further apart.

It started with a complaint on our first night in the new camp.

"You have caused me to set my ladies aside in more distant tents, it seems. So I have no one to rub my back and wash me. So you must do it and promise not to look. Will you promise?" *Say What?*

"Um. Er. .. Would that be wise, Your Majesty?" *I was almost speechless.*

"Of course. I am the queen and a widow. I can do anything I want. That is what Roger always tells me. And that is what I want. So do as you are told and proceed. I command it."

I followed the Queen's orders and, as you might imagine, things got out of hand rather quickly.

"A little lower, William.

"Um. A little harder please. Oh that is nice. Now around in front. Yes. ... More to the right. ... More .... Even more .... Oh yes. .. I have changed my mind, William; you may look.

******

Several days later a galloper arrived from Lord Mortimer carrying an order. The Queen and her son were to be immediately brought to Northampton where the armies of her supporters were gathering. I understood the need for speed so we immediately began striking the Queen's camp with the intention of getting underway the next morning as soon as the sun arrived.

And setting off the next morning is exactly we did. We got underway as soon as the Queen and her ladies finished getting ready and climbed into the wagon that would be carrying them and the young prince. The problem was that it was about three hours after dawn before the Queen and her servants were ready to go. We were already running late and time was of the essence. *Sheesh.*

I was very tired as a result of spending my nights getting to know the Queen and keeping her properly massaged so it was with both a strange feeling of relief and a great sense of apprehension that I was finally able to climb aboard my horse, point my hand down the road, and shout "forward" to order our march to begin.

Our convoy included only my thirty horse archers and the Queen, her son, and the Queen's dozen or so attendants and servants. Everyone was either mounted or riding on one of the three horse-drawn wagons that carried our tents and supplies.

No camp followers were allowed to accompany us except for one sutler whose wagon was filled with womanly things such as knitting needles, tiny little amphoras filled with face whitening powders and smelly flower oils, and lace pieces from the lowlands that were in need of embroidering. *Queen Isabella and her ladies had made such a fuss about my initial decree that no camp followers were to accompany us that I made an exception for the sutler which resulted in even more smirks and smiles from my men, all of which, as you might imagine, I chose to ignore.*

No one was on foot and the wagon horses were strong so once we got moving we were a fast-moving convoy with scouts riding several miles ahead and behind as well as a file of battle-ready outriders off to starboard under Thomas Corn and a similar file off to port under the Sergeant Major. The rest of the men and I stayed with the Queen and Prince Edward.

My plan of response if we were attacked was simple as all battle plans must be and, equally important, well-known and understood by my men: I would sweep up Prince Edward on to my horse in front of me and attempt to carry him to safety.

Archers Adams and Smith would ride with me with each man leading a remount for me along with his own. Lieutenant Goodman would try to do the same with the Queen and follow us. The Sergeant Major would command our rearguard with Thomas Corn as his number two. They would immediately launch a counterattack and concentrate on discouraging and delaying anyone who tried to pursue the prince.

The Queen's ladies and her servants and the sutler would be on their own in the event of an attack. In other words, if everything turned to shite we would abandon everyone except Prince Edward and the Queen and rendezvous an hour's hard ride back down the road from whence we had come. Anyone who could not make it to the rendezvous was to try to make his way to Northampton on his own and rejoin us there. If that failed they were to report to the Company's shipping post in London.

What brought home the seriousness of the matter and impressed the men the most, however, was that I gave each man six silver coins to spend if we were attacked and he got separated.

"Use them to buy food and whatever shelter and assistance you need until you can find us. If that appears impossible you are to make your way to London and report to the captain of our London shipping post."

It was a good plan but I was quite worried despite it. My fear was based on the very real likelihood that the King and his supporters had spies in Mortimer's camp. If so, they would almost certainly hear of the Queen's departure from the camp and her travel to join him—and it would not take an alchemist to figure out that the Queen and the prince would most likely be travelling on the only road that ran between Ipswich and Northampton.

In other words, if the King's men moved fast they might be able to ride up from where they were assembling at Windsor and intercept us before we could reach the safety of Mortimer's camp—and we had already given them an extra three hours due to our late start on the very first day.

We, of course, could defeat an effort to intercept us by getting to Northampton *before* the King's men could ride north from Windsor in time to cut us off. As a result the night before we departed I had gone out of my way to explain to my men and the Queen why we needed to start at dawn each day, move quickly without any stops or delays along the way. I also told them that we would continue travelling at night if there was enough moonlight.

My men were veterans so most of them both understood our need for speed and appreciated that I was trying to avoid a fight in which some of them might well be killed or wounded even if the prince escaped. I was counting on the sergeants to make those of my men who did not understand the need for speed begin acting as if they did.

But why had Mortimer not sent additional men to help guard the Queen and Prince Edward? Did he have so few horsemen or no one he could trust or was it something else or an oversight? I never did find out.

******

It began three or four hours after we had spent the night camping in a field a few miles west of Cambridge. Archer Williams who had been riding several miles ahead of our column with another archer came galloping back to report that a large number of men who appeared to be armed were riding down the road towards us and coming fast. Worse, he also reported that a lone rider who had been riding in front of them as a scout appeared to have ridden back to report that we were on the road and coming toward them.

But whose men were the riders—the Queen's coming to escort us into Northampton or the King's to coming to intercept us and seize the prince?

Chapter Twenty
They almost catch us.

I took no chances. I immediately shouted for the driver of the Queen's wagon to stop. As he did I leaned over and snatched up the prince and sat him in front of me on my horse. He was a pampered little shite and immediately began kicking and complaining and trying to climb down.

"Quiet damn you. We may have big trouble so behave yourself or I will spank you."

He looked back over his shoulder and gave me an incredulous look, and promptly stopped struggling. It was probably the first time someone had ever spoken sharply to him let alone swore at him or threatened to spank him when they really meant it.

******

Our problems began immediately when the Queen refused to climb from the wagon to board Lieutenant Goodman's horse and sit behind him. She had seen me pick up her son and knew there was trouble, but she wanted to stay in the wagon with her ladies.

I barked an order at her.

"Get your arse aboard the Lieutenant's horse behind him, Isabella, or I am taking your son and we are going to ride off and leave you to the King."

That did it. She gotten to know me well enough to know I meant it. A moment later we were moving back down the road a fast amble with our horse holders right behind us with our remounts and theirs. I was holding tight to the prince who was sitting in front of me and the Queen was holding tight to Harold. The three ladies we left behind began weeping and crying out beseechingly when they realized they were being abandoned.

There was no hesitation on the part of the ladies' wagon driver, however; he jumped down from his seat and began running out into the field next to the road in a desperate effort to escape. The rest of the Queen's servants and the sutler immediately ran after him such that in less than a minute only the Queen's hysterical noble ladies and the three wagons remained on the road.

As we rode off I looked over my shoulder in time to see the Sergeant Major and his men in the distance off to the starboard side of the road and Thomas Corn and his men off to port. They both had brought their horses to a fast amble similar to mine and were leading their archers on a course to intercept the oncoming riders who were now galloping down the road towards us whilst holding outstretched lances and waving swords over their heads. It did not take an alchemist to know that they were definitely not some of the Queen's supporters.

I could not see the arrow I knew he was holding because of how he was riding with his back to me, but I knew from the way the Sergeant Major was riding and holding his bow that he had his bow strung and an arrow nocked. The archers riding on either side of him were obviously similarly ready to push out arrows and fight.

What I could not *see* was what Thomas Corn and his men were doing. That was because their backs were to me, but I could tell from the way they were riding that they too would be pushing out arrows as soon as they got close enough to our pursuers. They were all good men and doing what they were obliged to do.

Three or four minutes later two women who were talking and a man and a boy on a loaded hay wain looked up in surprise as our horses thundered past a little village. The village was on a hillside next to the road. We had recently ridden past it when we were coming the other way.

We stayed on the road and when it began curving around the hill we could no longer see our pursuers. Several miles later I finally I saw what I was looking for—a wooded area towards the top of the hill that we might be able to get into and hide before our pursuers came around the bend and could see us.

"Go," I shouted as I started to kick my horse in the ribs to bring him up to a full gallop. But as I did I changed my mind and decided to stay on the road instead of trying to hide in the trees. Our horses were fresh and going strong, the boy was not heavy and neither was the Queen, and we had remounts; we would outrun them instead of hiding.

******

I finally pulled my horse to a stop four or five miles past the village. It was just short of the rendezvous point where we were supposed to gather if we got separated. The road behind us was fairly straight so we would be able to see any pursuers who came around the hill that was about three miles back. So far we had not seen any of them which was very encouraging.

Our remounts were breathing hard after their long run. But they were still considerably fresher than the horses we had been riding so I ordered everyone to hurriedly dismount and change over to their remounts. The four of us did so and then we waited.

The Queen started to say something but shut her mouth when I barked "not now" at her.

Whilst we waited and watched the road behind us we fetched water for the horses by taking a water skin from one of our supply sacks and pouring it into our leather caps for the horses to drink. As we did a strung out line of riders began to come into view behind us—our pursuers and their horses were beginning to come around the hill and become visible. There were more and more of them and they were strung out along the road because some of their horses were faster and stronger than the others.

"Shite," my remount holder muttered when he saw them. He immediately began wrapping the reins of the two horses he would be leading around his wrist and readied himself to climb aboard his remount.

"Wait," I shouted at him and to the others. "Let the horses rest a little longer to catch more wind."

I said it instinctively without thinking and it surprised me when I heard myself say it. Then I realized why I did: The nearest of the horses coming towards us appeared to be labouring. That was no surprise both because they had been ridden harder and much further than ours and because most horses were not as capable as our amblers for riding long distances. *And that gave me an idea.*

"Get ready to mount," I said less than a minute later as I picked up the boy and sat him on my remount. I did so without taking my eyes off the men riding towards us. This time the Queen did not argue when Lieutenant Goodman boarded his remount and pulled her up behind him. We would be in very serious trouble if the caught up to us and everyone knew it.

"Time to go," I shouted as I leaned forward and kicked my horse in the ribs. I held tight to the little prince as I did.

My horse began ambling further down the road with Lieutenant Goodman's horse and our other horses close behind. Beyond us I could see a long line of pursuers stretched out along the road and more and more of them coming around the hill. I also saw a wide-eyed man driving a horse cart look up in surprise as we flashed past him and farmers in the fields on both sides of the road who had stopped working and were watching us.

The next time I looked back over my shoulder the nearest of our pursuers was only five or six hundred paces short of catching up to our rearmost horse holder—but his horse was clearly labouring and slowing down after its long all-out gallop. It had already slowed to a trot and looked to be coming to the end of its strength. The rest of our pursuers were strung out along the road much further back and some them seemed to be pulling up as well.

A few moments later I looked back over my shoulder again and watched as the horse of the pursuers' closest rider slowed to a walk and came to a halt. Behind him other riders pursuing us were doing the same. Their horses were finished and our horses were still ambling smoothly. At that point I was sure our pursuers were not going to catch us.

I gave a great whoop of triumph, and my idea came back into my head, and I decided to keep riding as if our pursuers were right behind us.

******

We kept riding until I was sure that there was no one still trying to pursue us. Then I pulled up my horse and ordered one of our horse holders to join me.

"Give Charles the horses you are leading, Michael, and take the boy."

As soon as Michael had the prince sitting in front of him I leaned out of the saddle and took two more quivers from one of the horses being led and threw them over the two that had been riding on my horse in front of the prince. My bow had long ago been strung but I checked it once again to make sure its string was still usable.

"What are you doing?" the Queen suddenly demanded from her perch behind Lieutenant Goodman. "William."

"Now it is our turn and we need information," I said as I boarded my horse. "Everyone is to wait here until I get back," I shouted out the order as I pulled my horse around and started back towards our pursuers.

Chapter Twenty-one
The tide turns.

My brown gelding ambled smoothly back up the road towards our pursuers. The first one I would be reach would be their leading thruster, the rider who had come the closest to catching up to us. I was ready for a fight and he was dismounted and seemed to be doing something with his saddle. He looked up and saw me coming and went back to working on his saddle. I had almost reached him when it must have suddenly dawned on him for the first time that he might be in serious danger.

There was a look of surprise on his face when he suddenly turned to look at me and saw me riding straight at him with a longbow in my hand and already leaning forward to push out an arrow. For a brief moment he began hurriedly trying to finish doing whatever it was he was doing, but then he gave up trying and attempted to board his exhausted horse and ride away. It was much too late for him to save himself.

He was just starting to climb aboard his horse when I rode past him at a distance of about ten or fifteen feet. As I did I pushed out an arrow that took him in his thigh. It was an armour-piercing heavy and the arrow's sharp iron head must have gone all the way through the meat in the man's leg and stuck the horse. It was the only possible explanation because the horse instantly began screaming, lurched away hard to port with a stumble that almost caused it to go down, and then it bolted out into the field next to the road.

The thruster's starboard foot must have come out of its stirrup when my arrow hit his leg because he came out of his saddle and went overboard to port when his horse lurched and stumbled and almost went down. Unfortunately for the thruster, his port-side foot did not come loose from its stirrup when his other foot did. As a result, he was dragged a considerable distance into the field next to the road with his head bouncing along the rocky ground and being kicked by the hooves of his wounded and hysterical horse.

I saw all this in a brief instant as I continued on down the road without stopping to finish him off or question him.

******

The next thruster I reached had already turned his exhausted horse around and was walking it back to join his mates. But then he must have seen me ride past the thruster who had been ahead of him in the chase and the first thruster's horse then bolt and drag him across the field next to the road.

By the time I reached the second thruster he had managed to climb back aboard his exhausted horse and was desperately lashing it and kicking its ribs to make it run. And it did run; it broke into a ragged gallop that lasted all of about two hundred feet before I caught up with him. He was looking over his shoulder at me and screaming "no" when my arrow took him in the middle of his back.

As I went past him I heard him crying "oh oh" as he slowly tipped over to port and fell from his saddle. An instant later I was down the road and could no longer see or hear him.

A man walking his horse was next. But he had seen the fate of the second thruster and was smart enough to lash his exhausted horse into moving off the road and start running. I pushed an arrow at him and missed—and kept going.

Two riders riding side by side were next and I reached them very quickly. They must not have been very smart. They were walking their horses back to whence they came and had seen the fate of the second thruster and the third rider go off the road. But instead of separating and moving off the road to escape they tried kick their tired horses into a gallop and ride together back down the road to the safety of their mates who were further back. It was a bad decision.

I was only about twenty paces behind the rearmost of the two horsemen when I grunted and pushed out my first arrow. It went low and bit deeply into his horse's arse such that the horse staggered into the ditch running along the port side of the road, tripped over something, and went down hard. I quickly nocked another arrow and took second rider in the neck from a range of about ten feet as my horse and I clattered past him on the road. *It was a lucky push; I had been aiming at the middle of his body.*

My horse was still ambling strongly and I kept him on the road. I ignored several of our pursuers who were able to escape by riding off the road into the adjacent fields. Instead of pursuing them I kept riding and concentrated on picking off the riders whose exhausted horses were still on or near the road.

The next rider I reached was a lance-carrying knight on a very large destrier. As I came up on him he pulled his destrier around to face me, kicked it into a ragged gallop, and launched a charge as if we were facing each other in some kind of tournament.

The knight's effort to engage me one on one did not work; I merely swerved out into field next to the road and put an arrow deep into the side of his horse as the knight and I passed each other with at least twenty feet between us. The destrier was so big I would have been embarrassed to miss.

The exhausted and badly wounded destrier lurched off the road and ran a few more strides before it suddenly collapsed and went down on its side with its hind legs flying up in the air in a half somersault. I kept going.

******

By the time I reached the section of the road where it curved around the hill I had taken out nine of the pursuing riders and sent a dozen or more desperately scurrying off the road to save their lives. I had almost finished going through the arrows in my second quiver and was closing in on my tenth kill when ahead me on the road I saw someone in the distance beyond the man I was currently chasing. He was riding hard and obviously fleeing *toward* me. It was about then that I realized I was being watched by a family of astonished farmers who had been working in their fields near the road.

A moment later I understood why the rider was riding towards me when I saw a fast-moving rider coming up behind the fleeing man. The rider was wearing an archer's tunic and had his bow raised and an arrow nocked. I finished shooting my man off his horse a few moments later and then moved my horse off to the side of the road to rest for a moment whilst I waited for the arrival of the rider who was being chased by the archer.

I expected the rider being chased to see me and veer away. But he did not; he was so busy looking back over his shoulder at the archer coming up behind him that he did not see me as I waited by the side of the road for him to reach me.

The on-coming rider was wearing a breastplate and carrying a long sword so I knew he was almost certainly a knight. He finally saw me at almost the last moment when it much too late for him to do anything except stare at me with a look of shocked surprise.

Our eyes locked just as I grunted and put an arrow deep in his horse's side as it came galloping past me. The horse took three or four more strides and then veered off the road and turned a somersault about twenty paces off to my starboard. As it did it rolled over the knight or whoever he was.

The knight's horse was still screaming and trying to get to its feet a few moments later when the archer who had been pursuing what turned out to be my eleventh and final victory of the day pulled up his horse in front of me. Both he and his horse were clearly tired and breathing hard. It was one of the Sergeant Major's chosen men and we recognized each other instantly, but I could not remember his name. Then it somehow came to me.

"Hoy John White," I gasped as I took a number of deep breathes in an effort to get my wind back. "How goes it?" I managed to croak out as I raised my hand in greeting.

As I asked him I suddenly I realized I was so very tired that I could barely move and so, almost certainly, was the man I was talking with and our horses.

"Good I think, Captain, except for the men we lost," John managed to gasp out. "And how be you and the rest of the lads?"

"They be fine, John. Michael Green has Prince Edward aboard his horse and, thanks be to God, the Prince is unhurt and neither is the Queen. And what of the rest of our lads?" I asked anxiously.

He had an anguished look on his face and did not answer.

"Who is it that has fallen, John?" I asked again, this time very softly.

******

John and I walked our exhausted horses slowly up the road after we checked out the fallen knight and relieved him of his almost-empty purse. We also took off him a valuable wrist amulet of hammered copper with some shiny jewels attached to it in the shape of a cross. The knight had been wearing the amulet on his left wrist. It was supposed to protect him from danger and also, if he was captured, to act as a "tell" that he was rich enough to pay a ransom instead of being immediately killed or sold for a slave.

Unfortunately for the knight his horse had rolled over him and killed him when the horse went down. *The amulet had not worked; we would sell it for sure.*

I thought about riding back to the Queen and along the way checking out the dead and wounded pursuers I had put down. But then I changed my mind and decided to continue forward to meet with the Sergeant Major and Thomas. The questioning and looting of my kills could wait.

******

It was not until John and I reached our wagons that I realized how intense the fighting had been around them and that two of the Queen's ladies were missing. And I still did not know who amongst our men had fallen. John had merely responded "not sure am I? So best I not say" when I asked who of our men were casualties.

The Queen's third lady, on the other hand, was easy to find; she was lying by the side of the road with her eyes open and a great wound in her head.

A few of the Queen's other servants other servants had already returned and I saw more of them trudging back across the farmland to rejoin us. Some, however, were obviously still missing and so was the sutler. Surprisingly enough, the wagons were intact and the horses that had been pulling them were standing quietly in their traces and snuffling at the ground for something to eat.

More importantly, a half dozen or so archers were already dismounted at the wagons to rest their horses and I could see the Sergeant Major and some of the other archers riding in to join us.

We had obviously won the battle. But I still did not know for sure who we had lost whilst winning it.

.

Chapter Twenty-two
The joyous reception.

"Are any of the King's men still alive out there?" I asked bitterly when I heard that Thomas Corn and two other archers had been killed and three of the archers had been seriously wounded including a young archer who would almost certainly need a mercy.

"We need to question them to learn who besides the King and Despenser will be receiving our revenge." *Afterwards I remembered my words and regretted them; what would we do if King Edward won and he heard about what I said?"*

"Aye, Captain. Some of the prisoners who are still living are ready to be questioned. But many of the others are probably still sleeping," replied the Sergeant Major. "We had to hit them on their heads to put them asleep so they would not start jumping around and making noise whilst we were retrieving our arrows."

We spent the rest of the day burying our dead, stripping the enemy dead and wounded of their weapons and anything else of value, and questioning those of our prisoners who could talk. Then we abandoned the prisoners and dead to their fates without harming them further and set out with the wagons towards Cambridge to re-join Lieutenant Goodman and the Queen and her son.

Our reunion with the Queen was bittersweet and a bit embarrassing—because she ran to me and threw herself into my arms and began weeping for joy as soon as I dismounted. The archers, as you might imagine, were no help; they just grinned and snickered.

But then everyone's face turned mournful a few moments later when the Queen gasped and began weeping again, this time in distress, when I told her about the dead archers and her dead lady and that her other two noble companions were missing. It was hard to know if she was distressed for them or for herself or both. It was about then that I realized she had never in her life been without a bevy of noble ladies to see to her every need and wish.

Ah well, those of her other servants who re-joined us would have to do for her until she can find some suitable noble replacements to join her court. Everyone should have her troubles. It astonished me then and still does that she thought hers were so huge.

******

Three days later we rode triumphantly into Northampton with Lord Mortimer leading a great escort of over a hundred nobles and knights and the young prince riding behind me on his own horse and surrounded two and three deep by archers leading their remounts and riding with swords in their hands. We were now fully accepted as Prince Edward's guards and I was once again getting a full night's sleep.

Northampton was jammed full of soldiers inside the city's walls with many more camping outside them. There were lords, knights, and their levies everywhere. The Queen's army was large and getting larger every day as more and more lords brought in their knights and levies.

And, of course, camp followers of every type and variety were everywhere as well.

Lord Mortimer had been effusive in his praise when he heard the tale of our journey and the ferociousness of our defence of Prince Edward. To my surprise, he encouraged me and my men to pitch our tents in the bailey of Northampton Castle so as to be near the rooms in the keep that had been assigned to the Queen and the Prince. He came across to me as a wise and ambitious man who understood the importance to his future of keeping the Queen and Prince Edward alive.

Various versions of the story about our fight with the King's men on the road had spread like wildfire through the Queen's army; and then had been further enhanced when the sergeant major and Lieutenant Goodman took two wagons piled high with bloody armour, swords, and saddles to the market to sell them. Our victory was the first proof positive that the King's men could be defeated and, as you might well imagine, everyone seized upon it as meaning that God was with the Queen.

At first there were only rumours about the fighting and our victory. But then the wagons were followed by a great crowd of men and widely viewed as they were driven into the city and then many more people saw them as they waited on the street in front of Northampton's great market so the merchants could inspect them and evaluate their re-sale value. It caused the stories about the size of the force we faced and the alleged ease of our victory to grow by the hour. And that, in turn, caused the morale of the Queen's army to increase enormously.

"If a handful of archers defending the Queen and Prince Edward can do that to hundreds of the King's men and suffer only four dead and two wounded just think what we can do?" was the general view.

The Queen's knightly supporters began to reassess their prospects which suddenly looked very much brighter. The change in the change in the nobles and knights attitude towards us was amazing: Men who had previously ignored us and looked down their noses at us were now smiling and nodding pleasantly when we encountered them. It was a heady moment for me and I had to go out of my way to act as if it was nothing special.

Even more important, at least from the point of view of me and my men, our loot ended up fetching much more than I would have thought possible. Men who had not been sure they wanted to fight for the Queen suddenly became certain and wanted more and better weapons. As you might imagine, my men were elated at the prospect of receiving even more prize money than they had initially expected. So was I, for that matter, even though I had no idea what I would do with my share.

Northampton Castle itself was a quiet refuge amidst the chaos and confusion of the Queen's ever-growing and somewhat disorganized army that was camped haphazardly in the city and the farmland around it. The castle was just outside the city wall and the River Nene ran alongside it and provided its water from a tunnel well that opened into the keep. Unfortunately the well water had a slightly foul due to the all men and horses camped along the river.

What encouraged me most was that the masts of several large sea-going transports could be seen on the river from the castle wall. They almost certainly meant that the river was navigable all the way from Northampton to the sea. Indeed, seeing them changed everything. It meant a Company galley could come from Cornwall and get almost all the way to the postern gate on the castle's river side. Even more important, in case fate turned against us, it meant we might be able to use the river to escape in the event we had to run.

I also realized that I might be able to use the shipping on the river to get a warning message to Cornwall reporting on what had happened to date. I knew the fighting on the road was well received by the Queen's supporters; and that meant it was almost certainly *not* well received by the King's supporters who were assembling at Windsor.

In other words, there was a good chance our London shipping post and any Company couriers riding past Windsor might now be perceived of as the King's enemies and be treated quite harshly. It was something the Commander and George Wainwright needed to know as soon as possible.

Hopefully, the King and Despenser understood that the fighting on the road with their men was in defence of Prince Edward and they would not take offence. But the Queen had been there also and had escaped as a by-product of our efforts to protect her son.

Upon reflection I decided there was no doubt about it; Commander Boatman and the captain of our London shipping post needed to know that our careful attempt at remaining neutral may have failed. If so, the King's men might well now consider the men of the Company to be their enemies because they assumed our fighting on the

Northampton road to save the prince meant we were supporting the Queen and Mortimer.

Something needed to be done, and quickly, to warn Commander Boatman and our London shipping post of the potential danger. The boats moored on the river were the only answer I could think of since couriers riding to London and Cornwall would almost certainly have to pass through lands controlled by King Edward and his supporters.

I started to ride down to the river to where the transports were moored to see if either or them could chartered for a voyage to Cornwall with a stop in London either on the way or on the way back. But then the Queen beckoned so I sent Lieutenant Goodman to make the inquiries and arrangements. Pay whatever price their captains require, I told him; this is too important to haggle.

Lieutenant Goodman was successful in chartering a two-masted coastal trader so later that day I sent my most dependable outrider, Sam Atkins, to deliver my report to the Commander and to the captain of our London shipping post. I gave Sam a meaningless parchment message for anyone who captured him to find and told him what to tell the Commander and our London shipping post captain.

******.

"Are you William Courtenay, the captain of the Queen's guards?" the well-dressed lady of a certain age asked rather haughtily? I had never seen her before. She was new.

"No I am not. I am William Courtenay, the captain of Prince Edward's guards," I replied. "And who might you be?"

"I am Lady Margaret Byfield, one Her Majesty's new ladies; my husband is Sir Guy of Byfield. Her Majesty commands you to attend to her as soon as possible." *Commands does she? We will have to see about that.*

We marched together back into the keep and up the stairs to the Queen's rooms. Lady Margaret primly instructed me to wait whilst she attended the Queen to announce my arrival. I spoke with the sergeant of the archers standing about in front of the Queen's door as I did.

"A good hoy to you, Jimmy. How goes it? Has anyone giving you and your lads any grief? ... "That is good know" ...

Lady Margaret returned whilst I was talking to the sergeant. At first she had an angry and exasperated look on her face because I did not immediately run to the door when she beckoned. A moment later it turned incredulous when I told her what to do.

"Tell the Queen I will be there shortly," I said in response to her increasingly anxious beckoning. Then I turned back to the sergeant.

"There is one more thing, Jimmy. I know I have said it before but please remind your lads *and* your relief when it comes that no man is to enter the Queen's rooms or those of Prince Edward except Lord Mortimer. There are *no* exceptions no matter who they claim to be or what they say they are supposed to do."

Jimmy was grinning as he acknowledged my words and so were the men standing around in the hallway. Of course they were; nobody likes pushy women telling him what to do, especially women who think they are our betters.

*****

The Queen was not a happy camper despite her rooms being a bit drier and more comfortable than the tent she had been forced to sleep in whilst we were on the road from Ipswich. She was, it seems, in full pout. She sent her ladies away and got after me right proper.

"Where were you last night? The hallway in front of my rooms has been full of your men ever since we arrived but you have been nowhere to be found."

It was not the question I was expecting. It took me by surprise. So I hemmed and hawed and finally came up with a half-arsed explanation. I hoped it would be sufficient.

"I thought you might be busy talking to Lord Mortimer about, ah, your army's progress and plans, Your Majesty, and I did not want to disturb you." I finally got out.

She was having none of it and was standing looking at me with her arms crossed protectively in front of her breasts and tapping her foot angrily.

"I thought you knew that Lord Mortimer and I long ago stopped, umm, comforting each other," she said angrily. "Besides, he has no time to spend with me now because he has so many important things to do with the army and will soon be away with them."

Her explanation somehow made me angry.

"So Mortimer thinks his army is more important than spending his nights poking you or protecting your son, eh? Well I did not really know that, did I, you foolish cow."

My angry response made her both furious and strangely excited. It seems no one had ever been angry at her before let alone called her a foolish cow. She stamped her foot and glowered at me.

"I am a foolish cow am I, William? Well I am not as foolish as you think. Edward and his nanny are in the room next to mine and rightly so, eh? And you and your men need to close by to guard him, eh?

"So whether you like it or not whilst we are here in Northampton your men will have to continue to stand around in the hallway in front of his room to guard him. And since you will have to watch over your men I have also arranged for you to be staying in the room next to mine.

"And I am not as silly as you think, Dear William? I made sure you were given the room that has two doors and one of them opens into mine. So what do you think of that?" she asked triumphantly.

Chapter Twenty-three
Windsor and London.

Lord Mortimer began leading the Queen's army out of Northampton five days after the archers rode in with the Queen and her son following their fight with the King's men. The army began slowly moving south to engage the King's forces. It did so as more and more English lords got off the fence they had been trying to sit on and began bringing in their knights and levies to join it. The Queen, Prince Edward, and the archers guarding the prince did not accompany the army. They would remain in the relative safety of Northampton Castle until it was safe to travel.

Later that same day favourable winds resulted in William's message being delivered to Commander Boatman by one of the coastal trading cogs that had been at Northampton. And that evening there was full-scale rioting in the streets of London when the supporters of the King and Queen began fighting in the streets. The rioting was accompanied by widespread looting and arson. The next day our London shipping post issued more deposit parchments and accepted more coins for safekeeping than any previous day in all its years.

William neither remained at Northampton Castle nor joined the Queen's army. Three days after the Queen's army marched away he left ten men under the command of Lieutenant Goodman to guard Prince Edward, bid farewell Northampton and the Prince, and rode to London with Sergeant Major Arthur Donaldson and his twelve remaining horse archers. His intention was to deliver the prize coins that had resulted from the archers' victory in the battle of the road to the Company's shipping post and then remain in London to help safeguard them and the other coins the post had accumulated in its chests.

The night before he left William had informed the Queen of his intentions to leave for London. He had done so in a quiet moment after they had spent some time getting to know each other. She had become quite furious and haughtily announced that if he was going to go to London she was going to re-join her army. Then everything settled down and in the morning he agreed to escort her to her army before proceeding to London with his men.

Unbeknownst to William, Commander Boatman himself was already on his way to London aboard a Company galley that was newly arrived from the east. He had heard about the fighting on the road and decided to go to London for the same purpose—protecting the coins that had been rapidly accumulating at the Company's shipping post.

James Thorpe, the elderly Bishop of Cornwall, accompanied Commander Boatman. When he reached London Bishop Thorpe intended to seek out King Edward's influential supporters amongst the churchmen—and enlist their help to convince the King that the efforts of the mercenary company's archers on the road were only in the defence of the Prince and did not mean they were supporting the Queen. He hoped to do so by offering pouches filled with gold and silver coins to the Papal nuncio and several of his fellow bishops who were known to be particularly close to the King.

Even more important, if questions came up came up about the fighting on the Northampton road, Bishop Thorpe wanted the churchmen to help him explain to King Edward that the defeat the King's men had suffered had nothing to do with Cornwall's loyal Company of Archers.

The two men immediately set sail for London. It was the Commander's intention that the galley would, as usual, be rowed up the Thames and moored at the Company wharf on the river in front of the post. The ninety archers on board would then be immediately available to reinforce the shipping post and help guard the coins that had recently been deposited with it for safekeeping. Commander Boatman had already decided to move most of them to the galley where they would be easier to defend and more easily carried away if worst came to worst and the Company's shipping post was overrun.

Why were William and the Commander and everyone else so anxious about the coins at the shipping post? The answer was because the uncertainty of the war's outcome and the current troubles in London were causing more and more coins to be deposited with the Company for safe-keeping. As a result, record amounts of coins were accumulating at the shipping post in addition to the coins that were normally kept there to be available to buy back the money order parchments that the Company issued in exchange for the coins.

Paying a fee and handing over one's coins in exchange for a parchment receipt that could be presented to get a slightly smaller amount of coins at a later date or at another of the Company's shipping posts was one of the Company's major coin earners. It was increasingly being done by rich landowners and merchants because they knew it was a good way to safeguard their wealth from robbers and vengeful kings and queens.

It was no surprise that the troubles and anarchy in the city resulted in more and more Londoners with coins were willing to pay a fee to the Company to hold their coins to keep them safe from robbers who might invade their undefended homes and market stalls. The post's earning had never been so high.

Indeed, at one point in past week the Company's London shipping post had accepted so many coins that it temporarily ran out of the blank parchments on which were scribed the terms of their return, less a fee, at either the Company's London post or one of its other posts. It also caused the post captain, George Wainwright, to significantly increase the fees his post charged for holding the coins safely until they were claimed either at his post or one of the Company's other posts elsewhere in the world.

In other words, it was business as usual and the Company would greatly profit from London's unrest and riots *if* it was able to prevent the coins it would need to pay off the parchments from being taken by robbers or the king.

There was reason to be hopeful. The Company's shipping post was well guarded with barred doors, an escape tunnel where the coin chests could be stashed or evacuated to a secret exit, and its wall openings too narrow for a man to come through.

But there were still major problems associated with storing them at the post. One was that too many people knew about the coins that had been pouring into the post for safe keeping. Robbers were always robbers and there were entire companies of them in London. So it was only a matter of time before a serious effort was mounted to try to take them.

Another very real possibility was that king might blame the Company for his men's failure to get his son away from the Queen and send his army to take the coins. Kings, after all, always needed coins to pay for their meaningless wars and displays of importance. If either event came to pass the Company would have to make good on the parchments it issued by coming up with new coins from its own chests.

There was no doubt about it so far as Commander Boatman was concerned, the coins in the London post either had to be moved away to safety or successfully defended or both. On the other hand, not all of the coins could be sent out of the country or to Cornwall or anywhere else for safe keeping. Some of them had to stay in or near London to be immediately available. That was because there were sure to be many parchments presented for coins as soon as the current troubles ended—something that would happen sooner or later. Then the deposited coins would have to be immediately returned minus the Company's fee for protecting them.

The Company's willingness to fight to defend the coins in its chests and its ability to immediately hand over the amount of coins specified on the parchment at any time and in multiple locations was why merchants and others were willing to exchange their coins for Company-issued parchments in the first place. On the other hand, failure to immediately return the parchment-specified number of coins whenever and wherever the parchments were presented would ruin the Company's reputation and might well cause it to fail for lack of sufficient customers and fee revenues in the future.

In other words, a substantial amount of readily available coins had to be kept at all times in or near the Company's London shipping post or its other shipping posts where the parchments might be presented—and that would be hard to do if robbers successfully raided its shipping post or if the full weight of the King's army fell on the shipping post and destroyed it because King Edward was pissed at losing the battle to retake his son and blamed the Company for his losses.

It was the Company's need to immediately pay out coins when parchments were presented that explained why Commander Boatman as soon as he arrived in London began using his archers to move the coins in the shipping post to the galley on which he arrived—so they could be more easily defended. It also explained why Bishop Thorpe immediately set off with his apprentice sergeant, a young lad by the name of Adrian Goldsmith, and a large pouch of coins to visit Saint Paul's Cathedral to try to meet with the Bishop of London.

It was well known that Stephen Gravesend, the Bishop of London, was one of King Edward's strongest supporters and most important advisors. A sufficient "gift" to Bishop Gravesend it was hoped, would encourage him to advise the King to blame someone else other than the Company for his army's losses when they tried to capture the Queen and Prince Edward.

In the end the King turned out not to be a problem.

****** *Bishop Thorpe of Cornwall*

News of the defeat of King Edward's horsemen when they tried to "rescue" Prince Edward combined with the approach of Mortimer's ever-growing army greatly distressed the King's forces assembled at Windsor. Some of them began quietly slipping away. Others began changing their minds about fighting to support the King when they heard about the defeat and the size of the Queen's army that was slowly but surely moving toward them.

I did not know any of this when I arrived in London and took a horse cart to Saint Pauls Cathedral with a pouch full of coins as a gift to "encourage" my old acquaintance, Stephen Gravesend, now the Bishop of London, to use his influence to help me protect the Company of Archers. I knew he would appreciate the coins because Stephen was an ambitious man and Cardinal appointments in Rome where the weather was nicer were getting ever more expensive.

What I specifically wanted was for Stephen to do whatever he could to focus the anger of King Edward and his supporters on the free company of archers that caused his army to fail to recover his son and *not* on the Company of Archers from which the men of the free company had been recruited. It seemed like a reasonable thing to do because the King and his supporters might be on the verge of winning the war and about to seek revenge on everyone they thought was responsible for their losses.

My thoughts were quickly put right by Stephen Gravesend.

"It is not a problem at the moment, old friend. King Edward has other things on his mind like trying to stay alive while he waits for the tide of the war to turn back in his favour—which it inevitably will because Edward is God's choice to be England's king and the Church is solidly behind him. But I will take the coins for use when the King is more successful and his mind turns to revenge."

My surprise at hearing that things were not going well for the King must have shown.

"Have you not heard? The Queen's army is marching this way and London is in flames. Bishop Stapledon, the Lord High Treasurer, was pulled off his horse and killed by a London mob when he tried to disperse it.

"There is chaos and danger everywhere. As a result, the King and that dear Despenser boy and their supporters have just come in from Windsor to the safety of the even more powerful Tower.

"I and many other bishops and the nuncio are going over there later this afternoon to stay with them until the rioting and arson are put down and the whoring Queen and her lover are defeated. One cannot be too careful these days, eh?"

I, of course, agreed with him. What else could I do, eh?

******

Bishop Thorpe returned to the shipping post and Commander Boatman in a slightly wobbly condition as a result of more than a few bowls of wine and too much good food at the cathedral's table. He promptly surprised the Commander and everyone else by announcing that the King had retreated to the safety of the nearby impregnable Tower and that the Bishop of London and many of the king's friends and supporters were in the process of moving there to join him there.

"What does that mean for us, James, the Commander asked the Bishop. Is there anything the Company can do to profit from the situation?"

The hours of talking and reflection that followed were quite intense at times until Commander Boatman announced some of his decisions. Then everyone fell in line—"Coming to Jesus" was what it was called in the Company.

Two days later Bishop Thorpe again visited the Bishop of London, this time in the nearby Tower. He did so this time to report that Prince Edward was safe after an attack by French knights and to ask Bishop Gravesend to help the archers in William's mercenary company get the success payment they were due if they successfully protected the Prince. *As the good book says somewhere it is always better to collect money that is due you too early than too late.*

Bishop Thorpe and his apprentice found Bishop Gravesend in one of the Tower's several halls along with Lord Despenser and the King and several other bishops and nobles. They were gathered around a map.

"How do you see our situation, Bishop Thorpe?" Lord Despenser inquired after the usual bows to the King and the other traditional courtesies were exchanged. He seemed more than a little tense and some of the men around him had worried looks on their faces. "The red stones represent the Queen's army under the command of Lord Mortimer; it is coming south from Northampton.

"I ask because I am gathering opinions and have been informed you were a very successful soldier before you became the Bishop of Cornwall."

Bishop Thorpe looked at the map and made a fateful observation.

"What I think, Your Lordship, is that that the you and the King and his supporters are about to be cut off from any hope of escape and endure a prolonged siege that might well succeed in starving you into a surrender because the King is so loved that you will have too many supporters in the Tower to feed. And why would you allow that to happen if there are as many coins in the treasury as London's merchants and money lenders say there are?

"With enough time and coins you and the King could buy the goodwill and armies of many of England's nobles and hire a significant number of mercenaries with the coins that are said to be in the Tower's treasure room. So why are you taking the risk of staying here in the Tower and being starved into an unnecessary surrender?

"The Company of Archers has a stable in the city and can quickly arrange the necessary wagons and draught horses for you and the King if you decide to leave and fight on. You can employ them to carry the coins to Wales and safety before it is too late, and then begin using the coins to raise a new and bigger army.

The King and Despenser and the Bishop just looked at each other. Then Despenser looked back at the map for a few moments and became increasingly enthusiastic.

"Bishop Thorpe is right. We could do it, by God; and we should do it quickly if we are to avoid being cut off."

Then after a pause he added 'It is our only hope'. He said it under his breath without realizing he had spoken out loud and that the others had heard him.

Bishop Thorpe was encouraged to make another suggestion.

"Should Your Majesty desire to employ them, I can arrange the wagons and horses to arrive in secret as soon as darkness falls tonight," he volunteered. "Some of my most fervent and loyal parishioners happen to be stationed at the stable. I am sure they will help since I know they are strong supporters of the King."

Then he smiled and added even more.

"The stable is outside the city walls and very near here and to the south. So they could bring the wagons and horse in through the south entrance to the Tower's bailey without being seen from the city walls. If they do that, His Majesty and his men could be on their way to Wales by the time the sun arrives tomorrow morning. You could stop at Windsor for something to eat and even spend the night.

"If the stones on your map are accurate the Queen's army will not reach London for several days and then it will take them several more to get to Windsor. You would be rested and well on your way to Wales by then."

"What a wonderful idea; God is once again smiling on the King," Bishop Gravesend said as he raised his eyes toward heaven and made the sign of the cross. "Wales is said to be beautiful this time of year and have many mercenaries who would be available for His Majesty to employ."

Everyone smiled and nodded to everyone else. The Company of Archers had just become King Edward's newest and best friend.

Chapter Twenty-four
King Edward flees.

William and his men rode into London from the south on the river road. They arrived to find a great bustle of activity underway at the Company stable. Archers were everywhere assembling a convoy of wagons and horse teams to take to the Tower that evening as soon as the sun finished passing overhead. And more horses and wagons were beginning to arrive such that the stable yard was soon overly full and the newest arrivals had to be held out on the narrow side street that ran in front of the entrance to the stable.

Surprisingly, William was the last man to see the hustle and bustle at the stable and learn why it was happening. He was the last to know because when he and his twelve men reached the side street that led to the Company's stable he decided to continue riding alone on up the Thames road in order to report his arrival to the shipping post and see if any messages were waiting for him.

He had done so, ridden on to the post that is, after watching his men follow Sergeant Major Donaldson into the side street that branched off from the main road along the Thames and begin riding toward the entrance to the Company's stable. They were to feed and water their horses, get something to eat if it was available, and wait there for him to return.

The door of the Company's shipping post opened on to the main road that ran along the river. It was further upstream from the narrow side street on which the Company stable was located.

William reached the shipping post in less than ten minutes. He was somewhat surprised when he found the post closed and its door barred. It was early on a late September afternoon and the weather was warm and sunny unlike the fog he and his men had ridden through earlier in the day.

For the past few days he and his men had spoken with travellers who had regaled them with all kinds of stories about the troubles in London and in the countryside around it. But the closed shipping post and the several columns of black smoke that were coming up from behind the city's walls were the first actual signs he had seen that suggested the city's troubles might be serious.

William dismounted in front of the post's door. As he did he became aware that people both in the post and in the buildings on either side of the narrow street were looking down at him from the window openings above him. That was not at all unusual; people were always curious when someone new appeared where they lived and worked. He was relaxed because there was nothing happening around the post that was in any way alarming. To the contrary, people seemed to be going about their everyday lives and the traffic on the river road and the Thames seemed normal.

"Hoy the post," William shouted as he used the handle of one of his wrist knives to rap out a friendly little tap tappity tap tap jingle on the post's outer door, the one that faced out toward the cobblestoned road that ran along the river. As he did he could see the Tower looming against the sky further up the Thames and some of the city walls that lay just behind it. The two columns of black smoke rising above its walls were somewhat unusual but fires were common in London and seeing the smoke from two of them certainly did not indicate that there were riots and the city was burning.

"A hoy to you down there," a man's voice shouted from one of the openings on the first floor. "I see your tunic. Be you an archer?"

"Aye, I am," William shouted. "I be Captain Courtenay late of Galley Ninety-two and the Queen's guards. Why is the shipping post closed?" *I was fairly sure I knew why but I asked anyway. If the post is closed the troubles in the city must be worse than I had been led to believe.*

"Wait there, Captain. We will be right down." *The post's men are in the safe space above the entrance rooms and warehouse? Things must be more serious for the Company than I thought.*

It seemed to William that it took overly long before the door opened. And when it did there were no less than four men in archers' tunics waiting beyond it. They were holding galley shields and drawn swords and obviously ready to fight to keep him from entering. One of them was wearing the three stripes of a sergeant. They relaxed and lowered their swords when they saw him and his stripes up close.

"You can tie your horse to the mooring post and we will let you in, Captain," the sergeant said. "Of course we will. But please be quick about it. The Commander's galley is up the river anchored in the pool before the bridge with most of the galley's lads if it is his galley you be seeking. Guarding the post's coins they are. Captain Wainwright and the rest of the lads are with the Commander at the stable getting the wagons and horses ready for tonight."

"Did you say Commander Boatman is here in London?" William was more than a little surprised.

"Oh aye, so he is. And the Bishop is with him too. At the stable I expects they are; getting the horses and wagons ready for tonight's big move I would think." *The Commander and the Bishop are in London? What big move?*

William was starting to climb back aboard his horse before the sergeant finished speaking. *Goddamn it!*

******

William kicked his horse into an amble and hurried the short distance to the stable. When he turned his horse off the river road and into the side street where the stable was located he could see archers pulling empty wagons out of the stable's yard by hand and parking them in the street. He rode past them, acknowledging their salutes as he did, and on into the yard.

The stable's yard was packed with archers, wagons, and horses and all their sights, smells, and sounds. In the background William could hear sergeants shouting at their men and the familiar sounds of a smith hammering on an iron horseshoe. He could also smell the smoke from the smith's fire. What he instantly understood was that he was seeing and hearing the sights and sounds of a big convoy of horse wagons getting ready to move out. *But why and going to where?*

"Hoy, William, glad you could finally make it," was the teasing shout of a jovial Commander Boatman as he waved a greeting and walked through the crowded yard towards where William had dismounted and was raising his tunic to take a long overdue piss. Some of the men in the yard smiled at the greeting. William heard the tone in which the Commander's greeting was delivered and saw the archers smile when they heard it—and instantly understood that things were going well. He relaxed.

William had finished pissing and dropped his tunic by the time the smiling Commander reached him and shook William's hand after they exchanged salutes. Major Captain Robertson joined them a few seconds later and so did a four-stripe captain he did not recognize who turned out to be George Wainwright, the captain of the Company's London post. Standing behind them in the background and grinning broadly were Sam and Tom, the two outriders he had sent to Cornwall to carry his report to the Commander. William raised his hand and smiled to let them know he was glad to see them.

"You and your men showed up just in time, Captain Courtenay, and it is a welcome sight you are. We have more than enough archers but they are all on foot because they came off the galley that brought me and Bishop Thorpe from Restormel. What we needed were horses and horse archers to ride them to help guard a convoy of wagons and the foot archers who are driving them and aboard to keep off looters; and now, by God, you have arrived and we have them.

"Come on, Lad; follow me and I will tell you all about it somewhere where we can talk privately."

The Commander led William and the other two men into the stable and to the horse stall on the far end where the Bishop of Cornwall was resting in a pile of clean straw. When they got there the bishop stood up and Commander sent away the men that were nearby whilst the bishop was getting to his feet. They were gone by the time the Bishop finished brushing the straw off his robe. Then The Commander and the Bishop explained to William what they had in mind and what his role would be.

Major Captain Robertson and the man who had been named to William as the shipping post's captain, George Wainwright, listened carefully even though they already knew the basic plan.

What William heard stunned him.

He immediately understood why even the rank and file archers could not be told any of it for fear the secret might leak into the wrong ears: King Edward and Despenser had contracted to pay the Company an absolutely huge sum of money to provide and protect the wagons and teams that were being assembled to carry all the coins in the Tower's treasure room safely to Wales. Moreover, the King and his supporters and the coin wagons had to leave that very night before the Queen's army could cut them off and prevent them from getting deep enough into Wales to be safe.

"Captain Wainwright and the men of our shipping post have been able to acquire the necessary wagons and teams from our stable and the other stables in the city. And we have enough archers from the galley that carried us here to guard both the post and the galley which is anchored just off the riverbank upstream from the post. But until you and your men arrived we had no horsemen to ride with King

Edward to protect the coins and our horses and wagons—and collect the additional success coins due to the Company if the King and his coins get through to Wales.

"If you and your men had not arrived we would have been forced to use even more of the galley's foot archers and have them ride in the wagons—and that would have spread us dangerously thin because we also have to protect the post's coins that are now aboard the galley and in the post itself. It would also endanger the men on the wagons because they would have no riders to warn them of attackers and to try to divert them."

William became more and more excited as he listened to the Commander and the Bishop explain their plan and what they wanted him and his men to do.

He liked the plan. But he was more than a little dismayed at what was *now* expected of him and his men. There was no surprise in that: In the space of a few days he and his men would be going from fighting desperately to keep the Queen's princely son from being captured by the King's supporters to possibly fighting desperately to keep the King's treasure-carrying wagons from being captured by the Queen's supporters.

Chapter Twenty-five
Chaos and confusion in the Tower.

It was a busy day at the Company's stable. Some of our men who knew something about horses, including Sam and Tom, spent it selecting from amongst the draught horses that various merchants and stables had offered to sell or rent to the Company "for use on a long trip." Others of the men spent it preparing the wagons our shipping post's captain, George Wainwright, had quickly rented or bought from various stables and merchants that very day.

According to Commander Boatman we had acquired enough additional wagons to take to the Tower and be loaded with coin chests but we still did not have enough draught horses. That was somewhat surprising since we could see that the stable's stalls used by its draught horses were full and other draught horses, newly acquired, were tied to the stable's mooring post or hobbled in the street in front of the stable.

"I may have misspoke," Commander Boatman finally admitted when he was asked about the horses in the stalls. "We probably have enough draught horses to fill our contract. What I am really concerned about is that there will not be enough room in the Tower's bailey for all the wagons if they all arrive with their horses already in their traces.

"So we will pull some of the wagons to the Tower by hand and bring the additional draught horses to the unhorsed wagons when the King's march begins and the bailey is less crowded. That will probably occur after the King and his supporters and the initial wagons have begun their trek to Wales. The rest of the wagons can catch up on the road if necessary.

"If anyone asks, you are to tell them we have the rest of the draught horses immediately available and will bring them in from the stable where they are waiting as soon as there is enough room in the bailey. I do not know how soon that will be or even if it will actually happen, not yet at least. But do not say anything unless someone asks."

If it will actually happen? Ah. He must have something in mind. But why is he not telling us what it is?

****** *William Courtenay*

Two-horse teams with an archer driving them pulled eleven of the empty wagons through the Tower gate and into the bailey behind it as soon as the sun finished passing overhead. Ten-man teams of foot archers from the galley moored in the river pulled the other six wagons to the Tower by hand. My little band of horse archers, now expanded to include Sam and Tom, rode alongside them.

Pulling wagons to the Tower by hand was not a problem. The teams of foot archers did it easily because the Tower was little more than a mile away and the wagons were empty. It helped that we had seventy or so of the galley's men to do the pulling and their arms and legs were strong from rowing and having enough food to eat.

There were also no problems getting the wagons to the Tower gate despite the darkness; the moon was out and there was a candle lantern on each wagon so the wagon behind it could follow it without running off the road. Four archers carrying candle lanterns walked ahead of the convoy to light the way and clear the road.

The Tower's south gate, the one that could not be seen from the city wall, was open and we were expected so we were passed right in by the guards. My men and I were mounted and bringing up the rear but we were not leading our remounts which had been temporarily left at the stable. Also mounted were Commander Boatman and the Bishop. They rode at the front of the column immediately behind the first wagon.

None of the archers from the galley's crew were mounted. Most of them would walk back to the galley and our shipping post to take up their guard duties when the night was finished. Several dozen of them, although they did not know it yet, would ride on the wagons all the way to Wales to help me and my horse archers guard their precious cargos.

******

What we saw in the moonlight when we rode into the bailey beyond the Tower gate was a scene of absolute chaos and hysteria. It seems the intended secrecy about the flight of the King and his coins ended as soon as the meeting with Bishop Thorpe broke up and everyone rushed off to get ready to leave.

However it happened, word of the King's intention to flee to Wales with the coins in the Tower treasury spread like a wildfire; everyone in the Tower soon knew that the King and Despenser intended to abandon England and ride to Wales with all the coins and jewels in the Tower's treasure room.

The result was inevitable: A great panic and innumerable rumours set in amongst the King's supporters. The asked each other what would become of their heads and their titles and lands when Mortimer and the Queen temporarily took over the kingdom whilst the King and Despenser were organizing an army to return and defeat them? The answers were not encouraging.

Some of the King's supporters fled the tower to return to their homes. Others decided they had no choice but to stay with the king and accompany him to Wales, especially since they understood that the coins he was taking with him would enable him to buy a great army and return just as the Queen and Mortimer had done.

King Edward and his most important supporters and their knights and servants had arrived at the Tower riding their own horses and he and a number of them had their own horse-drawn covered wagons containing their campaign tents and armour. In the moonlight as we rode into the bailey we could see some of their wagons off to starboard being hurriedly filled with supplies and equipment from the Tower.

We could also see and hear courtiers and priests without horses trying to climb aboard the wagons of the King and his supporters. They were arguing and fighting desperately with each other for the space on them. They were obviously doing so to avoid having to walk to Wales with the King or being left behind.

The high anxiety of everyone without a horse or wagon to ride was understandable because the Queen and Mortimer were not likely to treat the King's supporters kindly. In any event, as soon as we came through the gate we instantly understood that the bailey was packed with angry and desperate people; we could hear them even if we could not always see them in the moonlit darkness.

As you might also imagine, there was much shouting and pointing, and then cheers and shouts of joy, as we rode into the bailey at the head of our column of empty wagons. The mob surged towards us out of the darkness and immediately began desperately trying to climb on to *our* wagons even before they finished passing through the gate and entering the Tower.

There was noisy chaos everywhere in the dim moonlight with people shouting, pushing, and fighting with each other to get aboard and then for a space to sit. Most of the people in the hysterical mob were men but there were a number of women and children amongst them.

My men and I and the archers driving and pulling the wagons immediately found ourselves trying to fighting off the great horde of desperate men and women who had rushed towards our wagons and began trying to climb aboard them with their possessions. It soon became obvious that trying to stop them was an exercise in futility in the dim moonlight. They were climbing on board and sitting down faster than the archers or someone who wanted their place could throw them off.

Commander Boatman finally rode up and down the line of wagons shouting "let them board and leave them alone. Finish bringing the wagons in and park them against the wall over there by the door where our guides are standing with their candle lanterns. Then every archer who is *not* a wagon driver or on a horse is to climb down and join me at the door as soon as his wagon is parked. Drivers are to stay with their wagons and hold their horses."

A couple of minutes later the Commander led the archers on foot to the treasure room. I dismounted, handed the reins of my horse, to the horse archer who had been riding next to me, and followed the Commander. So did Bishop Thorpe. We climbed up some stone stairs and through a door; and then up another set of stairs to another door.

When we passed through the second door we entered a room brightly lit by a number of candle lanterns and filled by all sorts of crates and chests. It was the Tower's treasure room and, as I had just been learnt at the stable, it held much of England's great wealth.

A man who turned out to be Bishop Gravesend, the Bishop of London, saw us and rushed towards us shouting "Finally" even though we were not late. In a corner of the room off to my starboard I could see a man who turned out to be Lord Despenser surrounded by a crowd of a crowd of excited and loudly talking men who were waving their arms about, courtiers apparently. They all stopped and stared. King Edward was not there.

Bishop Gravesend was so anxious and excited that he was literally trembling as he rushed to greet us. Commander Boatman, an inherently good-hearted man, immediately tried to placate the poor fellow for fear that he would become so totally overbalanced that he would fall down and go to sleep.

"All is well, Eminence; all is well. We are here on time and have brought a horse for every wagon just as we promised. Even so we are short of horses and still gathering them. That is because it now seems that two-horse teams will be needed to pull the coin wagons because the coin chests are so heavy. But it will be no problem; it just means more of the King's supporters will have to walk. Not you and your priests, of course."

Chapter Twenty-six
The King flees.

The archers and the King's guards immediately began carrying the heavy chests down the stairs to the wagons in the lantern-lit darkness and loading them. They were so heavy that it took four men for most of the chests.

It went smoothly except for a few dropped chests once the first three wagons were cleared of their stowaways at sword point and then kept that way by archers who stood in the wagon beds whilst the chests were being loaded. The orders to the archers in charge of guarding the wagons simple: they were to chop anyone who did not quickly disembark and anyone who tried to come aboard.

Not everyone believed the archers' warnings, at least not initially. As a result several men who had already climbed into the wagons and a couple of thrusters from amongst mob who were attempting to join them took vicious sword slices to their arms and deep stab wounds in their arses.

Noise carries in the dark; it did not take long before everyone in the bailey understand that it did not matter who they might be, they too would be bleeding and screaming if they tried to climb aboard a wagon or in any way interfered with either the archers who were loading it or the wagon's cargo. When the first three wagons were loaded the archers similarly emptied the next three wagons of their passengers, left several archers on each of the loaded wagons to guard their precious cargos, and continued the loading process.

It took most of the night but long before sunrise the Tower's treasure room was empty and the crates and chests holding the King's coins were more or less evenly distributed between the Company wagons in the bailey. It was done properly because Commander Boatman himself had taken personal charge of the loading.

The Commander had been most careful. He opened each chest to make sure it contained something that should be carried to Wales and then specified which of the wagons should carry it. There were so many coin chests that by the time the last of the chests was loaded there was no room under the covers of the wagons for anyone except for the archers who were driving them and their sword-wielding archer guards.

******

King Edward and Lord Despenser found the chaotic scene and the great commotion and noise in the Tower's bailey both depressing and distressing. Even worse, a messenger arrived whilst the loading was underway with a report that the advance elements of the Queen's army were only two days away from London and being personally led by Lord Mortimer. The arrival of the Queen's army had been expected for some time, but it was still a shock and added to everyone's anxieties nonetheless, especially the King's.

The report that Mortimer and his army were coming for them was the last straw. Panic set in and King Edward and

Lord Despenser decided not to sit around and wait for dawn to leave the Tower. Night or not; they decided to begin riding to Windsor Castle as soon their horses could be brought to them. It would be the first stop on their flight to Wales and the subsequent rebuilding of a more powerful army.

Dawn was still several hours away when the King and Despenser and the thirty or forty knights, nobles, and royal guards in the royal retinue mounted their horses and climbed aboard their carts and wagons. Their departure through the Tower gate leading down to the road along the Thames caused a brief outburst of angry shouting and much consternation and confusion on the part of the king's now exhausted and subdued supporters who were still in the bailey. No one wanted to be left behind; they hurried to accompany the King. So did the archers.

The eleven archer-guarded coin wagons with horses in their traces were well back in the great procession that followed the King and his courtiers and guards out of the Tower's river gate. They were joined by their levies and the camp followers and sutlers who had been waiting anxiously outside the gate.

There was much confusion, angry curses, and stumbling about in the moonlit darkness. My horse archers and I rode alongside the wagons and it took quite a while for us to reach the gate and join the slowly moving column. We had barely reached the river road and turned to starboard to head toward Windsor by the time the sun appeared.

Bishop Thorpe was riding with us along with his apprentice sergeant and so was Commander Boatman's apprentice sergeant, Jack White, who had been temporarily assigned to me to replace Thomas Corn. There were at least three sword and longbow carrying foot archers on each of the wagons to guard them.

A great crowd of men and women joined us in coming out of the gate behind the riders and wagons carrying the nobles, courtiers, and priests who were fleeing with the King. It was large crowd but not as many people were in it as had initially been inside the Tower bailey or waiting outside it. There were fewer because some of the initial mob had already left the Tower to go home or to hide in the city. Others had remained behind in the Tower because they did not know what to do or where to go.

As Bishop Thorpe and I rode out of the Tower with our apprentice sergeants and all the available horse archers we could not see the six horse-less wagons still sitting in the bailey surrounded by their guards. But we certainly knew they were there.

****** *Commander Boatman*

Those of the archers who remained behind in the Tower's bailey with me and the horse-less wagons watched as Bishop Thorpe and Captain Courtenay led the captain's horse archers and the horse-drawn coin wagons out of the Tower gate.

I waited for the better part of an hour after the last of the King's supporters walked through the gate before I gave the order I had long ago whilst the wagons were still being loaded decided to give: "Move them out."

For safety's sake I decided that the who were remaining behind should pull the six remaining coin wagons down to the river road and load the coin chests they were carrying on to the Company galley waiting there. It was a reasonable thing to do since they would safer and easier to guard if they were on the galley and the galley was anchored in the river instead of tied up along the riverbank.

It was still dark in the bailey and almost everyone was gone by time I gave the order to begin quietly moving the last six wagons out of the Tower. Hopefully the chests they were carrying would be safely loaded aboard the galley and out of sight by the time the sun appeared.

Once the galley was loaded some of the archers climbed aboard it and anchored it in the river whilst the others went to guard the shipping post and the coins that were still in it. Both groups would remain in place as guards until the next two or three Company galleys reached London and could take on some of the chests.

We had to wait until some of the coin chests could be off-loaded because there were so many of them and they were so heavy that they would likely fall through the bottom of the hull and be lost forever if we sailed with all of the chests on the one galley and it encountered heavy weather.

****** *Following the King*

King Edward and his entourage rode away in the middle of the night and left the column of his mostly-walking supporters behind as soon they were outside the Tower gate. The road was open and they reached Windsor that same day. William and the Bishop and the wagons William and his men were guarding might have reached Windsor that same day if the road in front of them had been clear. But, of course, the road was not clear because it was clogged with the great crowd of soldiers and camp followers who were following the King and his courtiers to wherever it was they were going. Many of them were on foot.

"Damn; we should have had the wagons at the gate and ready to go right behind the King," William said to Bishop Thorpe as they rode side by side in front of the first wagon. It was slow going because the road in front of them was clogged with slow-walking men and women trying to follow the king.

"Perhaps not," was the Bishop's response. "If we had been too close behind the King and Despenser someone riding with them might have noticed that we were forced to leave behind the six wagons that had no horses in their traces to pull them."

It was many hours later and several hours short of Windsor when the archers and the wagons they were guarding finally pulled out of the slow-moving column and prepared to camp for the night in a pasture by the road. Some in the column had already stopped; others were still on the road.

Bishop Thorpe and William continued talking about the King and his somewhat desperate situation that evening as they sat around the archers' cooking fire. The Bishop mentioned the "success coins" that would be due if the crown prince was protected. He told William he was thinking about trying to go into Windsor Castle when we arrived the next day and requesting the bonus coins due for the services and successes of William and mercenary company.

"I might be able to get them paid early," the Bishop suggested with a yawn, "on the premise that the coins due for our services might be collectible now that the prince was safely away from Mortimer and "the French who twice tried to murder him so that a Frenchman could take the throne when King Edward went to heaven."

"We probably will not be able to get them since we are contracted to keep the prince safe for an entire year and the year is not up. On the other hand, as the Bible undoubtedly says somewhere—it is always better to ask too soon for coins that you are owed and be told to come back later than to ask for them too late when there may not be any left.

"Who knows, William, the King might even approve the immediate payment of the success bonus since he has so many coins available at moment and we are still marching with him and his rapidly dwindling number of supporters.

"If the King does approve releasing the coins to us we can take them from the chests in the wagons. Besides, visiting the castle to ask for them is a good excuse to talk to the bishops and courtiers to find out what they know—if they are still there by the time we arrive."

Another of the things the two men talked about that night were the large number of people who had been riding and walking ahead of them who had already either turned around to return to London or had turned off on side roads to begin travelling back to their homes or potential places of refuge.

"Not many of this lot will last the distance," a grizzled horse archer sergeant interjected when the conversation turned to their road mates. "They have no bottom." He had been sitting near the two men and listening to their conversation.

"Aye, you are right about that Sergeant Miller," the Bishop Thorpe agreed with a chuckle. "But neither will I unless the cooking improves."

William's new apprentice sergeant who had been listening from where he was positioned in the wagon above them giggled as he rolled over and pulled his sleeping skins higher. He was sound asleep a moment late despite the unevenness of the chests that made sleeping on top of them difficult. The apprentice was young but he was already a soldier.

Several of the archers heard the apprentice sergeant giggle and felt better for it; things must be going alright.

It is a strange fact of life that parchment scribers have commented on since the days of the Romans; real soldiers, even young ones, seem to be able to fall asleep instantly and do so whenever they have a chance. It has always been that way but no one knows why.

******

A great rain began in the middle of the night complete with thunder and lightning. Many of the archers including William and Bishop Thorpe were already in the wagons and sleeping under the sail-like wagon covers that protected the crates and chests they were carrying. The horses, of course, just stood impassively in the rain and got wet.

Within seconds of the rain beginning all the rest of the archers were in there with them under the wagon covers. In addition, although William never did know about it until much later, a young woman with three small children was sheltering in one of the wagons. The archers guarding the wagon had taken pity on them because of the children and had shared their food and let them sleep under the wagon. The archers had been awakened by the thunder and pulled them up into the wagon when the rain started.

It is another similarly strange fact of life that many book scriveners have also commented on since the days of the Romans; real soldiers seem to have a soft place in their hearts for children. It has also always been that way but no one knows why.

Chapter Twenty-seven
We reach Windsor Castle.

Windsor Castle slowly came into view through a lightly misting rain as William and I turned off the main road and rode towards it at the head of our column. Our horse archer guards aboard their horses and the convoy of coin wagons were following close behind us. We had gotten on the road early and made good time. It was only a couple of hours after dawn.

Off to our right as the castle came into view we could see a host of the King's supporters and their camp followers who had reached Windsor before us. They had set up a totally disorganized camp of wagons, tents, and makeshift shelters of all kinds.

Only a few people could be seen moving about in the camp. The King's supporters and their camp followers who had arrived before us were mostly out of sight in their tents and wagons as a result of taking shelter from the rain. But they were there; we could see smoke still rising from their campfires and knew the rain had only recently started. Beyond the encampment were the walls and roofs of Windsor Village where the castle's guards and servants lived.

There was also a somewhat similar and partially abandoned encampment filled with tents, wagons, and camp followers in a meadow off to the port side of the road. It appeared to be the remnants of the King's army which had been assembled there before the King deserted his men and ran for the Tower almost a week earlier.

William asked me how many of the lords I thought had led their men home instead of following King Edward to the Tower and then back to Windsor and on to Wales.

"Much more than half, I would wager," I answered. William nodded his agreement. "Aye Bishop," he said with a smile. "I think you are right. The King and Despenser are in deep shite for sure. It is no wonder they are running."

What was most noticeable and eye-catching thing of all as we approached the edge of the camp were the people gathered at the castle's main entrance gate. Some of them appeared to be walking back to where they were camping. Even so, there were at least thirty of them standing in the rain waving their hands about. They were obviously seeking admission.

Who might they be? We had no idea. They may have been supporters of the King or castle servants; there was no way of knowing. The only thing that was certain was that the castle's entrance gate was closed and the guards we could see standing out of the rain in the portcullis beyond the gate were not letting anyone enter through the door in the gate. That they were so desperate to enter that the castle that they were willing to wait in the rain was more than a little worrisome; I could not help but wonder who they were and why they were so anxious to enter.

Damnation. Will I be able to get in to pass out the coins in my "gift pouches" and ask the King for the Company's success payment for successfully guarding his son? And then

there was the even more important question I hoped to have
someone ask about the coin wagons.

****** *Bishop Thorpe of Cornwall*

Safety first is what the bible says is required under the dangerous circumstances such as we would surely be facing in the next few hours. Accordingly, being the good Christians that we are, we left our horses in their traces when we drew the wagons we were guarding into a circle and began setting up a camp close to the road with our horse archers' horses and remounts saddled and waiting inside the circle. We deliberately set up our camp some distance away from everyone else's.

Staying close to the road and being ready to leave on a moment's notice seemed like a reasonable thing to do because, if worst comes to worst, our wagon drivers could whip up their horses and try to make a run for it back down the road with William and his horse archers acting as their rear guard. *If that happened, as you might well imagine, all hopes of winkling more coins out of the King and his supporters would be lost and I for one intended to ride for Cornwall with my apprentice sergeant as if the devil himself was snapping at my arse.*

Hopefully, nothing like that would happen and only good would come out of our efforts to help King Edward get his coins to Wales, especially now that his son and heir, Prince Edward, was thought to be safely ensconced in Northampton Castle with some of our archers guarding him. The "good that would come of it", of course, meaning an early payment of the coins due to the Company for protecting the prince and an opportunity to get our hands on more of them in some way or another if we could.

My hope that we might get more coins in some way was not ill-founded. As the Bible says: Where there is a will there is a way; and we certainly had the will to get more coins. It had existed ever since one of our Company's previous commanders decided that we needed more coins to tide us over the rough patch when Jesus returned and there would be peace on earth and no way for us to earn coins carrying cargos and protecting people until he decided to leave again. *Not that I believed the bit that followed about the lions and wolves laying down with the sheep; they eat them you know.*

Ah well, we would find out what was happening with the King soon enough since I was in the process of riding to the Windsor Castle gate with my apprentice sergeant, Adrian Goldsmith. Adrian had put aside his sword and switched into his priestly robe during one of our early morning piss breaks. I, of course, was already wearing mine and my mitre. I was also carrying my crosier which I thought was a nice touch in that it would convey a certain dignity to my requests for admission and an early payment.

Two of William's horse archers rode to the castle gate with us to hold our horses. William, as you might well imagine, did not ride forward with us. It would have been much too dangerous for him to do so. The problem was that one of the King's men who had been at the battle on the Northampton Road might recognize him and point him out to King Edward. The King, after all, was likely to still be pissed and angry about his men being defeated so thoroughly by William and his men.

What we most feared, as you might well imagine, was that the discovery that William and his archers were now guarding the King's coin wagons would result in William and his horse archers being sent away with fleas in their ears, or worse, and some of the King's supporters would end up being assigned to guard the King's coins. That is why William and the archers had once again turned their tunics with their distinctive rank stripes inside out once again and had been ordered not to say a word to anyone that would suggest they were in the Company of Archers.

And, of course, what would make things even worse would be if I had to flee because I was associated with William and his men. It would almost certainly put an end to my efforts to get an early payment of the success coins due to the "mercenary company" for successfully protecting the prince.

The risk and dangers of William and his men being recognized had to be accepted, however, because so many coins were at stake and horse archers were needed to guard the King's coins. The foot archers riding in the wagons would put up a fight to save them, of course, but without horse archers to distract anyone who tried to take the coins they would inevitably be overwhelmed and killed without having any way of escaping.

Commander Boatman had understood this and without hesitating for a moment had ordered William and his men to guard the coin wagons. He had done so because he had no available alternatives; William and his men were the only riders he had available. It would have been much too dangerous to send only foot archers from the galley to guard the coin wagons because they would have no way to escape from mounted pursuers in the event the Company's relations with the King turned foul.

As it was, if everything turned to shite the foot archers would have to gallop away in the wagons with William and his men doing their best to hold off and destroy the pursuers just as they had done on the road to Northampton.

Because of the possible danger, and rightly so, William and the archers had been ordered to never talk about the fighting on the road and to deny emphatically that they had been involved. William himself was wearing the tunic of a two-stripe archer turned inside out and doing his best to stay out of sight. He had also changed horses and trimmed his beard in the latest courtly fashion of having it come to a point under his chin. I hardly recognized him myself.

****** *Bishop Thorpe at the Windsor gate.*

"Hoy there. I be Bishop Thorpe, the Bishop of Cornwall, and I am here to meet with Bishop Gravesend, the Bishop of London, and Lord Despenser on the King's business. Let us pass."

The sergeant of the guards at the gate was more than a little sceptical. "Are they expecting you?"

"Of course they are; I am bringing good news and coins to the king."

Chapter Twenty-eight
The Windsor Reception.

It took more time than it should but Adrian and I were finally allowed to enter Windsor Castle. I took it as a hopeful sign that the gate itself was briefly opened to admit only the two of us and we were allowed to bring our horses into the castle's bailey with us. The two archers who had ridden with us to hold our horses were sent back to our camp to dry out and resume their normal duties. We would ride back to camp. *I hoped.*

We led our horses into the portcullis and waited expectantly just inside the gate for about five minutes until we spotted one of the castle's clerics hurrying purposely across the bailey in the rain toward us. At least we were out of the rain unlike the crowd of people who were still waiting to be admitted. It was still fairly early in the morning.

The priest who splashed his way across the castle's bailey to fetch us was in his middle years and had the hood of his robe up as a result of the rain. I somehow knew he was coming for us as soon as I saw him hurrying across the bailey toward the gate. When he reached us he identified himself as Father Albert, one of the king's clerics, and said he had been sent to fetch us. But he did not say who had sent him.

Father Albert kissed my ring all right and proper and I made the sign of the cross and mumbled something in Latin to bless him. Then we followed him out into rain whilst leading our horses. We walked in the rain because it did not seem right to ride whist Father Albert walked; besides, I wanted to talk to him.

Father Albert was not at all friendly as we hurried across the bailey to get out of the still-misting rain as soon as possible. He said not a word and merely grunted when I asked him an innocent question about who was in the castle with King Edward.

Perhaps he had not heard me because we were walking rapidly or because it was raining, but I somehow got the impression he was afraid to say anything. That set me to worrying that he thought we might be spies or about to be arrested. It also worried me that a King's man had come to fetch us because I had asked to meet with one of the King's courtiers, Stephen Gravesend, the Bishop of London. Stephen was an old acquaintance and a long-time courtier. Adrian, of course, knew none of this.

Father Albert led us through the castle's extensive bailey to a door into the castle's similarly huge keep. I had ridden past the castle on several occasions when I served as a horse archer during my early years in the Company. That was before a position in the Church was bought for me and I was sent to Rome as a spy in the household of an English cardinal. This, however, was the very first time I had ever actually been in the castle.

There was no question about it; the castle was formidable and almost certainly could be held until its defenders were either gulled into opening a gate or had to surrender because they ran out of food and the firewood needed to cook it. It was easy to understand why it had never been captured.

Adrian and I wrapped our horses' reins about hitching post outside the door and followed Father Albert into the castle's keep. He led us down a long corridor lit by the narrow wall openings high above us on the starboard wall. We passed a servant who was sweeping the hallway with a shock of straw tied to a long pole; he carefully did not look at us as we walked past him. That was a bit surprising since Adrian and I and Father Albert were all three dripping water on the stones of the corridor's floor from walking in the rain across the bailey.

It was a great relief when the King's cleric opened a door for us and I found myself looking at an old acquaintance, Stephen Gravesend, the Bishop of London, a loyal supporter of King Edward as were most churchmen and so frequently attended the King's court that he had his own rooms in the castle. There was a plate of bread scraps, half-filled jars of butter and honey, and an empty bowl on a table. He obviously had just finished breaking his nightly fast.

Stephen had been at the Tower two nights earlier with the King and had almost certainly returned to Windsor with him on the previous day. Until I saw him instead of a band of the King's guards I was not sure about our safety. *No one was waiting to arrest us for leaving the six wagons behind; thank you Jesus and all the saints.*

******

"Hello James, how good to see you again and why are you here with this handsome young man?" Stephen said as he approached us with a smile and held out this hand most friendly to me and then to Adrian. *I relaxed somewhat as some, but not all, of my fears and apprehensions fell away.*

Now all I was, I suddenly realized, was terribly tired from two hard nights and hardly any sleep.

"Hello again, Stephen," I said with a smile as I shook his hand and moved towards the warmth of the summer fire in the room's little fireplace. Until I saw the fire I had not realized much how my wet clothes and the wind had chilled me.

"This is my assistant, Father Adrian. He was with me at the Tower the other night but it was dark and you were more than a little preoccupied. He and I have come to bring the King and his supporters both good news and bad news. I know it is early but can you get me in to see him as soon as possible?"

Stephen eyes went up at the notion that I had arrived bearing news for the King. He made a little "give me" motion with both his hands and nodded his head; so I told him.

"The first good news is that Prince Edward is safe in Northampton Castle and finally out of Mortimer's hands because he and the Queen are off to London with their army. The prince is being guarded by the men of the mercenary company that you and your friends and the King's other supporters employed to guard him.

"Even better, the Northampton Castle gate has been closed to Mortimer and his army and the Queen so the prince is now free of them for the first time in years. *I was not sure the gate was closed to them or that the Queen was still with her army and out of Northampton, of course, but she should still be where William left her and that was close enough for me to proclaim it as a fact under that circumstances.*

"The second good news is that all eleven of the big horse-drawn covered wagons that were packed full of coins at the Tower two nights ago have reached Windsor. They are so loaded that it takes two horses to pull them. I accompanied them myself because I know how important they are to King Edward. It is almost certainly the biggest single collection of coins in the world and now they are here for the King to use as he sees fit." *Not even close; we have much more than that cached in both Restormel and Cyprus for when Jesus returns.*

"The bad news is that a messenger has just come through on his way to Cornwall. He reports that Mortimer and the Queen and their army know that King Edward and his supporters have returned to Windsor. They now appear to be marching directly to Windsor instead of to London."

There was no messenger, of course; but Mortimer was no fool so it was almost certainly what a messenger would have reported if there actually had been one. In any event, it was the message Commander Boatman told me to deliver; he wants the King and Despenser and their coins to keep moving towards Wales as fast as possible. He did not say why but I am fairly sure I know.

"Well James, that is indeed both good news and bad news. I would imagine the King and Lord Despenser already know all that but I suppose we should tell them just in case, eh?" *We? Oh well; I can live with "we" if that is what it takes.*

"Yes, Stephen, we should inform him immediately. But I cannot meet the King looking like this, can I? It would reflect badly on the Church and me personally. The news is important but I need to dry out first and so does Father Adrian."

"No problem, dear boy. You do look a bit wet and frazzled for a court appearance come to think of it. But I have an extra robe you can use whilst yours is drying and I am sure we can find one for your, um, assistant as well. Your mitre looks very nice, by the way. It is very old, I think. Where did you get it?"

******

Adrian and I went off with Stephen to attend to the King after donning our newly borrowed robes, quaffing a much needed bowl of mulled wine, and standing under a roof overhang for a piss against one of Windsor's walls. As I knew he would, Stephen had decided to accompany us and led the way. I was feeling very tired but somehow excited.

Stephen stood up and did so, led us to the King that is, after cheerfully adjusting his robe by giving it a good shake. He clapped a mitre on his head, picked up his crosier from where it was leaning against the wall, and said "follow me" in a determined and officious voice. He seemed to be very pleased to have an excuse to meet with the King in the presence of a messenger bearing good news. *I wonder how cheerful he would be if he knew that I not only intended to ask the King for the "success" coins due to William's mercenary company for successfully guarding the prince, but also "reward" coins for getting him away from the Queen and Mortimer.*

We walked down the dimly lit corridor past both the door which we had used to out outside to piss and the door further down where we had entered with Father Albert. We kept going and then made a very short dash through the rain to get into another part of the keep, stepping in puddles as we did.

Our once again wet sandals made a sharp slapping noise as we walked briskly back down the passageway through which Adrian and I had initially walked to get to Stephen's room. It was covered by a roof and there was a stone wall all the way up to the roof on one side. On the other side of the corridor, however, the wall only came up to my waist and opened into some kind of mini-bailey with a sitting bench in it and four or five small puddles of water. The low wall and the corridor floor next to it were wet and slippery from the rain.

It suddenly dawned on me as we walked that we still not met or seen anyone except the floor sweeper when we first arrived, not a single guard or servant, not even in the rain swept bailey. The castle seemed strangely empty. Perhaps not letting anyone into the castle was how the King insured his safety. I decided not to ask; but it was interesting.

******

We walked briskly along several similar corridors around the edge of the inner bailey, probably to avoid crossing it in the rain, until we reached a door that was cracked open. The dim sound of voices could be heard on the other side of it. Stephen pushed the door open and entered and we followed him in. It was instantly obvious to me that we had entered the King's court without the King being present.

The room became silent as we walked into it and everyone turned to look. There were perhaps a little over twenty people in it; almost all men and all well dressed. Most of them were standing around talking in about in little groups of four or five and were no doubt talking to one another about those things that courtiers are said to think are important such as how many buttons someone was wearing on his tunic or who was poking whom and where. There was not a servant or guard in sight.

My first impression was that the room was so large that it appeared to be mostly empty despite the people in it; my second was that its emptiness did not bode well for the King.

All of the men except the priests were wearing swords and about half of the sword carriers were wearing breastplates and almost certainly had chain shirts on under their fine clothes. Numerous candle holders were placed all along the walls of the room. The only furniture was a single large and very empty chair at the far end of the room. There were no women present.

The candles were not lit. The light in the room came from narrow wood-shuttered wall openings that ran all along the room's four walls above the candle holders. Their shutters were open. The room itself smelled vaguely of piss. There was a carpet on the floor in front of the chair with a line of pillows across it. No one was standing on the carpet or near the chair. They were all at our end of the room.

Seven or eight of the men in the room were priests amongst whom I counted no less than four mitred bishops clustered around a priest wearing a red sash around his robe. The other priests appeared to be their assistants and were standing apart from them.

Then it struck me; of course, the priest with the red sash must be the papal nuncio from the amount of attention they seemed to be giving him. Nuncios are rare in Rome since they are representatives of the Pope and usually found wherever there is a Christian King or a powerful lord; but I remembered seeing one who was visiting Rome when I was posted there in an English cardinal's household as a Company spy.

Stephen led us straight to the bishops. But on the way he stopped and whispered something into the ear of a well-dressed man wearing a sword, almost certainly a knight or noble, who listened carefully and then nodded and left the room with a purposeful stride to his walk.

"A good hoy to you all, my friends," Stephen said to the bishops and the nuncio as we walked up to them. "This is James Thorpe, the Bishop of Cornwall. He has brought important news for the King. The Earl of Arundel has gone to inform His Majesty of James' arrival."

Stephen being Stephen and an experienced courtier said it in such a way that implied that *he* had played an important part in obtaining the news even though he had just learned of it himself.

Everyone bowed at us respectfully and gave me a careful look, and then every one of the bishops turned to look at the nuncio, to see how they should respond. Of course, they turned to him; a nuncio's recommendation was inevitably needed for advancement in the Church in addition to the necessary prayer coins to get the Pope to speak with God and get God's blessing for his promotion. *They must all be courtiers; I did not recognize any of them.*

"News is always welcome," the nuncio said in Latin. "Can you share it with us, Bishop Thorpe?"

I was, as you might imagine, taken aback by the request. Should I tell the court before I told King Edward and Lord Despenser? My uncertainty must have showed because Stephen jumped in to save me.

"Ah, here comes His Lordship, I think. Perhaps the King is ready to receive us," Stephen said as he took my arm and pulled me towards the door. Nobody was there and no one was coming out. Stephen explained what he had done as he took me by the arm and pulled me toward the door.

"It would never do to have the nuncio know before King Edward," he said quietly as we walked towards the closed door. "He would have tried to be the first to tell the King the good news and left it you to tell him the bad."

A few minutes later the Earl of Arundel stood in the doorway and beckoned for Stephen and me to follow him. I gestured for Adrian to come with us.

Chapter Twenty-nine
The Windsor Deception.

The Earl of Arundel led us to the door and through it. He was one of the King's many cousins according to Stephen's whispered comment out of the side of his mouth. Beyond the door was a much more luxurious smaller room with fine carpets covering its floor and King Edward sitting behind a nicely carved wooden table. Tapestries with various hunting scenes hung on its wall to reduce its draughts of air.

A slim and handsome young man dressed in the latest fashion with Anvers lace on the cuffs of his tunic was standing at the King's side. It was definitely the King and his good friend and England's Chancellor, Lord Despenser.

I recognized Dispenser immediately because I had met and spoken with him at the Tower less than forty-eight hours earlier. There was a young cleric sitting at a small table nearby with a quill in his hand and an expectant look on his face.

It was the first time I had ever been in the presence of any king, let alone the king that God had chosen to rule over me in my life outside the Church. Truth be told, I was instantly underwhelmed and rather disappointed—he looked like just another of England's high birthed nobles with a face that suggested a serious shortage of thinking space behind his eyes. But then, of course, he was not just another useless noble and he had Lord Despenser and his courtiers to help him with his thinking and decisions.

I went down on my knees and banged my head three times on the rug. It was finely woven with brown and blue designs. Stephen merely bowed deeply in the manner of a courtier with great flourishes of his right hand. Adrian copied me from where he had been standing in the back of the room by the door.

I had overly grovelled in my greeting because both Commander Boatman and Stephen had advised me to be sickeningly obsequious if I was ever introduced to the King. I had also required it of Adrian even though I am sure he would have preferred to stand in the back of the room and snicker at my behaviour. *Stephen was right; humouring kings and princes is sometimes necessary when meaningful things are at stake. It has always been that way and many a good coin has been obtained from them because of it.*

"Edward likes to see that sort of thing and he is unworldly enough to think it is important in judging the strength of a man's loyalty and his ideas." That was Stephen's comment when we had begun discussing how I should behave and what I should do and say when I was presented to the King.

"Bowing low whilst making a great flourish with one's open right hand is how courtiers always behave when they approach King Edward. He thinks it is very elegant. So that is what I will do whilst you are banging your head on the floor and making your knees sore. Besides, the dear boy already knows I am loyal and my courtly flourishes will make a nice contrast with you making a fool of yourself and taking the risk of doing an injury to your knees and making your head hurt.

What I understood and appreciated, of course, was that Stephen was being particularly helpful in return for my promise of a pouch with one coin in twenty from amongst whatever coins, if any, the King released to the Company that day. He had undoubtedly also taken at least that much of a portion from his friends and acquaintances when he sought coins from them to help pay William's mercenary company to guard the prince.

It was no wonder Stephen had been so glad to see me; I was turning into his coin cow and he was cheerfully milking me and the Company of Archers for all he could get. On the other hand, promising to pay Stephen a modest share of the day's takings was a case of money talks and ox shite walks or whatever it is that the franklins and merchants sometimes say. Besides, sharing a few of the King's coins with Stephen for his services and advice would be well worth it if they worked.

What are friends for if not to help each other get ahead, eh?

******

King Edward seemed greatly pleased by my extraordinary show of respect, he nodded approvingly. Lord Despenser, on the other hand, merely looked on and gave the impression of being slightly amused. Perhaps he was usual that way but it was certainly different from the look of desperation that was everywhere on his face when I saw him at the Tower. The face of the cleric at the nearby table, on the other hand, was impassive; he just sat there with a stony face and his quill poised over a parchment.

Stephen spoke first as we had agreed he would.

"Your Majesty, I am pleased to present your loyal subject Bishop Thorpe, the Bishop of Cornwall. This is James' first visit to the court and he brings good news as to the safety of your esteemed son, Prince Edward, and his successful removal after all these years from the clutches of his foul mother and her traitorous and misguided followers."

The King's eyes widened and lit up with excitement at the news about the prince. He jerked straight up in his chair with a gasp as if he had just been awakened by a bad dream. Lord Despenser put his hand on the King's table and leaned forward; his interest had also been greatly awakened— perhaps he suddenly realized that his future and the King's might not be so dark after all.

"Can it be true?" the King demanded excitedly as he stood up and looked down at me intently whilst I struggled to stand up. "My son has truly been gotten away from his mother and Lord Mortimer after all these years?"

"Yes Your Majesty, it is true," I replied as I tried to get my feet under me so I could stand up. *It is definitely harder to do when one is older.*

I continued speaking after Stephen grabbed my hand and helped pull me up on to my feet.

"Prince Edward is alone and safe behind the strong walls of Northampton Castle, Your Majesty. And the castle's gate is closed to everyone including the Queen and her army. The Prince is being guarded by the company of mercenaries that the Bishop of London and others of your loyal subjects had the honour to engage on Prince Edward's behalf."

I said it with a nod toward Stephen to acknowledge his help. The King was still having trouble believing what he had just been told.

"You say my son is safe in Northampton castle and the gate is closed and guarded against his mother and Mortimer by my loyal mercenaries? Are you sure? Truly sure?" The King and Lord Despenser were getting more and more excited before my very eyes. *I found it quite strange; it was as if they believed that their behaviour and Despenser's rapacious governing of the kingdom would be overlooked if the Queen did not control Prince Edward.*

"I am absolutely sure, Your Majesty. The mercenary company you wisely instructed your faithful subjects to employ to protect the prince has remained loyal to you and fully done its duty. It has shed blood and lost men to protect your son and now it has shed blood and lost men to liberate him. A courier en route to Cornwall came in to my camp this very morning bearing the news.

There was no courier, of course, but saying there was made my story more believable. And that is almost certainly what the courier would have said if there had been one. I knew for a fact that the Queen had left the prince and Northampton because she had done so when William did; he and his men had escorted her to her army's camp before riding on to London.

"The courier is one of my most faithful parishioners. He would not have lied to me and he had no reason to do so. There is no doubt about it, Your Majesty; your son, Prince

Edward, is finally free of the Queen and Lord Mortimer and is now being protected by the loyal company of mercenaries you were wise enough to order your subjects to employ."

"He is free; my son is free," the King said as he impulsively turned and gave a great hug to Lord Despenser. We are going to win, Hugh!" he exclaimed. His smile and good cheer filled the room. *It was definitely not the time to tell him that Mortimer and the Queen's army were on their way to Windsor. But now that the King is in such a good mood it was certainly the time to ask for the coins.*

"And there is even more good news, Your Majesty," I said with as much enthusiasm as I could muster. "All eleven of the wagons that set out for Windsor with the coin chests from the Tower's treasure room have arrived safely and are here at Windsor. They were brought here and are being guarded by the same mercenary company that is guarding the prince at Northampton and provided the wagons and horses to carry the coins."

"Yes, Yes, that is good news indeed," said the King enthusiastically. "The mercenaries will be well rewarded for their loyalty and wonderful successes. That is certain. Eh, Hugh?" Even Despenser was smiling. Good news, as the bible says, smoothes many rough edges.

"Your decision to reward the mercenaries properly is a very wise decision, Your Majesty," I said with an acknowledging slight bow. "Very wise indeed.

"Rewarding the mercenaries for their loyalty and successes and promptly paying them the coins they are now due is such a good decision that God must surely have guided you to it. It will surely also make it even easier for you to hire many more mercenaries when you reach Wales. They will flock to you to serve under your banner because they will believe your promises to reward them if they are successful.

"Your ultimate victory is now assured, Your Majesty. And I am honoured to be the first to congratulate you." *Lay the compliments on the King like you slather butter on hot bread was the advice I had been given.*

"Ahem. Am I authorized, Your Majesty, to take the payment now due to the mercenaries from one of the wagons and pay them what they have earned? And perhaps that much again as a bonus for their success in order to encourage other mercenaries to join you in Wales? Bonuses for great successes are a tradition with the mercenary companies and are expected under such circumstances as I am sure you know."

I held my breath; King Edward might know it is a tradition to pay bonuses to mercenaries if they are successful but I certainly did not. But they should be paid so saying that they must is close enough when one is trying to get the agreement of a king or noble for something he would rather not do if he can avoid it.

The King looked at Despenser and all went well: Lord Hugh nodded his agreement and added "Bishop Thorpe is right; it will encourage others to join us."

Right then and there I decided to wait until after we had the coins to suggest that the Queen's army was coming fast and they needed to run. First things first as the bible says.

And then Despenser asked the question I hoped he or King Edward would ask.

"Are you sure the coins got away safely, Bishop Thorpe?"

"Oh yes, Lord Despenser. They certainly did. Thanks once again to the archers of your faithful mercenary company there are eleven wagons full to overflowing with coin chests right here at Windsor. They are each so full that it takes two horses to pull them. At this moment they are being heavily guarded in the mercenaries' camp that is just off the road in front of the castle's main gate. You can see them from atop the castle wall.

"Moreover, I can safely swear to you in the name of Jesus that not a single coin has been removed from a single chest since your loyal men and mercenaries loaded them in the wagons. Indeed, the archers guarded them so carefully and honestly even though it was not part of their contract that perhaps a double bonus is justified."

The King was all smiles and enthusiastic. He nodded his agreement to my suggestion without even consulting Despenser.

At that point only one thing was absolutely certain so far as I was concerned—it was *not* the right time to spoil King Edward's good cheer by warning him that Mortimer and the Queen's army would have surely heard of the King's flight from the Tower and were now almost certainly going to bypass London and come straight to Windsor.

The "right time," I instantly decided, would be *after* the coins the King had just agreed to pay were safely out of the wagons and on their way to Cornwall. In other words, I had to be patient about informing the King of his danger and get the coins on their way to Cornwall before I did. Only when the coins were on their way would another "messenger" stop on his way to Cornwall and warn of the fast-moving army of the Queen that was coming this way.

Patience is a virtue as the good book says. And mine turned out to be quite costly for King Edward and Lord Despenser.

Chapter Thirty
We collect our coins and are on the road again.

We rode back to the archers' camp in a very good mood even though I was somehow so tired that I had trouble mounting my horse. The rain had stopped and I was excited and pleased because of the coins the King had agreed to pay us. Adrian was similarly pleased for another reason—because he could tell his mother that he had been at court and in the same room as the king. It will, he told me as we rode out through the portcullis and headed towards our nearby circled wagons, make her day and astound the village women.

William was waiting as we rode up and dismounted. "How did it go?" he asked as I wearily slid off my horse with a groan and almost fell over. "You were gone so long I was getting worried."

"It was very tiring, terribly tiring for some reason. But it went well, William; absolutely excellently in fact. We met the king and, to make a long story short, he has authorized a doubling of the "success" payment due for your company's protection of the prince—and also an additional doubling of that amount as a bonus for your success in getting the prince safely away from both the Queen and Mortimer. That is what carried the day.

"And that is only the half of it—it was clear to me that neither the King nor Lord Despenser have any idea as to how many coins were in the Tower. Their ignorance and the fact that Bishop Stapledon, the Lord High Treasurer, is known to be dead of trying to stop the rioting in London make it highly unlikely that anyone knows for certain how many coins were in the Tower or their value. And for sure no one knows which coins went into which wagon two nights ago in the darkness.

"Having said all that, we should not waste a minute in getting our payment coins out of here in case the King changes his mind. But here is the thing—we need to keep all eleven wagons to carry what is left of the coins to Wales. That way it will appear we only took a few coins in payment. So we will need to find another wagon to carry *our* coins away from here as soon as possible. And then we have to decide whether to send them to London or to Cornwall and who should go with the coins to guard them."

And it was about then as he stood there talking to William that Bishop Thorpe realized something was wrong. He somehow felt a bit weak and light-headed. *I need a rest; two days of travel and two nights with little or no sleep have done for me. And then the meeting with the King. And now...*

"William," the Bishop said suddenly. "You will have to get two wagons, two ... I cannot ... I think I need ... rest for a few minutes."

And with that Bishop Thorpe tried to grab on to the saddle of his horse to keep himself from falling on to the wet ground. He could not hold on to it and his legs suddenly had no feeling and began to buckle. Then, although he was only partially aware of it, his view of William sort of faded away and he began to wobble and go down.

Adrian had dismounted next to the Bishop and had been watching him closely ever since he had trouble climbing aboard his horse in the castle bailey. He was able to drop his horse's reins and get to the wobbling Bishop before he fell. He quickly grabbed the Bishop's right arm up high by his shoulder to help steady him and hold him up. But he was not strong enough; the older man was too heavy. His weight began to pull them both down.

"Help me hold him," Adrian said unnecessarily as William instinctively reached out and grabbed the Bishop under his other arm. But even the efforts of the two of them were not enough to keep the old man upright. He was just too heavy. The best the two men could do was lower him to sit his arse on the wet ground and try to hold him in a sitting position so his head would not fall back and hit the ground.

"He will be fine. He just needs a rest and some ale to drink," Adrian said loudly and somewhat defensively to the archers who had quickly begun gathering around them. "He had a hard morning and was already over-tired when it began."

All the archers who had been watching them ride in from the castle came hurrying over to help. Then there were even more. Someone whipped off his knitted cap off and put it on the ground under the bishop's head just before the Bishop was gently tipped over backwards so he could rest whilst lying flat.

Almost immediately someone else rushed up with a bowl of ale and he was raised back so he could take a few sips. There was a great outpouring of concern and compassion from all around; the old man was truly liked.

Bishop Thorpe's sudden collapse surprised everyone that morning. One of the wagons was quickly pulled into place and made ready with so many men trying to help that they began getting in each other's way.

The wagon's coin crates were hurriedly moved around and more than enough sleeping skins were hurriedly gathered so there would be a comfortable place for him to rest. But then the question arose as to how to get him over to the wagon and then up and into the comfy bed that had been so quickly prepared.

For a moment everyone looked at everyone else. Loading a sleeping man into a high-sided covered wagon was not as easy as it sounds.

"I think I can pick him up and hoist him up over the backside of the wagon if a couple of lads are up there to take him," a big and strong-looking archer sergeant offered. I nodded and agreed.

"Please give it a try Adam," I said. "It would be appreciated; we cannot leave him like this."

Adam pointed to another strong-looking archer, a two-striper named Jacob Smith, and gave him a "will you help me?" look without saying a word. Jacob nodded back and spit on his hands. A few moments later the two archers hoisted the Bishop to his feet. We all stood back a little to give them room.

When they were ready Adam nodded to Jacob and then with one great motion and a grunt swept his left arm under the Bishop's legs and picked him up and held him the way a mother would pick up a baby. Everyone hurriedly moved back give them enough room as the big sergeant used small and careful steps to carry the bishop to the rear of the now-nearby coin wagon.

By the time Adam reached the rear of the wagon with the Bishop Jacob and several other archers had hurriedly climbed into it and were waiting to receive him. The three archers sat on a row of chests with Jacob in the middle and leaned forward over the rear of the wagon. The apprentice sergeants Adrian and Jack White were right behind them.

When Adam reached the back of the wagon Jacob took a deep breath, spit on his hands again, slid them under the Bishop's body that was being held up to him. He moved his hands to where they seemed to best fit, and said "On three. ... One... Two... Three."

And as fast as you could say "easy peasy" the Bishop was in the laps of the three men in the covered wagon and unseen by most of the men outside it. Together the five men pulled and pushed to partially turn him so his head was pointed towards the front of the wagon.

As soon as the Bishop was pointed towards the front of the wagon, Adam gave the word and the five of them lifted and pulled the Bishop right on over Jacob's head and chest to get him to a flat space on a couple of coin crates immediately behind the three men in front. It had been covered with the hastily gathered sleeping skins of woven wool and had just become the Bishop's new bed. It was well done.

Some of the men standing around the wagon cheered softly and everyone was pleased.

Bishop Thorpe was barely into the wagon when I began giving the first of many orders. It was mid-morning and the rain had stopped. The last few stragglers of the King's supporters were still arriving from the Tower and others appeared to be leaving.

"Adrian, you and Jack are to come out of there. Let Sam and Tom tend to Bishop Thorpe. I need you two out here to help me." *What I really needed first, of course, was more information from Adrian as to what King Edward had said and agreed when Bishop Thorpe was in the castle.*

The two apprentice sergeants climbed out of the wagon and Adrian was soon telling me everything he could remember about Bishop Thorpe's audience with King Edward. Before he was even half way through his tale I knew that time was of the essence and running out.

Chapter Thirty-one
We take the payments we earned.

I had talked with Adrian so I did not need to wait for Bishop Thorpe to recover in order to know what needed to done—get the coins the King agreed to pay us away from Windsor as fast as possible. I filled a couple coin pouches with silver coins from one of the chests and gave the necessary orders to the two apprentice sergeants, Adrian and Jack.

"You two are each to take one of these coin pouches and go to the encampments of the King's supporters and *immediately* buy at least one good covered wagon with a team and at least one extra wheel; and preferably buy two of them. Two-horse teams for each wagon would be best but one horse will do if the horse is sound. Pay whatever it takes and try to be back within the hour—but do not come back until you have at least one wagon and team.

"If you cannot find immediately available wagons you are to buy two-wheel carts, but only if they have a back so the chests cannot slide out and at least one spare wheel. Take Sam and Tom with you. They know horses. Also each of you is to take a foot archer with his sword and shield with you to drive the wagons. Mount them up behind you whilst you are riding around looking for wagons to buy. Hurry, lads, hurry."

The two apprentice sergeants caught my sense of urgency and so did Sam and Tom who had been waiting nearby. I handed the pouches to the two apprentice sergeants and they all ran for their horses. As they did I pointed at a couple of foot archers and gave them their orders.

"You two run for your swords and shields and go with these men. Hurry. Run."

As soon as the lads rode off with a foot archer sitting behind them and holding on for dear life I went to see if the Bishop was awake and could talk. As I did I saw a hard-riding messenger come galloping up the road towards the castle's gate. The guards must have seen him coming and recognized him because the gate suddenly opened in time for him to gallop into the bailey. There were still a couple of dozen people at the gate trying to get in.

******

I gently raised the side of the wagon cover next to where the Bishop was laid to see if he was awake. I lifted the wagon's cover up so I could see in. His eyes opened at the sound and there he was. He did not look good.

"It is good to see you awake and resting, Bishop. Are you feeling better?" I asked as I tied up the side of the wagon cover so we could see each other as we talked.

"Just tired most terrible, William," He said weakly. "And my chest hurts too much for me to sleep. It feels like I have been kicked by a horse. Did Adrian tell you about our meeting with the King and the coins?"

"Aye, so he did, Bishop, so he did. You have truly outdone yourself. I have already sent him and Jack to the encampments of the King's supporters to try to buy a wagon or cart so we can get our share of the coins out of here and on their way to Cornwall as soon as possible. That way we can continue to ride with the King and still have eleven coin wagons for him to see."

"Good man. I knew you would understand what had to be done. Adrian does too. He was most helpful. Please watch over him if I am not around to do so."

"Oh aye, you can count on me until you are rested up," I said with a voice full of false good cheer. *Uh oh, he thinks he is not going to make it back to Cornwall; I wonder if there is a Greek barber amongst the King's supporters in the encampments or in the castle?*

"There is something else, William. Do you know that one of our eleven wagons was loaded with some of the gold coins at the Tower and that the other ten have mostly silvers?"

"No. I did not know. Is it true?"

"Aye, it is true. The third wagon from the front. It is the only one of the eleven in our convoy that is mostly carrying gold. We have it with us so the King and Despenser can find gold if they come looking for it.

"It is the only wagon with gold because the Commander made sure most of the chests with gold coins in them went into the wagons without horses, the ones that were abandoned and left behind in all the confusion. Hopefully, everyone has forgotten them and the chests that were loaded on the abandoned wagons are already on their way to Cornwall for safe-keeping until someone claims them.

"As you might imagine, it would be best if the King and Despenser did not find out about most of the gold coins being left behind and going missing. So you should not only take gold coins for our payment so that fewer chests are missing from the wagons, you should also exchange some of the gold chests in the third wagon with the silver chests on top of the other wagons and sprinkle some of the remaining gold coins on top of the silvers in some of the silver chests immediately under them, eh?

"Also you might want to spread out the silver chests amongst the wagons so the wagons all appear to be full and it does not look like we took more coins than we were due for our payments. Put the ones with the gold on top so the gold is seen if they are opened. Do you understand?"

My God, we do not have many of the gold coins from the treasury with us; most of them are off to Cornwall.

"I understand, Bishop. You can count on me; I will get on it immediately whilst I am sending the payment coins we earned to Cornwall."

"There is one more thing, William. Commander Robertson wanted me warn the King that the Queen's army was close behind and coming fast. He wants the King and Despenser to spend their time worrying about saving their arses instead of thinking about the coins they might have left behind.

"I did not want to be the bearer of bad news whilst the King was in a good mood about paying us our coins. So I did not tell him about the Queen's army. You will have to do it. And when he asks, you will also have to give the Bishop of London one coin for every twenty payment coins you carry off; that was our arrangement if he helped us and he did."

******

I waited with the Bishop until I saw Adrian and Jack returning at a fast amble. They were bringing a one-horse wagon and a horse-drawn cart with them. When I saw them coming I patted Bishop Thorpe on the shoulder most friendly and said I would be back soon. He asked me to leave the wagon cover partially rolled up so he could see what was happening.

We got to work as soon as Adrian and Jack pulled to a halt next to our circle of wagons. Three chests from the gold-carrying wagon were loaded in the new wagon and three chests in the cart. It was probably more coins than we were due but who was to say, eh? Besides, we had earned them so far as I was concerned.

Whilst the lads were off looking for wagons to buy and the Bishop had his eyes closed I had once again struggled over the question of who should accompany the new wagon and the cart and which way should I send them—towards London or Cornwall? I flip-flopped several times behind my eyes before I made my decisions:

My decision was to send the coins directly to Cornwall. I also decided they should be heavily guarded even though it would mean weakening our ability to defend the King's coin wagons and they would have to outrun the King and his courtiers.

Of course I decided to send a strong force to guard our coins. So far as I was concerned our coins were more important than the King's even though his were much more numerous. On the other hand I did not want to leave the King's coins totally unguarded in case there was a chance we might be able to get more of them without pissing him off.

As soon as the new wagon and cart were loaded I called for the men I had decided to send with our coins and told them what I expected of them.

"Adrian, I am promoting you to Sergeant Major with Jack as your number two and Sam and Tom as your sergeants. The sergeants will each be in charge of one of the transports and its chests. I want you on the road in the next five minutes and riding hard for Cornwall as if the devil is snapping at your arses. *Which he well may be.*

"You cannot risk losing the chests by swimming your horses across the Thames. So you will have to cross it on the Oxford Bridge and then turn off and head towards the southwest and Cornwall on the old Roman road.

"Bishop Thorpe and everyone else think the King and his followers are heading for Gloucester and on into Wales where they hope to use the coins in the wagons to raise an army of mercenaries. I think he is right because that appears to be the only way King Edward can keep his crown. If so, they will also be on the road to Oxford and you will not be safe until the King and his followers keep going west toward Gloucester after you have turned off to ride to ride to the southwest.

"In other words, it is likely that the King and his men will be right behind you until you get over the Thames at Oxford and can turn off on the old Roman road. So you will need to leave immediately and move even faster than they do until you get to the turn off towards Cornwall and get far enough down the road that they do not chase you. In other words, you must abandon any horses or wagons that break down and keep going; not the chests, of course.

"Take your remounts so you can use them to replace any of the wagon horses that go foul. I am also going to send ten of the foot archers off the galley with you as guards. They can ride in the wagon. I am also sending four of the horse archers from mercenary company with you. They can be your scouts.

"Use the coins in the chests to buy food and whatever else you need along the way, but no matter what you must move as fast as possible until you are well beyond the turnoff. You can explain it to your men after you get underway."

"Oh, and one more thing: Make sure every one of your foot archers has his sword and shield in addition to his bow and the extra quiver of arrows they each are supposed to be carrying.

Why was I sending Adrian and his men west towards Cornwall instead of east to London? Because the Queen's army was likely already in London and might even be already coming this way. We would almost certainly lose our payment coins if they met on the road. Going west on the road, on the other hand, gave Adrian and his men a chance to out-run the King and his supporters who would be behind them until Adrian and his men turned off for Cornwall and the southwest.

Chapter Thirty-two
On the road to Gloucester.

Adrian and Jack and their men clattered out of our roadside camp and began hurrying down the road less than five minutes later. As they were leaving the two just-promoted apprentice sergeants rode over to the Bishop's wagon and bid him a fast farewell. I barely saw them go; I was too busy rearranging the chests in all the wagons so the chests with gold coins in them would be on top.

It was mid-morning and they were down the road and out of sight by the time I finished rearranging the coin chests and began walking over to the Bishop's wagon and to see how he was doing. What I saw and heard when I reached him was somewhat encouraging; he was asleep and snoring in the bed that had been made for him on top of some of the coin chests. The archer who had been assigned to stay with him raised his finger to his lips and mouthed "he is sleeping."

As I leaned over the side of the wagon to look more closely the archer caring for the Bishop suddenly sat up straight and acted surprised as he looked past me. I turned to see what he was looking at and was surprised myself.

The castle gate was still opening when out came the King and Despenser leading a great crowd of courtiers on horses and riding in wagons and carts. There were at least a hundred of them and they had women and children with them. I was stunned: The King was suddenly leaving Windsor and he had not bothered to inform his supporters who had followed him from London and were camped outside the castle.

All I could think of was that the courier must have brought news that the Queen's army was on the road from London and coming this way. Well, if that turned out to be the case then at least I did not have to gull the King into moving with a stitched up story; it would be true.

******

The King and Despenser were at the head of the column and talking and waving their hands about as they rode up the road toward us. When the King reached our wagons he raised his hand to stop the column and rode over to where I had come forward to stand and watch. Everything was quiet around the wagons; the archers had stopped whatever they had been doing and were watching.

"You there. Why are these wagons not ready to leave and where is Bishop Thorpe?" King Edward asked rather petulantly even before I had a chance to finish bowing with a great flourish of my hand as I had been taught to do in school. *I knew it was the King even though the only time I had seen him previously was in the darkness of the Tower bailey when we were loading the coin chests into the wagons.*

"I am most terrible sorry, Your Majesty, but no one informed us that you wanted us ready to march. I am happy to report, however, that our company is always in a high state of readiness to march or fight. We can immediately begin moving the coin wagons on to the road to join you as soon as the order is given."

"And the Bishop of Cornwall; where is he?"

"Bishop Thorpe is with us but most unwell, Your Majesty. He fell off his horse and went to sleep as soon as he returned to us from the castle this morning. We have made a bed for him on top of the coin chests in yonder wagon. He is resting there now and will travel with us if it your wish that we accompany you."

The elegantly dressed man riding next to the King was not comforted by what he heard.

"Are the coin chests safe and ready to travel?"

"Yes Excellency, they are in the wagons and have been there ever since they were loaded in the Tower on Wednesday night."

It was a nice partially sunny day but getting chilly. The leaves had already begun falling from the trees. In the background I could see there was suddenly much activity everywhere in the camp of the King's supporters. They had obviously seen the King and his courtiers come out of the castle and realized he was returning to the road.

As I gave the orders for the archers to mount their horses and wagons and move out I wondered how many of the King's supporters would stay behind this time.

******

It did take much time at all for our wagons to move to the edge of the road. But then I deliberately kept them from immediately joining the King's column; I wanted to be as far back from the King and his courtiers as possible.

What I mainly did for the rest of the day was worry. I was worried that the King would once again decide to ride ahead of the main column. If he did, he might catch up with Adrian and his men who were somewhere on the road ahead of him with our coins. I tried to think of something to slow the King down—and came up with absolutely nothing except to ride forward myself and keep him in sight.

My problem was that I had no idea what I could do to slow down the King or anyone else if I saw them hurrying on ahead. As a result I spent my time alternating between thinking about what I might do to gull the King into slowing down and trying to compare the speed of our column with how fast Adrian and our coins might be travelling on the road ahead of us.

Many of my concerns fell away that afternoon when the King and Lord Despenser decided to stop early in order spend that night off the road in the relative comfort and safety of a courtier's castle somewhere to the west of Marlow. The rest of us camped alongside the road in a sheep pasture.

It had been an interesting day.

******

Bishop Thorpe had recovered enough to be able to sit with the driver of his wagon. I periodically rode alongside so we could talk. The size of our column had been getting smaller every day as more and more of the King's supporters peeled off to try to return to their homes or find someplace to hide. The archer driving the wagon never said a word but

I am sure everything we said was repeated around the campfires when we stopped for the night.

It was mid-morning and we were about a day out of Gloucester when the Bishop asked me take over as the wagon's driver for a few minutes so we could talk privately. I did and he told me about an idea that had come to him. I liked it immensely and promptly said I thought we should give it a try.

"But first we need to lay the foundation so it is believed," the Bishop said and made a suggestion. It was quite creative and I instantly agreed.

"I know just the man to do it," I told him. "John White, him what got himself promoted to sergeant for his successes whilst fighting on the Northampton Road."

I soon found John and we had a long talk, and then he went off to get himself ready. An hour or so later the road ran through a densely a wooded area. We had ridden a little ahead of the coin wagons and were stopped by the entrance to a cart path to wait on our horses for the wagons to reach us. John was leading his remount.

"This cart path will do, John; not many will see you if you leave us here," I told him.

When the coin wagons caught up to us and were moving past us a few minutes later John quietly began riding down the little used path leading his remount. No one saw him go except me and his fellow archers.

John was soon out of sight in the dense trees. He was carrying a bag of food and clothes and only armed with his longbow, one quiver full of arrows, and a courier's round leather pouch. In the pouch was a rolled up parchment message to me from George Wainwright, the captain of our London shipping post.

I thought the message addressed to me was rather well scribed, particularly since I had scribed it myself when the Bishop's wagon was forced to stop whilst its driver removed a pebble that gotten into the hoof of one of its horses. The wagon had to stop; scribing is difficult in a moving wagon. And I had to be in the wagon so its covers would conceal the fact that I myself was the scrivener.

******

After John disappeared into the trees I waited for about two hours and then began riding up to the very front of the column where the King was riding. It was the middle of a cool day in early October when I reached the King and Lord Despenser. I immediately reported that the coins were all still safe even though one of the wagons had to pull out of the column whilst a stone was removed from the hoof of one of its draught horses.

"It has already caught up and all the coins are safe. I thought Your Majesty should know," I said.

The King nodded his thanks and I slowly dropped back until I was riding amongst the courtiers and their knights who were riding immediately behind the King on horses and in horse-drawn wagons. Their supply wagons and the common soldiers of their levies were further back in the column.

The courtiers did not know who I was but I was acceptable because I had just talked to the King and whatever I had said seemed to please him. They, of course, immediately inquired as to the nature of our conversation. I obliged them and they too were pleased to hear that the coins were safe and well guarded. It gave them something to talk about.

I rode for about an hour with the courtiers and their knights. I was someone new and the men around me listened avidly as I told them a couple of stories that I made up about myself as a mercenary sergeant in the Holy Land and now as a lieutenant and my mercenary company's number two in England.

The men riding with me were enthralled and asked many insipid questions. But then a hard-galloping messenger riding one exhausted horse and leading another came pounding up along the side of the column shouting "Lieutenant Jackson, where is Lieutenant Jackson of the archers?"

"Hoy," I shouted. "Over here. What is it?" I asked as I moved my horse to the side of the column. By the time I did every eye in the vicinity was looking to see what was happening including the King's and Despenser's who were looking back over their shoulders to see what all the commotion and shouting was about."

I accepted the courier's pouch John handed me by the side of the road and continued riding as I started to open the pouch to read the message it contained. As I did the agitated courier waved his hands about and spoke urgently.

After a few seconds I stopped trying to open the courier pouch and just listened. What I was hearing so shocked me that my mouth gaped open. It was so obviously important that the King and his courtiers pulled up their horses.

"How many riders and how close?" I asked John rather loudly with a look of total disbelief on my face. "Are you absolutely sure it was Mortimer?"

Chapter Thirty-three
Panic sets in.

The King and Lord Despenser had seen the courier arrive and the disbelief and distress his message caused me. There was nothing I could do under the circumstances other than share the bad news with them. I obviously had no choice.

John followed me as I rode the short distance to the King with the most sorrowful and apologetic look on my face I could muster. The King and his Chancellor were waiting on their horses and looked extremely worried themselves. Of course they were worried; they had seen the exhausted state of the messenger and almost certainly seen my distress at hearing his report and heard me mention Lord Mortimer. There was obviously bad news about something.

I took a deep breath and made my report.

"Your Majesty, I am Lieutenant Jackson of the free company under contract to carry your coins to safety and guard the coin wagons. I regret to inform Your Majesty that a courier from my company has just come in with what might be very distressing news. He reports that this morning he had to ride around a very large army consisting of many hundreds of knights and other mounted men who are on the road behind us without a baggage train and coming fast in this direction.

"The courier says a party of Mortimer's men started to chase him and he only escaped because he was able to switch to his relatively fresh remount and outrun them in the farmlands and pastures next to the road. He estimates that the main body of our pursuers are only an hour or two behind us and coming fast without their baggage train."

The King was appalled and so was everyone else who heard my report.

"Oh my God, Hugh; what shall we do?"

I did my best to be helpful and encouraging.

"All may not be lost, Your Majesty. Far from it. My company's courier is a very reliable man. Even so he might have been mistaken about Mortimer's strength. There might, after all, only be a few hundred of them such that their attack will fail. Besides, our horses are still relatively fresh from not being ridden hard today and it sounds as though theirs are not; we can almost certainly outrun them to Gloucester.

"Even better, if we come to a place where the road is narrowed by running through a stand of forest my men and volunteers from amongst your knights and guards might be able to hold Mortimer's men off long enough for you to ride on to safety with the coins."

"Your loyalty will be remembered, Lieutenant," shouted the aghast-faced King Edward over his shoulder as he wheeled his horse around and put his spurs to it.

"Thank you, Your Majesty" I shouted at his back as he galloped away with Lord Dispenser and his attendants and courtiers following close behind. "And may God be with you." I am not sure he heard me.

What followed was nothing less than a catastrophe for the King and his chancellor.

******

The news that Mortimer and the Queen's army were coming and that the King and Despenser and their entourage had abandoned them and fled stunned everyone who heard it. They were able to believe it, however, because the King had twice previously done the same thing when he invaded Scotland and the Scots attacked his invading army. He had abandoned his soldiers and fled. It was one of the many reasons the Queen was so angry with him; he had left her behind when he fled and she had barely escaped being captured.

In any event, the story that Mortimer and the Queen's army was behind us on the road and coming fast rippled back through the column like a great wave in the ocean, It also changed along the way. By the time the story about the King's flight and Mortimer's on-coming army reached the rear of the column it had become that King Edward had fled because Mortimer and the Queen's army were only minutes away and about to launch a massive attack that would destroy them all.

Everyone who had actively supported the King in hopes of advancement also knew only too well the horrors the vengeful Queen would almost certainly lay on them if her men caught them. They panicked. Even worse, everyone seemed to have a different idea as to what they should do to escape being slaughtered by the army of the irate Queen. Mostly they wanted everyone in front of them to either move ahead at a much faster speed or move aside and get out of the way so they too could flee.

The people towards the front of the column immediately behind the fleeing king were all riders and did not hesitate for a second. If the King thought it was time to make a run to safety then who were they to disagree. They put their spurs to their horses and hurried down the road after the fleeing king. They included the archers and the coin wagons that had moved to almost the front of the column by getting back on the road early in the morning before most of the others. The king and the knights and other riders had then ridden around them to regain the lead.

It was in the middle and rear of the column where there were camp followers, walkers, sutlers, and hand carts mixed in amongst the levies of King's noble supporters that chaos and disorder reigned supreme. Almost immediately their forward movement came to a dead stop due to the hastily abandoned transports and goods that blocked the road. People desperately began leaving the column and fleeing into the surrounding countryside to either hide or to get around the blockage and back on the road so they could rejoin what was left of the column and follow after the fleeing king.

The inevitable result of the road blockage was that many of the people in the column spilled out into the fields on either side of the road and tried to walk or ride or drive their wagons and carts around it. Others tried to distance themselves from the chaos on the road and the forthcoming slaughter of the King's supporters by walking or riding deeper into the countryside in order to escape the deadly attack that was about to fall on them.

Everyone, in other words, was trying to get away from the attack that was about to begin and running every which way because they did not know what to do or where to go.

Those of us at the front of the column initially knew nothing of the chaos and confusion behind us because the wagons we were guarding and the riders we had been marching immediately behind were clattering as fast as possible along the road in an effort to catch up with the fleeing King and his entourage.

At some point the King or someone riding with him must have remembered the importance of the coin wagons to their future and slowed down so we could catch up. From then on we drove the wagons as fast as we could whilst surrounded by the King and his entourage of mounted supporters and guards.

It was an early October afternoon when Gloucester's walls came into view several hours later. Seeing them raised everyone's somewhat dejected spirits. That lasted until we got closer and realized that the gates in the city's walls had been closed to keep us out.

Apparently all the lord of the city and the captain of its guards knew was what they could see from the city walls— that an armed horde led by knights in armour was coming down the road from London and was about to descend on them. The captain promptly ordered the city's gates to be closed and the lord mounted his horse and fled to the relative safety of his castle which was further inland.

******

We parked the wagons and then a somewhat recovered Bishop Thorpe and I mounted our horses and joined King Edward and Lord Despenser and their milling mass of supporters outside Gloucester's main city gate to see what we could see. But before we did we circled the coin wagons on some vacant land near to where the fishing boats from the Bristol Channel fleet come in to delivery their catches and posted all the available archers as guards.

It was a tumultuous day as more and more of the King's followers got past the traffic jam on the road and reached Gloucester. In the end, however, most of his followers never did appear; they had either gone into hiding off the road or were trying to return to their homes. And for every additional supporter of the king who finally reached Gloucester it seemed that another decided to leave. We watched as several great lords gathered what was left of their knights and levies and led them away.

It did not matter that there were far fewer people in front of the wall than had followed the King and Despenser out of Windsor; the city would not let anyone in, not even the King whom the city's guards pretended not to recognize.

The people of Gloucester were quite canny as to how they refused to admit the King—a man who said he was speaking for the captain of the night watch shouted down from atop the wall that the gates were always closed at this time of day and he could not open them to anyone without his Lord's approval which, according to him, was impossible to get because "his lordship had gone off somewhere to a tournament."

There was no doubt about it Bishop Thorpe and I told each other as we watched and listened to the scene unfolding in front of us: the King and Despenser were coming to the end of the line. So we rode back down to the waterfront and started looking some fishing boats to buy.

The King be damned we decided; if we could buy or charter any boats we would load our men and as many as possible of the coin chests into them that night and sail down the Bristol Channel and around to the other side of Cornwall until we reached the River Fowey and could row up the river to Restormel. We also decided that if no boats were available we would not abandon the coins whilst there was still a chance we could get our hands on more of them; we would instead either follow the King into Wales or stay behind and wait for the arrival of Mortimer and the Queen.

But then the rumour changed as we sat on our horses watching the city's main gate and the increasingly ugly scene in front of it. Now there were said to be two of the Queen's armies closing in on the King and his ever-dwindling number of supporters: one coming in behind us on the road we had just travelled and one to the north that had already cut the road to Wales. As you might imagine, panic once again set in as the word spread that the King and what was left of his followers were cut off.

The King was clearly beside himself with worry but still sound enough of mind to concern himself about the coins. At least Lord Despenser was. Less than an hour later he and a couple of men who appeared to be minor nobles rode over to visit our circled wagons and ask about the coins. He seemed uncertain and suspicious so I went out of my way to be a religious simpleton and reassuring.

"The coins belong to the King and are being carried by the wagons our company has contracted with an oath to

God to provide along with their teams and drivers. We have a contract so we are obliged to keep the wagons safe for His Majesty so long as he wants to use them." *I made the sign of the cross as I spoke to emphasize my sincerity in case Despenser had gotten religion; people often do, you know, when they face great danger.*

And, of course, I had somewhat stressed the truth with my reassurances. We were obliged under the contract to provide the wagons and the teams and their drivers; but the contract said nothing about our being responsible to guard the coins and cargos the wagons were used to carry.

"The lieutenant speaks God's truth," agreed Bishop Thorpe with as much piety as he could muster.

In essence, I told the King's chancellor what he wanted to hear. The King may have been weak and getting weaker by the hour but we were still greatly outnumbered and would likely get chopped by the King's supporters if we told him our real intentions. Besides, Edward was England's king and he still might win. Miracles, according to the Church, are quite common if one prays and regularly tithes and buys dispensations as the King apparently did.

All we knew for sure was that the King and Despenser had reacted as we had hoped they would when John and I misled them as to how soon the Queen's army might arrive. What we did *not* know was how soon that would actually occur and what would happen when it did. *Why did we do it? Because it is well known in the Company, and even taught in the Company school, that the best time to separate a rich man from his coins is when danger lurks and there is great chaos and confusion.*

We also did not know what the King's plans might be now that the Queen's army was reported to be closing in and the road to Wales was cut. But we got the impression they might be similar to ours because after he left us Despenser walked down to the strand where the fishing boats brought their catches ashore.

Then the fishermen started to come in and they were obviously confused that no one was there to buy their catches. One of them actually walked over to our wagons and asked where everybody was. The bishop stayed out of sight whilst I spoke with him.

"There seems to be some sort of dispute and the city gates are closed," I told him. "It is said that they will open soon. I hope so because we are teamsters from London with a cargo of grain to deliver to one of the merchants."

The man merely grunted something in a dialect I could not understand and walked away. I said nothing to him about buying a boat or a passage because I did not want Despenser knowing our plans. Sure enough, Despenser was soon talking to our visitor who had snatched off his cap and seemed in awe at meeting one of his betters.

"Perhaps we should stroll down there ourselves after Lord Despenser leaves, eh William?" the Bishop had suggested as we watched the fisherman accept something from Despenser and walk back to the little one-masted fishing boat he had nosed into the strand.

When he reached his boat he started throwing fish over the side and on to the rocky sand of the strand. At that point we were fairly sure we knew the King's plan to escape.

On the other hand it might just be a contingency or even a deception.

Chapter Thirty-four

*The King flees, the Queen arrives, and
many of the remaining coins are lost.*

Bishop Thorpe was both disgusted and pleased as we
stood together and smiled and waved at the backs of King
Edward and Lord Despenser. They were riding back to the
royal encampment outside the walls of Gloucester after
visiting both our circled coin wagons and the nearby boats
of the Bristol Channel fishermen who had come up the River
Severn to sell their catches on the strand in front of the city
wall.

It had taken some doing and more than a little
exaggeration of the dangers, but it appeared we had
convinced the King and his Chancellor that the coins in the
chests should remain with us if the King and his Chancellor
decided to abandon their men and try to reach Wales in a
fishing boat. They had not come right out and said they
intended to abandon their men and sail away on one of the
fishing boats but it was fairly obvious from the instructions
we had been given.

"Start sending the royal coins to Cornwall as fast as you
can find boats and barges with a strong-enough hulls to
carry them, and then you are to guard them in Cornwall
until we send for them," the King ordered pompously.

"Oh aye we will be honoured to do so, Your Majesty," I
had assured him. "It is God's Will that we guard them so
you can certainly count on us." *It was probably more*

meaningless ox shite than I had ever delivered in my entire life, but he was a king after all and harder to convince.

Bishop Thorpe had helped by making the sign of the cross and promising that he and God would help keep the coins safe for the King.

"It is God's Will that your coins will be kept safe for you in Cornwall and waiting for you to summon them, Your Majesty. I myself will make it a point to be there to help God watch over them until you send for them."

Bishop Thorpe was much less encouraging and said what he really thought of the King a few minutes later as we stood together and watched him ride back to the royal encampment near the city wall.

"The King is going to abandon his men in the morning and run away to save himself once again is what he is going to do; Edward is a real piece of shite and that is God's truth."

The Bishop said it out of the corner of his mouth as we continued to smile and wave farewell to the King and Despenser even though they had their backs to us and were riding away. *Who knows who might be watching, eh?*

"I agree with you," I replied out of the side of my mouth as I quit waving and dropped my hand. "But I really do not care what God does with him now that the King is content to leave the coins in our keeping until he sends for them. Indeed, I hope he drowns so we can keep them."

"Running away is what he has always done whenever he feels threatened. It happened twice in Scotland, for God's sake. No wonder the Queen despises him; I certainly do," the Bishop said.

But then with a mean little chuckle and an agreeable nod of his head the Bishop added

"But you surely put a bee in his hair when you pointed out that the coin chests he wanted us to load on to the fishing boat were so heavy that they would almost certainly break through its hull and be lost along with everyone on the boat."

I smiled and agreed.

"Aye, and you are right about the King and Lord Despenser, Bishop. If they were in the Company we would hang them once for deserting their men and a second time for leaving the coins behind.

******

Early the next morning Bishop Thorpe and I stood on the coin chests in one of the coin wagons and watched as the little fishing boat carrying King and Despenser was pushed off the strand next to the riverbank and raised its single sail. It was obviously their intention to sail down the Severn to the Bristol Channel and then continue along the coast of Wales until they could find a safe place to land in the heart of Wales.

Once the fishing boat carrying King and Despenser had successfully gotten out into the river and raised its sails we mounted our horses and rode to the nearby encampment of the King's supporters to see what we could see. We were not alone.

A surprising number of the King's supporters had come to see him and his chancellor leave. They were walking and riding all around us as they made their way back to their camp. Most of them were quite angry and distressed. There had been many curses and angry threats directed at both King Edward and Despenser as they departed; not a single person wished them Godspeed.

We found the camp of the King's supporters to be virtually deserted. Some of the people, like us, hoped to flee in fishing boats. Others intended to remain and try to make peace with Mortimer and the Queen. Most of them, however, had already packed up and walked or ridden away to try to find a place to hide from the Queen's vengeance.

It was a nasty day. The wind was cold and blowing fiercely; a storm was coming in more ways than one.

"Shall we go down to the river and see if we can find some fishing boats to carry us and the coins home to Cornwall?" I asked the Bishop. It was something we could finally begin doing now that the King and Despenser were gone.

"Why bother? All the boats that were available have already been hired and set their sails either yesterday afternoon or earlier today. No new ones will be coming in until the weather improves."

******

The Queen and her army began arriving in Gloucester before the weather changed and the fishing boats could get up the River Severn to reach us. It was too late to load the coins and leave.

"Ah well, it was too much to hope for that we would get away with all of them," said the Bishop as we watched the Queen's army march up to city gate which had opened as it arrived. "As the bible says: a man should not get too greedy."

"Does it really say that Bishop?" I asked with a smile. We were standing together atop one of the coin wagons watching the Queen's army march into Gloucester.

"Mine does," Bishop Thorpe said with a satisfied look on his face. "And it also says it never hurts to ask for coins when they are due."

"Aye, and if I am not mistaken, here comes the woman who owes us some." I replied.

Sure enough here came the Queen clattering towards us in a horse cart with a guard of knights surrounding her.

"I heard about the covered wagons and the coin chests so I knew it was you the moment I saw them," she said as I jumped down from the wagon and welcomed her with a great flourishing bow.

Her eyes were twinkling with delight and neither Mortimer nor her ladies were with her. It was about then that I realized that I had missed having her nearby to worry about and comfort.

"We have been guarding them for you Your Majesty; particularly since some of the coins are owed to us. May I presume that it is alright with you if my men and I to take what we are owed for protecting your son?

She said yes and so we did.

The End of this Story

Epilogue
Some years later.

Queen Isabella lived for many years after the supporters of her son, Edward the Third, took control of the England away from her lover Lord Mortimer a few years later and had him brutally executed along with many of the Queen's supporters. Her husband, King Edward the Second, had been captured by Mortimer when ill winds blew the fishing boat carrying him and Lord Despenser ashore in England before they could reach Wales. He died in prison.

The Queen, however, escaped unharmed because none of Edward the Third's supporters were willing to take the risk of doing harm to the King's mother. She lived out her life peacefully in England and rarely visited the King and his court in the early years of his long reign. But she did not always live alone.

No one, perhaps not even the Queen herself, had known that she was pregnant with a second son when she sailed for France years earlier accompanied by the young prince who was now King Edward the Third. His name was Prince John and he had stayed behind in France when she returned to England. John had been mostly forgotten during the hectic years that followed the Queen's return and the subsequent arrest and life-long imprisonment of her husband in exchange for his abdication so their oldest son could rule England in his own right as Edward the Third.

It was not until some years later that the new King welcomed his younger brother upon his return from France and named him as the Earl of Cornwall at his mother's insistence—which was a more than a little surprising because Cornwall already had a hereditary earl, William Courtenay, the Commander of the Company of Archers who had succeeded to the earldom upon the death of his son-less uncle.

John was surprisingly small and immature for his age when he was finally reunited with his older brother the King. Indeed he was hardly big enough and strong enough to do more than toddle. But he had a growth spurt after he began eating good English food and ended up even taller and sturdier than the King. He was hard to miss with his flaming red hair.

- - - **The End of the Book** - - -

There will be more stories in *The Company of Archers* series as more and more of the parchment records found in the Bodleian Library are translated.

All of the books in this great and action-packed saga of medieval England are available as eBooks and in print, and some of them are also available as audio books. You can find them by going to Amazon, Google, Bing, or Goodreads and searching for *Martin Archer stories.*

A collection of the first six books of the saga is available on Amazon as *The Archers' Story*. A similar collection of the next four books in the saga is available as *The Archers' Story: Part II,* and the three books after that as *The Archers' Story*

Part III. And many more books and three more collections follow those.

A list of all the books in the saga follows along with many other books by Martin Archer such as the recent release of *The Wonderful New ERA Conspiracy,* which would have been made into a hilarious comedy by Mel Brooks if he had not passed away and *Cage's Crew,* a heist story featuring a very tough professional criminal. And then, of course, there are the five action-packed stories in *Soldiers and Marines.*

Finally, a word from Martin:

"I sincerely hope you enjoyed reading *The Windsor Deception* as much as I enjoyed writing it. If so, I respectfully request a favourable review on Amazon, Goodreads, and Google with as many stars as possible in order to encourage other readers.

"And, if you could please spare a moment, I would also very much appreciate your thoughts about this saga of medieval England and my other stories, and whether you would like to see any of them continue. I can be reached at martinarcherV@gmail.com."

Cheers and thank you once again. /S/ Martin Archer

Amazon print and eBooks in order in the exciting and action-packed *The Company of Archers* saga:

The Archers

The Alchemist's Revenge

The Venetian Gambit

Today's Friends

The English Gambits

The London Gambits

The Windsor Deception

Amazon eBooks in Martin Archer's epic *Soldiers and Marines* saga:

Soldiers and Marines

Peace and Conflict

War Breaks Out

War in the East

Israel's Next War (A prescient book much hated by Islamic reviewers)

eBook Collections on Amazon

The Archers Stories I - complete books I, II, III, IV, V, VI.

The Archers Stories II - complete books VII, VIII, IX, X.

The Archers Stories III - complete books XI, XII, XIII.

The Archers Stories IV – complete books XIV, XV, XVI, and XVII.

The Archers Stories V – complete books XVIII, XIX, and XX.

The Archers Stories VI – complete books XXI, XXII, and XXII

The Soldiers and Marines Saga - complete books I, II, and III.

Other eBooks you might enjoy:

Cage's Crew a "heist" novel by Martin Archer writing as Raymond Casey.

America's Next War by Michael Cameron and Martin Archer– an adaption of Martin Archer's *War Breaks Out* to set it in the immediate future when Eastern and Western Europe go to war over another wave of Islamic refugees.

And Martin's personal choices for everyone to read: Everything by Jacqueline Lindauer (*Joysanta*, etc) and Antoine de Saint-Euxpery (*The Little Prince*, etc).

Sample Pages from Book One of the Company of Archers saga *– The Archers*

.... We sometimes had to shoulder our way through the crowded streets and push people away as we walked towards the church. Beggars and desperate women and young boys began pulling on our clothes and crying out to us. In the distance black smoke was rising from somewhere in the city, probably from looters torching somebody's house or a merchant's stall.

The doors to the front of the old stone church were closed. Through the cracks in the wooden doors we could see the heavy wooden bar holding them shut.

"Come on. There must be a side door for the priests to use. There always is."

We walked around to the side of the church and there it was. I began banging on the door. After a while, a muffled voice on the other side told us to go away.

"The church is not open." The voice said.

"We have come from Lord Edmund to see the Bishop of Damascus. Let us in. We know he is in there."

We could hear something being moved and then an eye appeared at the peep hole in the door. A few seconds later, the door swung open and we hurried in.

The light inside the room was dim because the windows were shuttered.

Our greeter was a slender fellow with alert eyes who could not be much more than an inch or two over five feet tall. He studied us intently as he bowed us in and then quickly shut and barred the door behind us. He seemed quite anxious.

"We have come from Lord Edmund's castle in the Bekka Valley to see the Bishop," I said in the bastardised French dialect some people are now calling English. And then Thomas repeated my words in Latin. *Which is what I should have done in the first place.*

"I shall tell him you are here and ask if he will receive you," the man replied. "I am Yoram, the Bishop's scrivener; may I tell him who you are and why you are here?"

"I am William, the captain of the men who are left of the Company of English archers who fought in the Bekka with Lord Edmund, and this is Father Thomas, our priest. We are here to collect our Company's pay for helping to defend Lord Edmund's fief these past two years."

"I shall inform His Eminence of your arrival. Please wait here."

The Bishop's scrivener had a strange accent; I wonder how he came to be here?

Some time passed before the anxious little man returned. While he was gone we looked around the room. It was quite luxurious with a floor of stones instead of the mud floors one usually finds in a church.

The room was quite dark. The windows were covered with heavy wooden shutters and sealed shut with wooden bars; the light in the room, such as it was, came from cracks in the shutters and smaller windows high on the walls above the shuttered windows. There was a somewhat tattered tribal carpet on the floor.

The anxious little man returned and gave us a most courteous nod and bow.

"His Grace will see you now. Please follow me."

The Bishop's clerk led us into a narrow, dimly lit passage with stone walls and a low ceiling. He went first and then Thomas and then me. We had taken but a few steps when he turned back toward us and in a low voice issued a cryptic warning.

"Protect yourselves. The Bishop does not want to pay you. You are in mortal danger."

The little man nodded in silent agreement when I held up my hand. Thomas and I needed to take a moment to get ourselves ready.

He watched closely, and his eyes opened in surprise as we prepared ourselves. Then, when I gave a nod to let him know we were ready, he rewarded us with a tight smile and another nod—and began walking again with a determined look on his face.

A few seconds later we turned another corner and came to an open door. It opened into a large room with beamed ceilings more than six feet high. I knew the height because I could stand upright after I bent my head to get through the entrance door.

A portly older man in a bishop's robes was sitting behind a rough wooden table, and there was a heavily bearded and rather formidable-looking guard with a sword in a wooden scabbard standing in front of the table. There was a closed chest on the table and a jumble of tools and chests in the corner covered by another old tribal rug and a broken chair.

The Bishop smiled to show us his bad teeth and beckoned us in. We could see him clearly despite the dim light coming in from the small window openings near the ceiling of the room.

After a moment he stood and extended his hand over the table so we could kiss his ring. First Thomas and then I approached and half kneeled to kiss it. Then I stepped back and towards the guard to make room for Thomas so he could re-approach the table and stand next to me as the Bishop re-seated himself.

"What is it you want to see me about?" the Bishop asked in Latin.

He said it with a sincere smile and leaned forward expectantly.

"I am William, captain of the late Lord Edmund's English archers, and this is Father Thomas, our priest and confessor." *And my older brother, although I do not intend to mention it at the moment.*

"How can that be? Another man was commanding the archers when I visited Lord Edmund earlier this year, and we made our arrangements to pay you."

"He is dead. He took an arrow in the arm and it turned purple and rotted until he died. Another took his place and he is dead also. Now I am the captain of the Company."

The Bishop crossed himself and mumbled a brief prayer under his breath. Then he looked at me expectantly and listened intently.

"We have come to get the money Lord Edmund entrusted to you to pay us. We looked for you before we left the valley, but Beaufort Castle was about to fall and you had already fled. So we followed you here; we have come to collect our Company's pay."

"Of course. Of course. I have it right here in the chest.

"Aran," he said, nodding to the burly soldier standing next to me, "tells me there are eighteen of you. Is that correct?" *And how would he be knowing that?*

"Yes, Eminence, that is correct."

"Well then, four gold Constantinople coins for each man is seventy-two; and you shall have them here and now."

"No, Eminence, that is not correct."

I reached inside my tunic and pulled out the Company's copy of the contract with Lord Edmund, and laid the parchment on the desk in front of him.

As I placed it on the table, I tapped it with my finger and casually stepped further to the side, and even closer to his swordsman, so Thomas could once again step into my place in front of the Bishop and nod his agreement confirming it was indeed in our contract.

"The contract calls for the Company to be paid four gold bezant coins from Constantinople for each of eighty-seven men and six more coins to the Company for each man who is killed or loses both of his eyes, arms, legs, or his ballocks.

"It sums to one thousand and twenty-six bezants in all—and I know you have them because I was present when Lord Edmund gave you more than enough coins for our contract and you agreed to pay them to us. So here we are. We want our bezants."

"Oh yes. So you are. So you are. Of course. Well, you shall certainly get what is due you. God wills it."

I sensed the swordsman stiffen as the Bishop said the words and opened the lid of the chest. The Bishop reached in with both hands and took a big handful of gold bezants in his left hand and placed them on the table.

He spread the gold coins out on the table and motioned Thomas forward to help him count as he reached back in to fetch another handful. I stepped further to the left and even closer to the guard so Thomas would have plenty of room to step forward to help the Bishop count.

Everything happened at once when Thomas leaned forward to start counting the coins. The Bishop reached again into his money chest as if to get another handful. This time he came out with a dagger—and lunged across the coins on the table to drive it into Thomas's chest with a grunt of satisfaction.

The swordsman next to me simultaneously began pulling his sword from its wooden scabbard. Killing us had been prearranged by the Bishop. .....

**** End of the Sample Pages ****

The Archers and all the other stories in this medieval saga are available only on Amazon and can be found by searching there or on Google, Bing, and Goodreads. Search for *Martin Archer fiction*. And, if you could please spare a moment, I would also very much appreciate it if you would review this story and give it as many stars as possible in order to encourage other readers.

I would also most sincerely appreciate your thoughts as to whether or not there should be more stories in this saga about the Company of Archers. I can be reached at martinarcherV@gmail.com." Cheers, and thank you once again. /S/ Martin Archer

Printed in Great Britain
by Amazon